DECODE MY DESIRES HARRIS & KAT PART II

STEELE INTERNATIONAL, INC. - JACKSON CORPORATION A BILLIONAIRES ROMANCE SERIES CROSSOVER BOOK 5

CHARMAINE LOUISE SHELTON

CONTENTS

FREE BOOK

Get the start of the STEELE International, Inc. A Billionaires Romance Series with *Discover My Desires Sebastian & Lola Prequel* FREE!

Click Cover Below or visit **bit.ly/CLBooksNewsletter** to subscribe to my newsletter for latest news and launches, books from my author friends, and sizzling reads in book promotions. Plus, start reading the steamy billionaire romance *Series Prequel* of Sebastian Steele and Lola Lewis.

Their stories. Their discovery of unknown desires…

FREE BOOK!

EXCLUSIVE FOR SUBSCRIBERS!

STEELE INTERNATIONAL, INC. - JACKSON CORPORATION

A BILLIONAIRES ROMANCE SERIES CROSSOVER

ABOUT STEELE INTERNATIONAL, INC. - JACKSON CORPORATION A BILLIONAIRES ROMANCE SERIES CROSSOVER

Welcome to the titillating world of the multibillion-dollar global companies and the love affairs of the families that controls them.

STEELE International, Inc.- Jackson Corporation is a series of interconnecting Billionaire romance. Follow the Steele and Jackson families as they fly around the world chasing the women they love and their happily ever afters. Get ready for glitz, glamour, and steamy romance books. What's better than that? The Jet-set Lifestyle has never been hotter...

The Desires Series is not for the tea set; it's for the top-shelf vodka straight up in a pretty crystal glass coterie!

Don't miss any of the sizzling romance books in the STEELE International, Inc. - Jackson Corporation A Billionaires Romance Series Crossover:

Tempt My Desires Lachlan & Haley Part I

Tease My Desires Lachlan & Haley Part II

Grant My Desires Lachlan & Haley Part III

Intrigue My Desires Harris & Kat Part I

Decode My Desires Harris & Kat Part II

Honor My Desires Harris & Kat Patt III

A Trilogy of Desires Lachlan & Haley Parts I-III

A Trilogy of Desires Harris & Kat Parts I-III

Series Extras

Series Playlist

Visit CharmaineLouiseBooks.com for the complete list.

Decode My Desires Harris & Kat Part II

Welcome to the titillating world of the multibillion-dollar global companies and the love affairs of the families that control them.

Harris

Who's the sucker now? Me, that's who. The One really took me—not to mention my family—for a ride. I never should have given up my playboy card. Well, it's back in hand, and I have to make up for lost time.

Kat

What's that saying about best laid plans? Yeah, tell me about it. Hopefully my new goal to figure out Harris and what I feel for him works out better...

Can Kat redeem herself, or has she lost the opportunity for The One?

Travel with this playful pair as Kat makes her moves on Harris from sky-high penthouses on Fifth Avenue and the Sunset Strip to a private villa beside a lush Hawaiian lagoon and more in their sizzling, second chance billionaire romance.

Anthem: "Come Back to Me" Janet Jackson
https://www.youtube.com/watch?v=-5ecZWwO_hQ

Playlist:
https://www.youtube.com/playlist?list=
PLXwYvn0e218CGttnEJo1AjzohDVB0NGdd

Visit CharmaineLouiseBooks.com

KAT

"*I*'m so glad you guys came with us. I know it's best for society's expectations and all. But I do *not* enjoy engaging with Princess Fiona the Fair..."

Haley Jackson, the Countess of Aboyne née Steele, grimaces as we stand with her husband Lachlan Jackson, the Earl of Aboyne, and her twin brother Harris Steele. We're at Duchess of Montrose Fiona Graham's Ridel Art Gallery in Aberdeen for an exhibit opening.

Me, Katrina Roberts, the lass from the less-than-favorable upbringing who clawed her way from a dingy flat in Glasgow to the hallowed halls of the University of Edinburg on a full academic scholarship. I worked hard to escape poverty from the premature death of my father through graduation with an MA Business Management degree to administrative positions for C-suite executives. The latest Lachlan Jackson. But the position with the CEO of Jackson Corporation does more than train me for the best way to learn about business—straight from the source, the higher ups who actually run it. No, that position serves one purpose. And one purpose alone.

Revenge.

My eyes flick from a painting on the wall to Harris as he chuckles at Haley's reference to Fiona. Haley compares the woman who wanted to marry Lachlan to a willowy, mythical creature. Fiona with her ash blonde waist-length hair, violet eyes, and Scottish lilt appears as one who graces the heather meadows.

"You're more than welcome," Harris responds. "Hopefully Callum stays over there with his wife."

Harris inclines his head in the duke's direction, and Haley nods.

"Absolutely!" She says.

Ah, Harris Steele, my fledgling boyfriend, multibillionaire at thirty-two, the last single of The STEELE Quaternity. The four brothers and heirs to STEELE International, Inc. Sebastian, Malcolm, Roger, and Harris dubbed such by the media as the most sought-after of the world's eligible billionaires. Handsome; six plus feet; ebony hair; shades of gray eyes; powerful Alpha Doms and males.

And I made the last one fall for me in a few short months. I've said it once and I'll say it again. My red hair, pretty face, and curvy body get 'em every time.

Now not only am I in the prime position to ruin the Jackson's but also the Steeles. The power rests in my hands.

I flick my gaze to Chester Stewart, aka Chet, the forty-year-old vice president of Stewart Scotch. His family's company is Jackson Corporation's top competitor and has a centuries-old bitter rivalry over a title. Chet glares at me.

He hates me.

I hate him.

But we each serve the other's purpose.

Revenge against the Jacksons.

Now, he wants the Steeles, too.

But I question, do I want to take both clans down? Even after the families welcomed me like one of their own into their world of luxury, love, and loyalty?

Then again, I need to remain loyal to *my* family and the correction of the dirty deed that put us on the polar opposite of both clans.

I scowl at Chet, then turn my gaze to Harris.

Even though he lives in New York City, he has stayed in London working from his offices in STEELE London, jetting me around the globe for weekend getaways, or coming to Aberdeen. This is one such time. He returned from a business trip to Geneva to surprise me.

After our toe-curling marathon reunion, Haley asked him to come tonight—no pun intended. I agreed—whether or not pun with that walking sex on a stick. The plan to make an appearance, then go to dinner. Have some real fun, as Harris says.

I let my gaze wander. The paintings a mixture of landscapes featuring the fields above the North Sea and the rolling countryside of Aberdeenshire. Others capture women.

The hairs on the back of my neck rise.

No!

My eyes narrow on the painter's signature in the corner of the closest piece. The beam of light from the fixture above shows it clearly. IJ.

Is it possible?

I shift to get a better view of the next painting. IR.

A few more marked by either set of initials.

There's no denying it.

What the bloody hell do I do?!

"Great, it's a full house," Lachlan snorts. "Chet Stewart is here. The wanker."

"What's his problem now?" Harris asks.

"Who the bloody hell knows?" Lachlan asks rhetorically.

"Looks like Princess Fiona the Fair is about to speak," Haley says. "All bow down in her presence..."

I watch—frozen in place—as Fiona moves to stand in front of a piece covered by a white drape. The murmur of the crowd lessens as she calls for everyone's attention.

"Ladies and gentlemen, I am Fiona Graham, Duchess of Montrose. Welcome to Ridel Art Gallery this evening," she announces.

Haley giggles and whispers, "Fiona loves her new title."

Harris chuckles.

"Now, now, Countess of Aboyne, play nice with your noble peers," he chides his twin.

"It pleases us to share the paintings of an unknown artist. The new owner of an abandoned factory in Glasgow discovered the vast set of works in a loft. My team restored the ones you see around the gallery. The others will make their appearance soon. We know no history of the artist. Only the initials IJ on the earlier paintings and IR on the later ones appear. We know from the style and the strokes, the two are the same person. More than likely a man based on the subject and the age of the paintings."

Fiona pauses for dramatic effect.

My breath catches in my throat.

"The portrait behind me is the most extraordinary of the entire collection. The size larger than the others. Attention to detail superb. He draws you into the intimate sanctuary of the scene. The vibrancy of the colors speaks to his love of his muse. See for yourselves. May I present to you… *Siren in Repose*."

Fiona pulls the tasseled rope with a flourish, and the white drape slips to the floor.

The portrait displays a striking red-haired woman with a white silk sheet artfully arranged around her curvaceous body as she lies on a red velvet chaise. Sky blue eyes set in a face of flawless, porcelain skin stare seductively at the viewer.

I gasp and cover my mouth with my hand as the blood drains from my face, making the alabaster skin more pale. My pupils dilate. I have to get out of here before I faint.

"Wow! If not for the eyes, Kat looks just like the woman! Crazy, huh?" Haley exclaims.

"Yes, they do resemble one another," Lachlan says, then chuckles. "Kat, are you reincarnated?"

The three laugh and turn to face me.

My gaze flicks from the portrait to them. My knees wobble.

"Hey, are you okay, Kat?" Harris asks as he reaches for my arm. "Babe?"

Tears fill my eyes, and I shake my head. I glance at Lachlan, then bring my emerald green eyes to Harris.

"I—I'm so sorry…" I force out the words before I rush for the door, blinded by tears.

Well, I guess I have my answer.

No, I don't want to take both clans down.

The new question: is it too late to save myself from *their* revenge after all I've done?

"Kat! Wait up!"

I continue to the doors, intent on putting as much distance as possible between Harris and me.

What the bloody hell can I say or do now?

Mumbled apologies fall from my lips as I push through the crowd awed by the paintings, then burst through the gallery's front doors. Out on the street, I glance left and right for the fastest route away.

Harris' Rolls-Royce sedan sits at the curb with his driver inside. Can't go straight. I dodge around a couple staring in the gallery's front windows. Perhaps if I get around the corner before Harris sees me.

A hand grabs my elbow.

My back collides with Harris' firm chest as he bands his arms around my waist. Locked against him, I can't move. His familiar scent washes over me. A sob escapes my mouth. I struggle to free myself.

"Kat, babe. Talk to me," he says frantically as his grip tightens.

"What happened?"

"Is she all right?"

Lachlan and Haley's questions urge me to get away. I cannot face them. Not now. I renew my efforts. But Harris will have none of it. The Alpha male comes to the forefront.

"Kat! Enough! Tell me what happened," Harris says as he spins me around to face him. His dove gray eyes—obsidian in the glow of the streetlamps above us—scan my face. A frown mars his masculine beauty.

I swipe at the tears and press my teeth into my lower lip to bite back another sob. My eyes flick from his face to Haley, then to Lachlan. His emerald green eyes so like my own fill with concern.

I lower my head and mutter a curse under my breath.

"What?" Harris asks as he slips a finger beneath my chin to align our gazes. Softly he adds, "Talk to me, Kitty Kat."

My resolve breaks as a great sob crests the surface from the depths of my soul and knocks down the last vestiges of my defenses. I've held so much anger, bitterness, and pain for decades. Fought my battles and those of my mother Allison, elder brother Payton, and younger siblings Michael and Charlotte.

The only time I've ever found peace has been in the arms of my lover—Harris Steele.

And here I am on the brink of destroying not only his extended family but his too.

"Harris, wait a minute. Kat, honey, do you want to speak to me without these guys around? We can go to the restaurant and sit at the bar for a Girls' Chat. They can sit at the table or go home and to the hotel. Whichever you prefer. Okay?"

I glance over at Haley. Her dove gray eyes reveal the sincerity in her words and make my heart ache even more. Perhaps she's right. If I confess to her—alone—maybe it won't be as bad to see the pain I'll cause Harris and Lachlan. She's been nothing but kind to me. So maybe she'll be less upset.

She's super close with her sisters-in-law Lola, Starr, and Leonie, married to Sebastian, Malcolm, and Roger, respectively. They refer to each other as sisters and bond whenever the guys get overly protective. For a moment, I felt a part of their inner circle. But now…

As I open my mouth to respond, a movement beyond Haley catches my eye.

Chet.

Bloody *hell!*

He left the gallery and stands glaring at me with such animosity I shiver as the waves of his anger hit me full blast.

"Babe, you're shivering. Go. Go talk to Haley. She'll listen," Harris says worriedly as he presses me towards his twin. Then he nods to his driver who stepped out of the Rolls-Royce sedan when he noticed us on the sidewalk. "Ride in my car. I'll go with Lachlan."

"Yes, Kat. Harris and I will wait at the penthouse flat. Come over when you're ready. Take your time," Lachlan adds.

Neither notice Chet as he puts his index finger to his mouth in a shushing motion, then brings it down to slash at his throat as his evil glare intensifies.

My eyes widen at his threat, and I turn away.

What have I gotten myself into? Chet dares to threaten me with *death*? In public for anyone to witness?

I shudder at the thought, realizing he has the means to do so and no one would ever know.

Oh, Kat Roberts…

My mind scrambles to backtrack. No way can I admit what I've done now. Not with Chet and not knowing what he'd do to me. I need time to figure out this bloody mess. As much as I hate to do it, more lies slip from my mouth with ease.

"Haley, Harris, Lachlan," I start as I lick my dry lips and glance at them in turn. "Thank you so much. I—I was a tad bit overwhelmed. Forgive my outburst. I don't want to ruin our evening. Let's go back inside—"

"Kat."

"You ruined nothing."

"No need to apologize, Kat."

The three of them speak at once. But Haley raises her hand, and the guys go quiet.

"Kat Roberts. You will not stand here and tell us *lies*," Haley says adamantly.

My heart stops as my mouth gapes. Fuck!

Haley is a top-notch hacker. I have to admit she's far better than my self-taught skills, as good as they are for my needs—although they're unaware of my tech savvy. Harris is an expert coder. Together, they formed STEELE Technology & Cyber Security and known as the Dynamic Duo. Brainiacs, to say the least.

If my spell—or Siren's call, as Harris refers to it—didn't distract him, I'm certain he would have noticed something by now. Their subsidiary handles Jackson Corporation's technology systems. Once Lydie Jackson—the eldest of the siblings and COO—increased my security access, I delved into their files to uncover intel Chet could use to destroy them. Periodically, I fed it to him over the last few months in exchange for six-figure sums wired to my Swiss bank account.

But I'm not selfish.

The money goes towards a monthly allowance I give to

my mother, who cleans the homes of rich people in Glasgow. One day soon, she won't have to get on her knees for anyone ever again. I help my younger siblings too. Michael works but loves to sketch the architecture in Glasgow. I want to enroll him in a formal program. Charlotte is at university on a full academic scholarship and works too. She needs to focus on her coursework fully without concern over money for food or textbooks. I try to make their lives a little easier, too.

I think of the reasons for my actions—including the dirty deed—take a deep breath and straighten my spine.

Okay, Katrina Roberts, *smiogaid suas, nighean*!

"Ha! Haley, you got me! It's a tad bit embarrassing. So, I'd rather not say at the moment. You're right. Why don't we go have our Girls' Chat and meet the guys at your flat afterwards," I say with a smile. I do my best to make it reach my eyes.

Haley grins and loops her arm through mine.

"Perfect!" She says to me, then turns to Lachlan and Harris and wiggles her fingers. "Tootles, fellas. We'll catch you later."

Lachlan leans over and kisses her as she waltzes past him. He whispers something in her ear, and her face flushes scarlet. He chuckles and steps back.

"Okay, babe. Take your time. I'll be there when you need me," Harris says before he bends down to kiss me.

My throat constricts as my heart stutters from his sweet words. They're all so caring it adds to my discomfit.

"Thank you, Harris," I whisper as I squeeze his forearm. I can't quite make eye contact, but I offer a wan smile.

He kisses the top of my head and motions for his driver to open the sedan's back door.

Haley and I slip into the luxurious interior. Once the door closes with a light thunk, she turns to me.

"First, I want you to know you can trust me with whatever you have to say, Kat. Harris is my twin, and I love him with every ounce of my being. But I know how my brothers can be. So if he did something, do not hesitate to tell me," she says earnestly as she squeezes my hand.

I return the gesture with a smile.

"Thank you, Haley. I truly appreciate you. I admire how close you, your sisters-in-law, and friends are to each other. How I wish we could have had the same—" I stop as I realize the tense I used. Damn!

Haley notices it too and frowns. Before she can question my choice of words, I squeeze her hand.

"What I mean to say is I hope I can be a part of your inner circle," I clarify and say a silent prayer she believes me.

Haley studies my face for a minute, then nods her head.

"Of course! Us girls have to stick together," she responds, then winks. "And I'll take any excuse to get a night out with my girls! So thank you."

We ride to the restaurant in a comfortable silence. At the bar, we settle into a corner semicircular booth with a low table. I glance around at the posh eatery. The patrons resemble Harris, his twin, and her husband—well dressed, wealthy, young, gorgeous.

A server who could be a male supermodel takes our orders and returns moments later.

"Mmmm. Delish!" Haley says after she takes a sip of her Manhattan cocktail made with Jackson Special Blend Scotch—naturally.

I can't help but to grin at her reaction as she smacks her full lips. Her dove gray eyes twinkle in the warm golden light from candles artfully arranged on the tabletop and sconces on the walls. She tosses her waist-length ebony hair over one shoulder as she leans back against the buttery soft suede banquette.

"So, spill," she says.

I take a swig of my Old Fashioned to wet my suddenly parched mouth. No point in dragging it out. I take a deep cleansing breath as Starr taught me in a yoga session. Showtime as Harris says…

"Sometimes, I get a bit overwhelmed… rather intimi-dated by others. Well, more specifically of those who come from affluent backgrounds," I start, then take another sip of my cocktail. "Over the years, I've done my best to blend in with those kinds of people and not let my less-than upbringing make me feel less than them—"

"Oh, Kat," Haley starts.

I raise my hand and continue with a shake of my head.

"It's hard for me to talk about. And I know you mean well. But if you'd be so kind as to allow me to finish?" I ask as I squeeze her hand and smile. When she nods, I continue. "Tonight and the last few weeks, Harris has immersed me in your world—not that I dislike it—and it's hit me harder than usual. That's all. I'll get over it."

Haley blinks and bites the corner of her lower lip. Her gaze goes beyond me as she considers my confession. Slowly, she nods and turns back to me.

"I can't say that I understand your experience, Kat, as I was born into a family with multigenerational wealth," she says. "However, my mother and my Aunt Lucie come from middle-class families. Not quite your situation, but they share with us the challenges they faced growing up and blending into this world. Hell, I had to learn from Aunt Lucie about being a Countess as I'll step into her role of Marchioness of Huntly—hopefully no time soon. So I understand and respect you, Kat."

I thank her and take another sip of my drink.

"Wait a minute," Haley says as she sits up with wide eyes.

I lower my glass to the table and shift in my seat to face her again. My heartbeat speeds up and my underarms tingle. What could she think??? Bloody hell.

Haley narrows her eyes at me.

"Did someone make you feel a certain kind of way while you were with us?" She asks.

Her ferocious expression makes me giggle. Harris said she's become a mama bear since having her babies. And now she displays it as she's protective of me too.

The scowl morphs into a grin. Then she laughs.

I shake my head.

"No. Everyone treats me very well, thank you!" I respond.

"Good! Or else someone would have to answer for unacceptable behavior," Haley says as she wags her index finger. "Now, let's order another round and some artichoke dip and sliders. What else?"

I pick up the menu and add some tater tots with their specialty sauce.

That's another thing I love about the girls. They enjoy their food and drink! Sessions with Starr and their personal trainers keep them fit. Besides, the guys really love their curves, and Harris is no exception.

Haley and I spend the rest of the evening talking about the upcoming holidays the Steeles and Jacksons spend together in Capri and in Verbier, the next Girls' Getaway, and Lola's fashion show during Paris Fashion Week.

The way Haley includes me as part of the family gatherings makes my heart hurt. I so hope Harris and Lachlan will forgive me.

A few hours pass, and we leave for her penthouse flat off Union Street—a ritzy area in Aberdeen.

Harris rushes over to pull me into his embrace. I rest my head on his firm chest as I wrap my arms around his waist. Lost in the compellingly sensual scent of his cologne —floral, earthy, and vanilla—my body melts against him with a sigh.

"Feel better?" He murmurs as he strokes my back.

I nod and tighten my grip on him. I never want to let Harris go. Ever.

"Words, Kat. I will have your words," he says as his warm breath skitters across my cheek.

"Yes, Harris, I feel a whole lot better thanks to Haley," I respond to the Alpha male's command.

He rumbles soothingly, then leans back to gaze down at me.

"Do you want to share with me? If not, as long as you're okay, we can leave it alone," he asks.

I assure him all is well and best to move on. Put it behind us.

We bid Haley and Lachlan goodnight and leave for STEELE Aberdeen. Once in the President's suite, Harris scoops me into his arms and carries me through the palatial rooms to the primary bedroom. He strides past the double doors and deposits me on my feet beside the king-size bed.

Without hesitation, he strips my silk wrap dress and lingerie from my body and drops them to pool at my feet. I step out of my slingbacks just as he tosses me onto the bed. I squeal as I land amidst the sumptuous linens and plentiful pillows. My legs splay open to give Harris a full view of needy pussy.

He growls as he shrugs out of his suit jacket.

I snap my knees together, embarrassed he'll spy the moisture gathering along my lower lips.

A growl of displeasure has me shuddering and my legs falling apart.

"Open!" He commands. "Do not hide yourself from me, naughty lass."

I mewl in response as I lean back on my elbows. My hooded gaze rakes over his body that puts Adonis to shame as he sheds his clothes and toes off his shoes and socks. As he stands to his full six-feet-one-inch height, his massive cock thumps against the happy trail along his eight-pack abs.

My pussy softens in anticipation of Harris' girth breaching my folds. Another mewl slips from my slack mouth.

He rumbles deep in his chest as he planks over me.

"I always want to see you bare to me, Kitty Kat and comfortable telling me anything on your mind. I'll let it go tonight. But know we will keep no secrets from each other," Harris says as his dove gray eyes bore into my emerald green gaze.

My eyes widen at his words, and my heart bangs against my chest.

Bloody—

Harris' mouth crashes over mine. As he takes complete possession of my mind, body, and soul, I give into his passionate lovemaking one last time.

HARRIS

Go to Haley's now. We're having a meeting in thirty minutes.

I frown at my mobile screen with the cryptic text message from Baz.

What the hell is that all about?

I scrub my hand over my face and roll onto my back amidst the rumpled bedding. I glance to the right at the cold, empty space beside me. Only an indentation in the pillow and the faint scent of her perfume give any sign My Kitty Kat was here.

She left before I woke up. Without a word.

Presumably she didn't want to wake me. Not that I would mind, especially with my morning wood. I groan at the thought of her writhing beneath me just hours before. My cock tents the sheet as my erection grows. My Siren drives me crazy.

I sit up on an elbow and type a quick text message to

her, then wait for a response. Nothing. Well, no worries since we have plans for dinner tonight. I toss the mobile onto the bed and head to the shower. Might as well get ready for the *meeting*.

On the ride over, I shoot a text message to Haley for any insight she can give to me. While I wait for her to answer, I scroll through my work emails. Since I'm in the UK, I'll spend some time in our STEELE London offices. Haley returns full time next week. So, I'll make sure all is ready for her.

As I ride up in their private elevator, I send another text to My Kitty Kat. The doors ping open onto their entry foyer. Without glancing up, I step off.

"Hey."

I lift my gaze from the mobile screen to find Haley at the open double doors to their penthouse flat. A frown knits her eyebrows together as her eyes scan my face. Her hair piled atop her head in a messy bun sags to the side.

"Hey. What's up, Hal? You look like you've been through it," I say as I lean over to kiss her cheek.

She shakes her head and glances up at me. Her dove gray eyes full of concern.

"It's not good, Harris," she whispers.

"Haley? Is that Harris?" Lachlan calls out.

"Yeah," she shouts back, then pulls my arm. "Come on."

I draw back and frown at her. But she shakes her head and tugs at me. I give in and follow her inside their flat.

Lachlan stands, arms folded, with Lydie beside him.

Both stare at me the same way Haley did a moment ago as though judging my reaction—to what I do not know.

"Okay. What the fuck's going on?" I ask as I fold my arms across my chest and plant my feet. "Somebody better tell me why I'm getting a silent third degree."

"Har—"

Lachlan's mobile rings. He pulls it from his jeans pocket and glances at the screen before he accepts the call.

"He's here now," Lachlan says, as he brings his indecipherable gaze back to my face. "Okay, we're headed to my office."

He ends the call and motions for us to follow him. Lydie keeps pace with her brother. Haley remains by my side as we walk down the corridor to Lachlan's home office. Inside, he settles on a leather chair at the seating area. Lydie takes the other chair, leaving the sofa for Haley and me.

The oversized flat-screen television splits into three views. Baz sits at his desk in his home office at The STEELE Tower on Fifth Avenue in New York City. Malcolm appears to be at Steele Southampton Village in his mansion's office. Roger sits on a sofa in the home office of his Paris triplex penthouse. Each one stares at me.

What the fuck?!

"Spill it," I say, addressing Baz.

"My guy thought his research on Kat was too clean. Not so much as a traffic ticket or a late library book. Her social media imprint nonexistent as were searches of her on the Internet. Nothing appeared prior to the accident with her parents. No school grades, nothing on her parents' jobs. Nothing. A complete enigma. So he dug deeper, and he followed her—"

"Hold the fuck up, Baz!" I shout as I leap to my feet and stalk towards the television. "You mean to tell me you found this out and didn't even bother to tell me *anything?* Then you have *your guy* follow *my woman?!* Without fucking telling me?! Not cool, Baz!"

He cocks an eyebrow and watches me in silence. When I finish, he leans forward and pins me with an intense gaze more powerful than Roger's signature stare.

"First off, back down, Harris," Baz responds coolly. His platinum gray eyes brook no room for argument.

I growl and pivot on my heel. Once I'm seated again, Baz continues.

"Harris, as your eldest brother and the CEO of STEELE International, my responsibility is to you, our family, and to our company. I chose not to tell you right away because I wanted to have full details and irrefutable proof of any wrongdoing before I drew any conclusions. Do you understand?" He asks.

He's right. Baz takes on the mantle of our third parent and cares for us beyond measure. After family, STEELE ranks as his next priority. When our father named him as his successor six years ago, my siblings and I accepted and respect his leadership role too. So I know without a doubt he has my best interest at heart.

"Yes," I respond.

Baz nods and goes on.

"My guy followed Kat for a period of time. He saw her with Chet Stewart"—my head swivels to Lachlan who watches me intently, then to Lydie who purses her lips—"They spent time in the back of his Bentley before she got out and he drove away. That incidence made me call Lach and Lydie. Also, my guy uncovered Kat's real background."

Baz lifts a manila file folder from his desk, and Lachlan slides a similar one across the coffee table towards me.

"This contains his complete report, photographs, and documents. You can read the summary on the first page. We will wait," Baz says.

I glance at the manila file folder like it's a cobra weaving back and forth, set to strike a devastating blow. Haley nudges me with her knee, and I pick up the folder warily.

In all honesty, I wish this shit wasn't true. For one brief moment, I had a taste of what my twin and our siblings enjoy every day—the love of the soul mate. I thought Kat was The One for me. The One I would spend the rest of my life, have children, a little family of my own. Fuck.

I open the file and stare at the summary sheet held by a paper clip to the top of a sizable pile of what I presume to be damning evidence. My stomach knots.

Haley—as though sensing my distress—rubs my back. The calming touch of my twin allows me to refocus. I detach the sheet and read the summary.

Fuck. Me.

Katrina Roberts, 27, of Glasgow, Scotland

Father: Ramsay Roberts, deceased at 37 of a heart attack, unemployed

Mother: Allison Roberts, 49, domestic maid

Siblings: Payton Roberts, 30, unemployed; Michael Roberts, 24, kitchen porter; Charlotte Roberts, 21, university student

Prior Residence: Glasgow, Scotland; shared with parents and siblings

Current Residence: Aberdeen, Scotland

Known Associates: Chester Stewart, Vice President, Stewart Scotch; Isla Ritchie, former administrative assistant to Lachlan Jackson, CEO, Jackson Corporation

As I scan the rest of the page, the roaring of a train grows in my ears.

I flip through the photos.

Sure as shooting, the four-color images capture Kat with Chet. She stands on a sidewalk beside a Bentley sedan. In another, she scans the street surreptitiously before she slips inside. She steps out. Chet sticks his head through the window to speak to her. He pulls off. She stares after him.

Last night at the gallery, Chet watching Kat; her looking at him.

All the fuck while on my arm.

Damn!

I toss the photos onto the coffee table and run my fingers through my hair, then yank.

Harris Steele, you dumb ass! How the hell did I fall for this trick? Siren's call my ass. And Chet Stewart? My family's competitor and rival? Hell no!

Once again, I leap to my feet. This time I pace the floor. My mind reels. Thoughts run wild.

"Let me guess, she colluded with Chet to fuck with Jackson Corporation. Why? What did she give him? I didn't get an alert about invalid access. Haley, did you?" I think aloud as I try to make it make sense.

Haley shakes her head and glances at Lachlan, then at Lydie.

"Lydie can give you more details," Lachlan says, as he nods at his sister.

"We don't know why. But we intend to find out tomorrow when we confront her at the office," Lydie says as her emerald green eyes blaze. *The Shark* is out for blood. "You didn't receive an alert because I upped her clearance to access fake information. I noticed Stewart Scotch was getting the jump on some of our launches and news. Plus, I overheard Chet bragging about us getting our comeuppance. It took a bit of time to figure it was coming from Lachlan's office. Our heads of technology and security ruled out his personal assistant—Gladys. Then we turned to Kat."

Lydie hands another manila file folder to me before she continues.

"We wanted to get her on enough shared information to ensure any action we take sticks. Her mining activity lessened, then stopped. At first, we thought she realized we knew about her activities. Then I saw how serious the two of you became with her attending the foundation galas with you. I wanted to tell you but didn't want to risk her finding out. Not that I don't trust you, Harris. Kat is the questionable one."

"So this chick faked us out the entire time?" Malcolm asks incredulously.

"Hung out with us in our homes. Embraced by our families. Not good," Roger adds.

"How the *fuck* did I miss it?" I yell at the ceiling with my fists raised.

Everyone turns to me.

"Listen, Harris. It's not your fault, and no one blames you in any way," Haley says as she stands in front of me to stop my pacing. "None of us detected any hint of deceit from Kat. Okay?"

I scan my twin's face and those of the others to confirm her words. They agree with her wholeheartedly. With a ragged sigh, I plop onto the sofa and throw my head back against the cushion.

"So now what?" I ask, staring at the ceiling.

"Lydie and I will meet with Kat tomorrow when she arrives at my offices. She better tell us everything we ask. Then we'll determine the extent of the damage before we decide her fate. Not to mention dealing with that fucking wanker Stewart once and for all," Lachlan says, eyes flashing like his sister's fiery orbs. With a shake of his head he adds, "A great first day for my return from paternity leave."

"If you find she did anything to harm Harris or STEELE, I will handle her," Baz states.

"No, *I* will handle Kat Roberts *and* Chet Stewart," Malcolm *The Enforcer* corrects with a steely expression.

Roger nods.

"Fine," Baz and Lachlan say at the same time as Lydie voices her agreement.

I shake my head as I think back over the last three months. What a fucking mess I've gotten our companies, family, and myself into. Never again will I allow a woman to use me. Ever. I groan.

"And you have jokes when I say I hold on to my playboy card like a life preserver in a tsunami…" I grouse as I scrub my hand over my weary face.

Well, back to the basics for this playa.

KAT

orning, Kitty Kat. Where did you run off to? The bed's too cold without you... H.

As I read Harris' text message, my heart clenches. I miss him so much already. Last night was a whirlwind of emotions. Too many for me to process. I need space and time to figure out this bloody mess. What the *hell* am I going to do?

As much as I want to come completely clean with Harris and Lachlan, I'm scared to death of the repercussions. I don't want to lose Harris or the respect of Lachlan—not to mention both families hating me. I've grown attached to Haley, too. And once again, she comforted me as though I were already a part of their family and her inner circle of girls.

Bloody hell!

Think, Kat Roberts, dammit!

Once I arrived at my flat, I showered. But too keyed up

27

to eat breakfast. As I sip my morning tea, my mind races to find a way to avoid the wrath of not only the Jacksons and Steeles, but the death threat of Chet.

I shiver at the memory. How adamant he was as he slashed at his throat. Would he really go that far? I suppose so since what we did was highly illegal, and he stands to lose a hell of a lot more than I do. He and his brother Bram vie for the coveted positions of CEO and Chairman of the Board of Stewart Scotch. Magnus—their father—encourages the competition and will only announce his successor when one of the brothers "proves their worth." Naturally, Chet wants the role so much he was ripe to get intel to ruin Jackson Corporation and the family. So, yeah, I'm sure he'd find a way to hurt me greatly—or worse.

And if Chet ever found out about my family, I'm certain he would exact revenge on them, too. It's bad enough for my mother, Michael, and Charlotte, as it is without one more problem. Payton, well, he's another story. Not that I wish any harm to befall him. No. He just doesn't want to do anything more with his life than hang out at the corner pub and talk about his latest idea guaranteed to make him loads of money. Just like our father did before he died. Dreamers through and through. I need to protect all of them.

But how, Kat Roberts, when you can't protect yourself from Chet???

I circle back to the initial question: what the hell am I going to do?

With a sigh, I rise from the couch to pace the floor.

The fake life I created is solid. All documentation of the car accident and the deaths of my parents in proper order. The details of my youth afterwards match up to public records, too. The guy I dated from the records office helped me to cover all angles since I told him I had a stalker. Again, the power of my red hair, pretty face, and curvy body never fails me.

So even if Chet goes digging to get info on me, he won't stumble upon my family or any connection between them to me. They're safe.

Comforted by that realization, I think about my initial desire for revenge. The dirty deed won't ever go away. The enormity of it proves too extreme. It would be hard to forget it and move on with my life. But I'm torn now.

Aargh!

I rack my brain for how I can hold on to the fledgling relationship I have with Harris.

Is it so bad for me to want it all?

Don't I deserve some happiness at last?

Think, Kat Roberts, dammit!

One thing I know for sure. I'm tired of the lies.

My mobile dings a text message alert. My heart skips a beat. It's Harris' ringtone. I scramble back to the couch and lift my mobile from the cushion and drop onto the seat. My hands shake as I type in the unlock passcode, then tap the message app.

Guess you're busy. I'm at Haley's for a bit. I'll call you later. We're still on for dinner, Kitty Kat. H.

I close my eyes as I throw myself back against the

couch. My heart thuds. Tears well up behind my eyelids and trickle into my ears. I swipe at them with one hand while the other clutches the mobile to my chest. A sob bursts past my lips.

Dammit, Kat Roberts!

* * *

As I walk through the lobby of Jackson Town House, my gaze slides to the seating area where I first met Harris. Lachlan asked me to bring Harris up to his offices since he had a last-minute phone call that delayed him meeting Harris downstairs. The corners of my mouth curl into a woeful smile.

Harris never called me yesterday, and we didn't have dinner.

I left voicemails and sent text messages to him. At first, I assumed he was still with Haley. He loves his niece and nephews and spends as much time as he can with them.

But as time passed with no response, worry haunted the fringes of my mind. It's not at all like Harris to ghost me. He'd sent two text messages about missing me and dinner. So what happened?

Later in the evening, I went to STEELE Aberdeen. The front desk informed me they could not provide details on Mr. Steele and asked me to leave the premises—escorted or on my own. I blinked at their rebuke and backed away to hurry out of the hotel. I felt their eyes like daggers on my back as I rushed to the doors.

Outside, I stood on the sidewalk as tears slipped down my cheeks. I sent a text message to Harris asking him to please tell me what's wrong. No response.

And nothing this morning. Not a word from Harris.

With a sigh, I turn away from the seating area and head for the private lift to the executive floor.

Jackson Town House is the landmark property on Union Street built by the company's founders of the famous Aberdeen granite. It's the second largest granite building in the world.

As I step off the lift, my gaze wanders anew. The executive floor has offices for their legal, finance, operations, and technology departments, along with various conference rooms. Their other divisions have designated floors below. Employees move about busy with their tasks. The buzz of their conversations and activities mixes with the soft classical music piped in through the surround sound system.

The decor highlights the Old World feel of Jackson Town House. A palette of caramel and Bordeaux hues with gold accents reminiscent of our Scotch and wines blend with the dark mahogany woods and leather furniture, crystal light fixtures, original artwork, and Aubusson rugs. The reception area has a spacious desk. Three attractive receptionists with headsets in their ears and custom-tailored caramel-colored dress suits and skin-tone heels that serve as uniforms sit behind it. I smile and nod at them as they greet me.

Portraits of past generations who founded and helped

continue the legacy of Jackson Corporation line the walls as I make my way to Lachlan's suite of offices. The first portrait of the founder and the creator of the finest single malt Scotch Whiskey. He set Jackson Corporation on the path to the most renowned liquor company in the world. After him, successors of each generation have portraits ending with one of Lachlan.

As I approach his private reception area, I notice the desk for Gladys sits empty across from mine. That's odd since she usually arrives before me, and it's Lachlan's first day back from paternity leave. I glance at the closed double doors leading to his office. It's soundproof, so I can't hear if he's inside.

I place my coat in the closet behind my desk and my handbag in the bottom drawer. After I boot up my computer, I rise to get a fresh cup of tea from the break room. Then I stop when the doors to Lachlan's office open. He stands just inside.

"Ms. Roberts, kindly come in," he says.

The formality of his request gives me pause. Then I relax since he probably wants to keep the personal separate from the business.

I smile and walk around my desk.

"Good morning, Mr. Jackson," I say, maintaining the professional demeanor. "Welcome back to the office."

He merely nods as he steps back to let me pass him.

My smile falters when I see Lydie, their General Counsel Ryan Dixon, Lars Gustave Head of Technology, and Sam Fisher Head of Security seated at the elliptical-shaped conference table.

"Have a seat," Lachlan says behind me.

My heart races, and my armpits tingle.

Oh, no!

I do my best to blank my face, but heat rises in my cheeks. With deliberate steps, I walk to the only empty seat at the conference table—between Technology and Security. Lachlan takes his seat across from me between Lydie and Ryan.

I am fucked.

So much for trying to figure out what to do or say.

I swallow and await the first move.

"Ms. Katrina Roberts, this meeting is being videotaped and audio recorded. Do you object?" The General Counsel states.

I shake my head, my throat too dry to form words.

"Ms. Roberts, kindly respond verbally," the General Counsel says.

"Yes, sir. I mean no, sir, I do not object," I answer as I lick my lips nervously.

Come on, Kat Roberts. Get yourself together! I chide.

The General Counsel presses a button, then turns to Lachlan.

He stares at me from across the table. Unable to hold his unblinking assessment of me, my gaze flicks to Lydie. She, too, stares at me in silence. I avert my eyes to the center of the table. Another minute passes before Lachlan speaks.

"Ms. Roberts, we have irrefutable proof you met with Chester Stewart of Stewart Scotch and provided him with confidential information about Jackson Corporation," Lachlan pauses to gauge my reaction.

I school my face in an effort to avoid giving even the slightest sign of guilt. Then I wait for him to continue. Meanwhile, I fear my heart will burst right out of my chest.

"Disclose all you shared with him," Lachlan demands.

I shift in my seat.

What the hell am I going to do?

My gaze lifts to Lachlan. He's immovable. A glance at Lydie reveals the same stoic expression. Last, I peek at the General Counsel. Another controlled stare.

Bloody hell!

Well, as they say, the cat's out of the bag. All of my hard work to seek revenge ends now. The concern for Chet's death threat looms large. If I confess, they will know and destroy Chet and me. Fuck! The revenge seemed good in theory, but now…

"Ms. Roberts, kindly answer the question."

The General Counsel's words snap me back to the office. The magnitude of the situation nearly breaks me.

I nod, then correct myself and respond affirmatively.

Kat Roberts, you have no other choice.

Words spill from my mouth as I recount each bit of intel I stole and gave to Chet. The Head of Technology taps on his tablet. The General Counsel jots down notes on a yellow legal pad. Lachlan and Lydie continue to stare at me.

By the end, I sit back, exhausted. However, relief washes over me like a soothing balm. I take a deep cleansing breath à la Starr and await my fate.

"Ms. Roberts, that covers the extent of your activities?" The General Counsel asks.

I blink and swallow.

Bloody hell. The cameras and audio equipment I installed in Lachlan's office suit.

I clear my throat and add to my list of confessions.

The Head of Technology nods at Lachlan.

"Our team found the devices. Any others anywhere?" He asks.

I confirm no others.

"One final question. Why?" Lachlan asks.

"*One final question. Why?*"

The question reverberates in my head. It increases in volume until all I hear is a roar.

My eyes close as I try to push the sound from my head. I need to clear my mind. Focus, Kat Roberts!

I swallow and shake my head. One last attempt to shake myself free of the guilt, remorse, pain. My eyes open. They settle on Lachlan with a plea for understanding.

His gaze is cool, assessing.

A deep cleansing breath and my lips part.

"Lachlan, what I'm about to say is extremely personal to the Jackson family. It would be best to limit those who hear to you, Lydie, and the General Counsel, as he cannot disclose your affairs," I respond. And wait.

Lydie glances at Lachlan, who continues to stare at me. His eyes narrow slightly at the mention of affairs. Despite his poker face, I sense his mind working to figure out what the bloody hell I mean by my cryptic response. Lydie returns her equally cool gaze to me. She waits for her brother's lead.

"Give us the room," Lachlan commands. Once only the four of us remain, he continues. "Answer the question, Ms. Roberts."

Okay, Katrina Roberts, *smiogaid suas, nighean!*

"Iain Jackson," I state with my chin held high.

Lachlan cocks his head.

Lydie frowns.

They glance at one another. Silently, the siblings ask if the other knows the name. Lydie arches an elegant eyebrow. Lachlan looks at me. And waits for me to explain myself.

"I assume neither of you knows the name," I say as my eyes flick from one to the other. Then I try a different name—perhaps more familiar. "Angus Jackson?"

Lachlan and Lydie glance at one another again. This time, recognition blooms in their emerald green eyes. As one, they turn their gazes to me.

"Not that we're here to entertain you with our family's history. However, Angus Jackson is our father, Connor's great-great-grandfather, and a former head of Jackson Corporation," Lachlan responds. "Get on with it, Ms. Roberts."

I nod, sensing I better wrap it up, or risk Lachlan losing his patience. But he'll want to hear what I have to say. So I don't let his demeanor deter me. This isn't my fault in any way.

"You do not know Iain Jackson because his father disowned him and decreed his name would never be mentioned by the family or anyone else ever again. Angus obliterated Iain from the Jackson family record," I say. Then pause to allow them to process that bit of information, as the rest is sure to shock them.

"His father is Angus Jackson. His brother is Errol Jackson—the second son—who took his place after Angus banned Iain from the family," I add, for further clarification.

Lachlan focuses on me even more intently. Lydie scans my face.

"Iain—as the heir apparent—was expected to step into his father's shoes as the head of Jackson Corporation and as the Marquess of Huntly. Iain chose to follow his dream of being a painter. In fact, his studio was the watchtower at Jackson Castle. Angus destroyed it when Iain forsook his hereditary place. You restored it beautifully, Mr. Jackson," I say.

Lachlan's mouth opens, then he closes it as his eyes narrow to slits. His brain begins to process my words and my recent actions.

But I'm not finished. Yet.

"Iain left the family seat with his lover and muse without a pence from the Jackson fortune. They moved to Glasgow—the culture capital of Scotland—to pursue his dream. Angus forbid Iain to use the Jackson name," I say.

Further dawning appears on Lachlan's face. He sits forward and appraises mine.

"Iain changed his last name to his mother's maiden name," I say, then pause as my eyes move from Lachlan to Lydie and back.

Lydie starts to speak. But I raise my hand to stop her.

"Iain changed his last name from Jackson to Roberts. Iain Jackson cum Roberts is my great-great-grandfather and your great great granduncle," I finish with my chin raised higher.

Let them challenge me. I'm ready.

And just like that…

"What is the meaning of this, Ms. Roberts?" The General Counsel bellows as he sits forward in his chair. "What proof do you have of these claims?"

"Where do you get such information?" Lydie asks at the same time.

I ignore them and lock eyes with Lachlan.

Further recognition fills his emerald green eyes so like mine. Where his hair is sable brown—like my siblings and father—my Titian hair comes from Iain's muse and lover. The woman in the portrait that hangs prominently in Ridel Gallery. The portrait of the woman Lachlan mused resembled me. How rightly so.

My entire life, I wondered why my red hair differed from my family. Later, I discovered the reason.

"The unknown painter with initials IJ and IR at Ridel Gallery. You want us to believe the painter is Iain Jackson, then Iain Roberts, the woman his lover, and you their descendant? Thus a distant cousin of ours?" Lachlan asks with an unreadable expression on his face.

Come on, Katrina Roberts. Don't allow his cool demeanor to ruffle you. You have the proof.

I sit straighter in my chair and maintain eye contact as I respond.

"Yes, Lachlan."

Lydie snorts.

The General Counsel blusters more outrage.

Lachlan returns my stare.

"What proof do you have of these claims?" He repeats the Counsel's question.

"Iain's journals, his signet ring, and his sketchbooks," I respond.

"Where did you get Iain's items?" Lachlan asks.

I close my eyes for a moment to collect myself. Emotions wash over me.

"My father—Ramsey Roberts—died of a heart attack. When I went through his personal effects, I found a key to a safe deposit box at the Bank of Scotland in Glasgow. The bank manager told me someone paid for it in perpetuity, and no one visited the box for decades according to their records. I was the first to open it in some time," I answer, then take a breath.

Lachlan waits for me to continue.

"What I found shocked me. The bank manager assured me the contents were untouched," I say.

"Who else is aware of the safe deposit box's contents?" Lachlan asks.

I shake my head, then correct myself and respond verbally when the General Counsel taps the recorder.

"No one," I respond.

Lydie frowns.

"You mean to tell us you did not share the information with your family or with Chet Stewart?" She asks.

I shift my gaze to hers and respond, "Yes. I did not tell anyone."

"Why not?" Lachlan asks.

I sit back and close my eyes. These past few days, my emotions run like a rollercoaster. One minute I'm high on —dare I say—love. The next I plummet with the fear of being found out. A reprieve, now this low of lows.

Bloody hell.

I open my eyes and pin my gaze on Lachlan's face. The pain and anger of being stuck on the poor side while he and his siblings grew up in the lap of luxury, pampered, catered to by the world. The fact darkens the light of happiness I experienced with Harris. A brief pleasurable moment in their world. Betrayal by my great great-great-grandfather for disowning his blood simply because his son wanted to follow his dream.

Dreams…

All the Jackson cum Roberts men had their *dreams*. Never solid and responsible. Quick schemes, flighty. My father and Payton included on the list. The women in their lives left to suffer for falling in love with dreamers.

"When I read Iain's journals… The pain he felt from being tossed aside by his family. No one contacted him. Not one letter he wrote returned with a response. He lost contact with the rest of the Jackson *family*. The only person he had was his muse and lover. But he never recovered from the loss of his loved ones. One of his entries broke my heart…" I trail off as tears fill my eyes.

I swipe at my cheeks and glance out of the window.

"It was this very office in which his father told him to go," I say. Then for Lachlan and Lydie's sakes, I recall from memory Iain's viewpoint of the last time he saw his father and brother.

"Hello, Father, brother."

I nod at each of them when I enter my father's office.

My brother greets me with a sorrowful smile.

"Glad you can join us," my father responds gruffly. His dissatisfied scowl takes me in from head to toe, not at all pleased with my attire of a smock shirt, trousers., and paint-stained brogues. "You could not find an appropriate suit? Never mind. Sit."

Once I'm seated beside my brother, our father settles behind his massive wooden desk. My artist's eye takes in the ornate carvings appreciatively. A master craftsman's finest work.

"Have you come to your senses and will take your proper place as the next to run our family's company?"

My father's question draws me from my musings.

I glance over at him.

We stare at one another for a heartbeat.

I look away first.

He sighs.

"With all due respect, Father. We have had this conversation many times before. I intend to follow my passion. I do not care to

follow in your footsteps," I respond as I bring my gaze back to his angry one.

My brother cringes beside me. He knows the roof is about to blow off the building. Again.

Surprisingly, our father remains silent. He studies my face for any sign of a change of heart.

I remain steadfast and hold his gaze.

He rises to tower over me.

"From this day forward, I disown you and no one will speak your name ever again. Your presence erased from this family's history completely. As I speak, your studio is being destroyed and your harlot removed. Leave this city with what you have at this moment. Do not let the sunset find you here. Never return. Contact none of us again. Ever. Do you understand?"

His pronouncement sends a chill through my very soul.

The sense of doom comes to fruition.

I scan his face, hoping to find a crack in his countenance. Nothing. I turn to my brother, and he glances away from my imploring gaze. My eyes shift back to my father. He stands indomitable and raises his hand to point at the door.

"Leave now, or I will have you escorted from the premises," he commands.

I never guessed my father would go so far as to banish me. To obliterate me from our family. Ruin my dreams.

I open my mouth to implore him. But as he rounds the desk with an expression of such detestation, I flinch. Then suck in a breath when he grips the back of my shirt and lifts me from the leather chair.

Forcefully, he pushes me towards the door.

I stumble before I catch myself.

One last glance over my shoulder reveals his imposing figure glaring at me and my brother's stiff back as he stares straight ahead. No remorse. No sympathy.

"Goodbye, Father, brother."

I turn my gaze back to Lachlan, then to Lydie.

Emotions swirl on their faces.

"I hated the Jacksons and sought revenge for Iain's sake. I wanted you to pay for the pain and hardship Angus Jackson caused not only his son, but also his descendants through the years. The last with my father, who died a dreamer at a young age, leaving my mother to take care of their four young children on the salary of a cleaner for rich people. Countless lives impacted because Angus was angry his son didn't want to follow in his footsteps as head of Jackson Corporation. To disown him? Obliterate him from history? A travesty," I say with a shake of my head.

I lean forward and continue.

"I decided to use Chet Stewart to help destroy your family and to get paid millions by him for the intel I provided. I had no remorse whatsoever. Perhaps it's the cold blood in my veins inherited from Angus. But then I got to know you and the current Jacksons. You treated me well as you do your employees. I saw a different side of the Jacksons than what history proved. I grew to admire you—particularly you, Lydie. A strong, intelligent, polished woman who can go toe to toe with men, run a business, and maintain her femininity. In fact, all the Jackson and Steele women I admire. Women I dreamed of being like when I was a child working odd jobs to help my Mum take care of my siblings."

Lydie tilts her head as she watches me.

"Then there's Harris. At first, I saw him as a means to get closer to the Jacksons and to avoid detection. But he took me by surprise, and I fell for him. Now... Who knows? He'll hate me, I'm sure..." I add with a sad shake of my head.

"Towards the end, I realized revenge was wrong. It wouldn't take away the pain. Only cause more of it for others who also don't deserve heartache. I was going to tell Chet no more, especially after he demanded I give him intel about STEELE Technology and Cyber Security. To use Harris or to access files on his computer. I decided no way would I go that far and no more on Jackson Corporation," I say, then swallow as the memory of Chet's threat looms large. Particularly since I confessed it all.

"The other night at the gallery, Chet indicated he would kill me if I told—"

"He what?!"

"That's absurd!"

"No!"

I bite the corner of my lower lip and nod.

Even after all I told them, Lachlan and Lydie have concern for me. Oh, Katrina Roberts, what have you done?

"Kat, we will handle Chet Stewart," Lachlan's statement draws my attention back to him. "However, we need to examine Iain's items, and you and your siblings will need to provide DNA for familial proof along with whatever our

General Counsel requests. What you did is inexcusable despite the circumstances. We will decide next steps and let you know the outcome of our decision shortly. A security detail will escort you from the premises and follow you around the clock. So do not try to flee. Do you understand?"

I nod since tears clog my throat.

Lachlan repeats the question for a verbal response.

"Yes, I understand," I answer shakily as the enormity of the situation hits me in the chest.

He rises from his seat and strides toward the doors of his office. Moment later, the Head of Security and two guards dressed in dark suits with ear communication devices escort me from Jackson Town House.

I take a moment to stare up at the beginning and the end of my family's involvement. My dawdling spurs the guards to take me by the elbow and lead me to a Range Rover for the ride to my flat.

Once at home, I give Iain's items and my hairbrush in a plastic baggie to them. They'll collect the rest from my family. The General Counsel forbid me to speak with them. He'll use a ruse to get their DNA samples. One guard leaves to take the package to Lachlan while the other remains outside of my flat's front door. Completely drained, I collapse on my bed and cry.

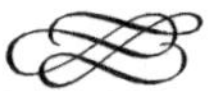

"What do you mean Kat's a *Jackson*???" I shout as I jump to my feet.

Lachlan called me to his and Haley's Aberdeen penthouse after he and Lydie met with Kat. Once again, we gather with my siblings along with their spouses, our parents, Lucien, and Laurent on the oversized flat-screen television. Uncle Connor, Aunt Lucie, and Lydie join us in Lachlan's' home office.

He told us about the confession and unexpected revelation Kat made. Then showed Iain Jackson's journals, signet ring, and sketchbooks to us. I stare at them on the coffee table in utter disbelief.

"Well, we *cannot* accept what Kat said without the DNA proof. I have no recollection of an Iain Jackson. Angus and Errol, yes. We were always told the watchtower crumbled from lack of upkeep and the harsh elements. We need more than what the duplicitous lass says since she lied to us all this time," Uncle Connor states adamantly.

"Exactly. She even lied about her parents' death in a car accident caused by a drunk driver, just like mine. I bet she only said that to gain sympathy from me. Terrible," Lola says sadly.

Baz puts his arm around her to pull her close to his side. She leans her forehead against his shoulder, but not before I catch a glimpse of tears in her hazel eyes.

I clench my fists.

Dammit!

Kat hurt not only me but also my family. Lola doesn't deserve to relive the anguish of her parents' death at a young age. This is beyond fucked up.

"What have you decided to do about Kat?" Baz asks. "And it's a damn good thing she didn't give that fucker Stewart any information on STEELE, or I'd have her ass. What's worse, she upset my wife with her bullshit, and she used my brother for her own gain. Not cool, Lach. At. All."

Lachlan shakes his head in disgust.

"Yeah, Kat fucked up big time. Aside from an initial launch plan and some other fixable information, she gave Stewart fake intel, thanks to Lydie. The Head of Technology is already working with Haley's team to shore up our cyber security," Lachlan responds.

"This is all my fault for thinking with the wrong head," I grumble as I pace the floor. You big dummy.

My mind works overtime to make sense of what we learned and line it up with Kat's behavior towards me. No wonder we connected so quickly. She saw me as a dolt she could charm with her Siren's call to gain access to our family and our tryst as a smokescreen for her illicit activities.

I thought she was a Bond Girl. Turns out she's 007 himself with her expert subterfuge…

On top of it all, she's a Jackson??? A long-lost, disowned, and forgotten relative??? Who sought revenge??? For real? Give me a break.

I cannot believe I fell for the okey-doke…

The last forty-eight hours have been torture. I ignored Kat's calls and text messages. Even when she progressed to desperate pleas. The front desk staff at STEELE Aberdeen followed my directive and turned her away from the property. I awoke from a wet dream with jizz all over my abs and my pecs. What am I? A horny teenager? It's been surreal to say the least.

And Kat's a *Jackson*!

That's why she lingered in front of the watchtower at Jackson Castle when we rode past it. She knew it was Iain's studio. Even then, she held her feelings in check with a blank expression on her face. I thought it odd when I took her on a tour of the Castle, and she had so many questions. She claimed it was the history buff in her, and her love for the great houses and castles of Scotland.

I scrub my hand over my face and stop pacing.

Un-fucking-believable.

"Harris, sit. You're making me dizzy," Haley says as she pats the spot on the sofa next to her. When I throw myself down, she continues. "No need to beat yourself up about it. Kat is the one who's in the wrong. Hell, she had us all fooled. But being a Jackson is definitely wild."

"I agree with Haley, Harris. You did nothing wrong. I'm truly disappointed because Kat fits in so well with you and the rest of the family," our mother says. She shakes her head and smiles at me with motherly affection.

"As they say, Karma is not kind to those who do wrong," Starr—forever the yogi—adds. "Wish her the best and let the Universe handle her fate."

Malcolm snorts.

"My Angel, then call me Mr. Universe because *I* will handle Katrina *Roberts*," he retorts. "Lachlan, just say the word, bro."

Lachlan nods at *The Enforcer*.

"Thanks, bro. We expect to have the DNA samples by the end of day today and results rushed. With that in hand, we'll know the veracity of her claim to the Jackson name—"

"Not that she or her family will get a bloody thing from us!" Uncle Connor interjects vehemently, then continues as his Scottish accent thickens with his anger. "Had she come forward with her findings like a civilized lass, we could have had a proper discussion. Blood is blood. I may not agree with banishing a child for their decision to not carry out their familial duty—or attempt, Lachlan. But those were different times."

Lachlan's face heats at the mention of his initial reluctance to take on the mantle of CEO and Chairman of the

Board at Jackson Corporation upon Uncle Connor's retirement. It wasn't until he and Haley began to date did Lachlan use his title Earl of Aboyne. Undoubtedly, he can relate to Iain's desire to follow his passion. Albeit, Lachlan had a different reason.

"I agree with you Da. And as you say, *blood is blood*. So I'm less inclined to press charges—"

"What?!"

"Are you kidding me right now?!"

"Say what?!"

The room erupts into an uproar as everyone speaks at once. Those on the television screen voice their opinions just as vociferously as those in person. I too can't believe Lachlan's proclamation. Then I think of Kat in jail. She'd never survive it. I shudder at the thought of her in a cell.

Haley whistles, and silence descends.

"I'd like to hear Lachlan's reason," she says once she has everyone's attention.

We turn to him and wait.

He kisses the side of her head and murmurs in her ear. She grins.

Lachlan faces us and goes on.

"The initial assessment of the information she stole shows no major impact on Jackson Corporation. The surveillance videos and audio prove I'm a hard-ass worker" —we chuckle along with him—"I empathize with her and her line of descendants' plight."

Lachlan pauses to glance at each of us before he continues, "I propose Kat leaves Scotland in one week and she never returns without our advance knowledge. Her family —if truly uninvolved—can remain. She can keep the money Stewart paid her since she used it to support her family. However, we will monitor her activities. Should she hack anyone else, we will press charges. Thoughts?"

Again, everyone speaks at once. But Lachlan calls for Leonie first.

"Kat's comments about the *posh life* and how impressed she was by the things we do make sense now," she says. The girls nod and murmur their agreement. "I noticed she became less guarded the more time she spent with us. She was wistful when we last spoke about the upcoming holidays in Capri and Verbier during Labor Day. Kat listened raptly. Perhaps she saw her error but didn't know what to do to fix the situation. And for Chet to threaten to kill Kat so publicly, well... *Mon Dieu!*"

Aunt Lucie speaks next and agrees with Leonie's assessment. But adds she doesn't trust Kat, and she would have to prove herself before she could gain it back. Our mother expresses a similar sentiment.

Lachlan hears everyone out, then turns to me.

"Your thoughts, Harris?" He asks.

I nod and respond.

"On a personal level, Kat fooled me once and will not have the opportunity to do it again. From a business perspective, I take responsibility for not paying attention to Jackson Corporation's tech activity. So, as much as I want to blame Kat, I have to share some with her. Fortunately, she didn't access pertinent information. To press charges makes it public, and you don't want Jackson Corporation to appear vulnerable. That would give hackers ideas. At the same time, it reflects poorly on STEELE Technology and Cyber Security's ability to protect our clients. So, from a selfish standpoint, you should not press charges. Banish her. I did already."

Haley rubs my arm. Our mother and Aunt Lucie tsk in sympathy.

I shrug and put a cocky smile on my face.

"So don't blame me if I don't get married any time soon, Mom. It's playadom for this old chap," I declare. "I hear LEVELS London Calling."

KAT

"*O*h, Kat, honey! Why did we have to come here? Is this where you work? Why did those men bring us here?"

My Mum whispers rapid-fire questions to me as she sits on the couch in Lachlan's private reception area. Her eyes scan the room as she twists her fingers in her lap.

Charlotte leans across me to whisper her concerns, too.

Michael sits in a chair. His eyes bright with awe as he scans the room, but for a different reason. He loves architecture and design. Jackson Town House must strike him as a masterpiece inside and out.

Payton scowls at me from the other chair. As usual, he's put out. Not that he's missing work or anything important. Once again, he's between jobs.

I haven't been able to speak with them since Lachlan forbid any contact. As much trouble as I'm in, I didn't want to provoke him by disobeying. I did not know they would be here today.

Lachlan had the security guards escort me to his offices an hour ago. He told me his decision to ban me from Scotland without returning unless with his advance knowledge. Thankfully, my family can stay. Relief washed over me twice. When he said he wouldn't press charges, and when he told me I could keep the money from Chet. The caveat of no more hack jobs or face prosecution from Jackson Corporation and whomever I was to infiltrate.

I thanked him and asked about Chet. Lachlan told me not to concern myself with him. So I relaxed. But I'll make sure Chet can't find me wherever I go. I have one week to figure out just where that will be…

"Listen, I don't have time to sit in this hoity-toity office all day. I demand to know what's going on."

Payton's irate voice pulls me from my musings. He stands before Gladys as she sits at her desk.

One of the security guards steps to him, and Payton glares back. As he opens his mouth to speak, the double doors to Lachlan's inner office open. His eyes flick amongst us before they settle on Payton. A nod and the security guard moves away from Payton to resume his stance by the wall beside the other guard.

"Payton, kindly come in," Lachlan says, then turns to us sitting on the sofa and chair. He gestures towards the office. "Mrs. Roberts, Kat, Michael, and Charlotte."

We follow Payton—who grumbles under his breath into the office. The elliptical conference table extends to accommodate my family, Lachlan, Lydie, the General Counsel, and me. We take our seats.

"Before we begin, this meeting is being videotaped and audio recorded. Do you object?" The General Counsel states.

My Mum and siblings glance at me, and I nod. We give our consent.

"Mrs. Roberts, allow me to introduce ourselves. I am Lachlan Jackson, CEO and Chairman of the Board of Jackson Corporation and the Earl of Aboyne. This is my sister Lady Lydie Jackson, COO and First Vice President of the Board. And Jackson Corporation General Counsel Ryan Dixon," Lachlan states.

My Mum glances at me nervously. I smile to reassure her, and she turns to each of them and murmurs a greeting.

"My, my, my, what impressive titles you have. Congratulations. Now, what is the purpose of this meeting?" Payton cuts in as he glares at Lachlan.

Lachlan flicks his gaze at my obnoxious brother and assesses him coolly. Unruffled, Lachlan takes a moment before he continues. Payton squirms under the intense stare. Satisfied, Lachlan shifts his gaze back to my Mum.

"M—My Lord, I'm so sorry. Please excuse my son's behavior—"

Lachlan shakes his head.

"Mrs. Roberts, no need to apologize. He's a grown man who's free to speak his mind and face whatever consequences come of his actions," Lachlan says.

Payton snorts.

I close my eyes and sigh. Bloody hell. For once, can he just not embarrass us?

When I reopen them, Lydie stares at me. What seems to be a sympathetic look appears briefly in her emerald green eyes. Then her face blanks again, and she glances away. She studies my Mum and siblings while Lachlan speaks.

"We brought you to Jackson Town House to inform you of news we received recently. We were aware Angus Jackson—our paternal great-great-great-grandfather and the former Marquess of Huntly—had one son named Errol. What we learned is Angus had a first-born son named Iain. Angus disowned Iain since he declined to follow in his father's footsteps. Iain chose his art—painting. Errol became the heir. Our line branches from Errol.

"Iain changed his surname from Jackson to Roberts and moved from Aberdeenshire to Glasgow with his muse and lover. Your husband—Ramsay Roberts—is his descendant, as are your offspring. The DNA results confirm the lineage. Were you aware of this information?"

My Mum swallows and shakes her head.

"Mrs. Roberts, kindly respond verbally," Ryan says.

"S—Sorry. No, I was not aware," she responds as her eyes flick from Lachlan to me.

"You mean to tell me we're actually Jacksons, as in the name of this building and company? We should be filthy rich with fancy titles like you lot? What do you do here, anyway?" Payton leans forward and peppers Lachlan with questions.

Please let the floor open, and I fall through the hole.

Better yet, shut Payton up.

My silent prayers go unanswered as he continues to drill Lachlan. The dollar signs practically bulge from my brother's greedy eyes.

I offer a prayer of thanks I—not Payton—found Iain's items. Payton would have sold everything to the local pawnshop for a few pounds. Fortunately, the paintings are safe at Ridel Gallery. Although I wish we could keep Iain's works in our family.

The General Counsel answers Payton's questions succinctly, and Lachlan continues.

"We cannot make up for the past. However, we can offer all of you the opportunity to have stability and growth in your lives. If you so choose to do so," Lachlan says and looks at Payton for the last bit. With only knowing my brother for a few minutes, Lachlan can already tell Payton is shiftless. How bloody embarrassing.

Charlotte clears her throat, and Lachlan moves his gaze to her.

"So we're cousins?" She asks, then continues when Lachlan confirms. "Do we change our names back to Jackson, or do we remain Roberts?"

"Or do we have a choice?" Michael asks.

"What's the offer?" Payton cuts in. "And it better be worth it."

Lydie snorts and pins Payton with a withering glare.

"Your track record proves you fail to maintain any job, and you limited your level of education by dropping out in your sixth year. And not to help your family. No.

Then and now, you spend more time in the pub around the corner from your mother's flat than you do helping to support her. So whatever the *offer*, it corresponds to what you deserve," Lydie scoffs as her eyes flash green fire.

Payton shrivels beneath her scathing remarks. *The Shark* took the bite out of him. Finally.

"The eldest Jackson alive—our father Connor Jackson, Marquess of Huntly—acknowledges you as Jacksons, despite his great-great-grandfather's disownment of Iain. Therefore, the choice is yours for your last name," Lachlan responds to Charlotte and to Michael, while ignoring Payton.

"Mrs. Roberts, STEELE Glasgow has an opening for a housekeeping supervisor. With your years of experience, you qualify for the position. The salary is over three times your current pay plus superb benefits with paid time off. If that interests you, the hiring manager will meet with you this week. My personal assistant, Gladys, will schedule the appointment," Lachlan says.

My Mum gasps as she brings her calloused fingertips to her mouth that hangs open in shock. The skin on her hands leathery and wrinkled from the harsh cleaning solutions she uses every single day despite the lotions I give to her. Wide eyes flick to me, then to Lachlan.

A slight smile plays at his lips. He nods in encouragement.

"Why, thank you Mr. Jack—"

"Lachlan," he interjects.

My Mum nods and clears her throat before she accepts the offer.

"Charlotte, since your university covers your fees, we will pay for your expenses until you graduate. You may continue to work. But I advise you to focus on your studies to maintain your impressive grade point average. After this meeting, you will sit with Gladys to review your expenses and to determine a monthly allowance," Lachlan says.

Charlotte gasps.

He continues, "If you wish to work within a Jackson Corporation or a STEELE International, Inc. division after you graduate, let us know. We will arrange a meeting between you and the appropriate parties to determine the best fit. Take time to consider your goals and to research both companies."

"Thank you so very much!" Charlotte exclaims. Her emerald green eyes shine with unshed tears of gratitude.

Mine fill it too, and I swipe at the corners.

"Michael, you've helped your Mum and sister through your jobs and time. But you should hone your innate talent in architectural renderings and your passion for the field through coursework. The University of Strathclyde in Glasgow ranks amongst the highest in the UK for the study of architecture. If you wish to attend, we will arrange for a tutor who will prepare you for the application process. Should you gain acceptance—which we believe will happen—we will pay for your studies and expenses. STEELE International has divisions that require designs for residential and commercial projects. They handle

Jackson Corporation's projects. Internships and a permanent position could be available to you should you wish to pursue a career at STEELE. Again, take time to decide, then get in touch with Gladys," Lachlan says.

"No need for time, Lachlan. I thank you and accept your offer!" Michael says as he stands and extends his hand across the table. His emerald green eyes spark with joy. At last, he'll have the opportunity to focus on his love of buildings without hinderance.

My heart clenches at my younger brother's happiness. Like me, Michael spends most of his life helping our mother and Charlotte. Never a complaint, only a smile. As he does now with a grin bigger than the Cheshire Cat's smile.

Lachlan rises and takes Michael's hand in a firm grip as he nods at him.

"Very well. After Charlotte meets with Gladys, you may speak with her," Lachlan responds with a smile.

They sit. The room grows silent. Our eyes turn toward Payton, who leans forward. Expectation makes his emerald green eyes glow.

Instead of addressing Payton, Lachlan brings his gaze to my Mum.

"Mrs. Roberts—"

"Allison, please," she cuts in with a more confident smile.

Lachlan returns her smile and nods.

"Allison, since Charlotte lives on campus and Michael will soon, we arranged for you to choose from three one-bedroom flats in Glasgow. We will purchase one in your name and cover your moving expenses and the cost of furnishings," he says.

My Mum shakes her head.

"Lachlan, you've offered so much already. No need for you to burden yourself any further," she says. Pride straightens her spine.

Then it's his turn to shake his head.

"No burden whatsoever. You should live in comfort," he insists.

My Mum glances at me, and I smile in encouragement. She turns back to Lachlan and thanks him.

"Last, we purchased Iain's paintings—those displayed at Ridel Gallery and the others they found. We will investigate any further works of his and acquire them should they exist. All reside in the Jackson family archives along with his journals, signet ring, and sketchbooks," Lachlan states.

Surprised by his decision, I jerk in my chair. My eyes widen as I stare at him in disbelief.

How could he just take everything? They're *our* family's heirlooms!

Lachlan cocks an eyebrow.

I meet his stare, then lower my eyes in defeat. Can I really blame him? No.

"Well then. Any questions?" Lachlan asks.

"Yeah! What's in it for me? What's my offer, *Lachlan*?" Payton demands. Fire replaces the glow of expectation in his eyes as they flash.

Lachlan hardens his expression.

"Nothing," he responds. "Should you take from your mother or move in with her, you will answer to me. The time is now for you to assume responsibility for yourself."

Lachlan passes his business card to my Mum, Charlotte, and to Michael.

"You may reach me via the number and email here and my mobile number on the reverse side," he says. "Any questions?"

His gaze flicks from one to the other as he repeats his question and ignores Payton.

"Where the bloody hell am I to live?" He asks.

"Your current flat," Lachlan responds. Then he stands. "Gladys will meet with you now."

Everyone except for Payton rises and thanks Lachlan and Lydie.

"Fuck you, Lachlan Jackson! Bloody wanker!" Payton shouts. "You won't get away with this—"

The two security guards enter the office and take Payton by the arms. They drag him from the room as he continues to hurl insults.

Again, my face reddens as I plead for the floor to engulf me.

HARRIS

"Why, hello there, Harris Steele. It's been a while, darling. Care to play?"

A statuesque blonde with a killer, lithe figure stands before me. Her cerulean blue eyes skim over my body, from my face to my crotch and back. A heavenly gleam fills her orbs. She's more than satisfied with my package. I must say even flaccid, it's magnificent. A sight to behold.

I smirk.

She takes my look as permission to engage. The pointy tip of her red-polished fingernail trails over my pec down the ridges of my eight-pack abs to rim my navel before continuing her pursuit of perfection.

My cock thumps at her erotic touch.

But my mind leaps back to the conversation with Haley yesterday afternoon.

"Harris, I know guys process breakups differently from women. We sit around with the shades drawn and eat pints of

butter pecan ice cream as we vent about the pain to our girl-friends. For days. Hell, even for months. No interest in another relationship for a while. But guys? You jump right back into the dating or fucking scene within a blink of the eye. Whiplash," my twin tells me as we talk on the phone.

She pauses when I grumble but goes on. Unstoppable when she gets on her soapbox...

"Don't try to deny it. I'm quite confident you've spent nights at LEVELS London. And no, I did not hack into their systems to check your attendance. I. Know. You. Harris Steele. Don't go overboard. You fell hard for she who shall not be named in a short period. Give yourself some time to recover. And I don't mean by jumping into bed with any of the more than willing members of LEVELS. Especially those who want to get their claws into the last bachelor of The STEELE Quaternity.

I'm telling you this because I love you and your pain is my pain. Also cut the crap about not marrying. You almost gave Mom a coronary. Okay?"

I hate to admit it. But Haley called it. Naturally.

Still, I'd rather partake of the fruit I gave up for months in favor of a tantalizing Siren. Besides, what I felt for Kat *Jackson* wasn't love.

On to the next one and all that.

I slip my hand around the blonde's slim hip and cup her firm ass, then give it a squeeze.

For a brief second, my mind registers her hip is more narrow and ass less round than the Siren's ample curves.

Ah well.

"Play or fuck?" I respond in a deep baritone as I pin the

sexy blonde with my most panty-melting smile.

Her pupils dilate to dark pools, leaving only the edges tinged blue. The tip of her tongue darts out to moisten her glossy lips.

"Is your pussy as wet as your mouth?" I ask with another squeeze.

The sexy blonde nods and her silky mane bobs.

I cock an eyebrow.

"Words. I will have your words," I correct her.

"Whatever you wish, Sir," she responds breathily.

I shake my head.

"Not Sir. Harris will do," I say as I rise from the barstool. With a hand on her lower back, I lead her past other members as we cross the floor of LEVELS London Peepshow.

One of the global, high-end BDSM/dance clubs created by Malcolm and Lucien. Built over several levels for dining, dancing, and to satisfy sexual desires open to members and their guests. Occasionally, non-members frequent the restaurant and party at the dance clubs. Some hoping to obtain an exclusive membership. It's a rigorous process. But oh so worth it.

I direct the blonde to a hallway with rooms on either side where behind floor-to-ceiling windows members engage in acts of role playing, Shibari, threesomes, and more. Whatever sexy fantasy one can imagine comes to life within the four walls of each room. Other members—mainly the voyeurs or those seeking foreplay inspiration—gather to watch, or peep.

I open the door to an empty room. The blonde sashays in ahead of me. With a smirk, I close the door.

No butter pecan ice cream for me.

I intend to fuck the pain away.

"HEY, cuz. When do you return to New York City? Haley went back to work, so no need for you to stay in London. I'm planning a Guys' Getaway to Puerto Rico in a couple of weeks. You game or what?"

I grin at the thought of hanging out with Laurent. It's been a while since he's busy with Yessenia, and I was with the Siren. A trip to Puerto Rico with my boys sounds like just what I need to keep that troublesome redhead out of *my* head.

"Oh, I am so game, cuz. Count me in," I respond.

"Finally, you'll get your head back on straight and let that girl go already," Laurent adds. "I don't give a damn she's my newfound cousin…"

He grumbles some more about the Siren. I don't blame him. She got to all of us.

When he stops, I cut in and tell him to send the details over. After we hang up. I get back to work at my office at STEELE London.

Haley returned full time. But she splits her days between here and Aberdeen. So it's true I do not need to remain in the UK. It's been almost a week. Time to get da steppin', as Martin says.

"Hey, Hal. Before I ask my pilot to set the flight plan for my return to the City, I want to check in with you. Do you still need me here or no?" I ask when my twin answers her mobile.

"Hey! No, I'm all good. Tomorrow I fly in for the weekly status meetings with my team. You don't need to attend. Lachlan mentioned Laurent's Guys' Getaway. Are you going? Please say yes, Harris!" She responds.

I can picture her holding her breath as she waits for my answer. She hasn't been on me about my post-relationship activities since our conversation earlier this week. But I know she still thinks about it. The mother in her makes Haley worry even more about me, aside from our twin connection.

I'll ease her stress. With a grin, I confirm I'm going to Puerto Rico and look forward to hanging with my boys. Her relief is palpable as she exhales and claps her hands.

Now I can see her shimmying in delight. Silly girl.

"Excellent! Well, safe travels. Call me when you land," Haley adds before we end our call.

I ask my personal assistant to arrange for a maid to pack my things at STEELE Mayfair and contact my pilot for the flight plan, then get back to work.

As long as I remain busy, my mind doesn't have a chance to fall back on the loss of that redhead. At least that's what I keep telling myself.

Good luck with that, Harris…

All the fucking in the world just doesn't compare to the lovemaking my Kitty Kat and I shared.

"Thank you for your more than generous gift, Kat! I mean, your volunteerism at Aberdeen Children's Center has been marvelous, and we're grateful. But your donation… Well, it's so unexpected…"

I smile at the director as she gushes on about the money I gave to the center.

It's my parting gift before I leave Aberdeen. I made it in the Jackson name with Lachlan's approval. Using the money I received from Chet Stewart pleased Lachlan. And it just felt right to me. I'd rather have a clean slate to start my new life.

My new life as Katrina Jackson.

I chose to take the name not only for the fact it is our true name. But because Katrina Roberts is finished. No more scheming. No more lies. Plus, Chet knows me by my former name, and I'd rather he not pursue me once Lachlan gets at him.

I shake my head to clear the thoughts so I can focus on the director. I tell her I'll spend another day with the kids to have a chance to say goodbye to them, the staff, and to the other volunteers. The rest of the day goes well. The lads and lasses give me big hugs, and the staff surprises me with a cake. I leave the center to a round of applause and best wishes.

Afterwards, I take the bus to Glasgow.

As I glance out the window, the realization Iain left Aberdeen for Glasgow at the direction of another Jackson as I do now saddens me. However, I deserve it. Iain wanted to follow his passion, and I sought revenge. One for a good reason. The other bad. History repeats itself in strange ways.

I awake to the bus driver shaking my shoulder. The past week took its toll on me. Worry led to no sleep. The rhythmic motions of the bus lulled me to a dreamless slumber until we arrived in Glasgow. I thank the driver and take a taxi to my Mum's new flat.

True to his word, Lachlan arranged for her to select one in a posh neighborhood and for her new job at STEELE Glasgow. The same for Charlotte and Michael. We're spending the rest of the weekend together before I fly to London.

I swallow back tears and watch the streets of my youth pass beyond the window of the taxi. Memories flood my brain. Even thoughts of my father fill my mind. I sigh and lean back in the seat. Tears spill from beneath my closed eyelids.

New beginnings, Katrina Jackson. Embrace the new and let go of the past.

"GOOD EVENING, MISS."

"Good evening, ma'am. How may I help you?"

The first smile since I left the center spreads across my face as the doorman then the concierge for my Mum's new flat greets me. The photos she sent only hint at the fabulous building. Crystal chandeliers hang from the triple-height coffered ceiling with matching wall sconces. My shoes sink into the plush wool rugs scattered over the travertine floors as I walk to the desk. Seating areas cluster about the lobby. A family of four sit by the window overlooking the courtyard garden.

"Good evening, I'm here to visit Mrs. Roberts, her daughter Katrina," I respond to the concierge.

My Mum kept the last name since my father isn't alive to change his or not. She wants to maintain their connection in any way she can.

The concierge rings the flat and announces me. He directs me to the private lift, and I take it to the penthouse.

"Kat, honey! You made it!" My Mum greets me when I step into the foyer. She gives me a hug and tugs my hand to lead me past the double doors into the flat.

My mouth drops open at the impressive view before me. Glasgow lit up in the night glows beyond the windows. The unobstructed panorama of the city captivates me.

"Incredible, isn't it?" My Mum asks with a broad smile.

It lights up her face as much as the stars in the inky blue sky. It's the happiest she's looked since before my father passed. And I'm happy for her.

"Absolutely," I breathe, then put my arms around her.

We stand for a moment, lost in our thoughts as we stare out the wall of windows.

"There you are, Kat!"

I glance over my shoulder to find Michael with Charlotte beside him walk into the massive living room. Charlotte dances over and bumps her hip against mine.

"Awesome, huh?" She says with a giggle.

"I say more than awesome! This is the high life!" I exclaim as I loop my arm around her waist.

Michael drapes his arms around us and rests his head on my shoulder.

"What a world of difference from our other flat," he says with a grin. Then he whispers in my ear so our Mum can't hear. "Too bad for Payton. He tried to sneak in. But Mum told him no."

"About time," Charlotte huffs.

I nod in agreement while our Mum tells me she wants to give me the grand tour.

The one bedroom, two bath flat spans half the top floor split with another penthouse accessible from a separate private lift. A terrace off the flat's front rooms extends the living space to the outdoors with chaise lounges, tables, and shrubbery. Each room decorated tastefully in classic furnishings and warm colors. The kitchen is a chef's dream. We settle in the room next to it by a roaring fire.

"So, where did you decide to go, Kat?" Michael asks. "I really wish you would stay here in Glasgow with us."

I didn't tell my family the reason for my abrupt departure, only about my desire to travel for a while. Which I will for a couple of months before I move to New York City. The director of Aberdeen Children's Center told me the nonprofit her friend works for has a position available in their offices on Fifth Avenue. With her referral, the hiring manager scheduled an interview in a few weeks. With hope, I'll get the job. If not, another opportunity will come up. New York has thousands of companies.

Most of all, it has Harris. And the chance to win his heart again.

My heart flutters at the thought. I smile at Michael and tell him it's time for each of us to follow our dreams.

HOW THE SCENE FLIPS.

I first laid eyes on Harris in the lobby of Jackson Town House as he sat on a leather chair waiting for Lachlan. The sight of Harris took my breath away. But I played it cool and professional. He was my boss' brother-in-law. Then he became my smoke screen and later my unpredicted lover.

Now, I glance around the well-appointed lobby of STEELE London as I sit on a tufted leather couch in one of the seating areas. Workers and visitors buzz about chatting amongst themselves or focused on their mobiles as they stride to and from the banks of elevators. It's just after one in the afternoon.

I expect the meeting Harris had ended, and I can catch him before he leaves for the airport. One tiny deception—and the last, I swear—garnered the information for me. There's no way I can leave the UK without apologizing to him in person. To plead for his forgiveness. And perhaps his love again?

Before I left Glasgow, I wrote letters to each of his family members—Steele and Jackson. I opened my heart to them in hopes they would understand and forgive me for my erroneous ways. Their easy acceptance of me will forever remain in my heart. I never knew people like them would care for someone like me. Carriers delivered each letter to arrive at the same time so no one would get theirs before another family member.

I tried to write the one for Harris again and again. But failed to express the depth of my feelings for him and my sorrow for hurting him so much. Words are simply not enough.

I rub my chest to ease the ache as I blink back unbidden tears.

The sound of a woman's melodious giggle followed by a man's robust laugh draws me from my musings. A glance to my left reveals a beautiful woman dressed in a navy and cream-colored Chanel suit with matching handbag and crocodile pumps. Her ruby red lips curl in a flirtatious smile as she stares up at the handsome man beside her. Her eyes dance as he grins.

Harris!

My stomach and heart clench at the same time. A gasp escapes my mouth. The hand rubbing my chest fists against my sternum.

Frozen in place, I watch as the happy couple strolls from the elevators towards the doors. Her laughter sounds brittle to my ears. Despair fills me.

Harris moved on already.

I slump back on the couch and close my eyes to erase the hurtful image of the pair. Yet it remains etched on my corneas. Burned into my brain.

Then I shake my head and admonish myself. *Smiogaid suas, nighean!*

Get it together, Katrina Jackson! Enough with the self-pity. You brought this on yourself, you liar!

A deep breath propels me from the couch. I hurry after Harris and the woman. As they walk to the door, I grasp Harris' arm.

He glances at the hand, surprised by the forcefulness of the out-of-the-blue gesture. When his eyes lift to mine, they widen, and his firm jaw falls slack.

My body comes to life in the presence of my former lover. I fight the urge to stroke his clean-shaven cheek and kiss his full lips. My nipples pebble against the silk blouse as my pussy moistens the gusset of the lace thong. I bite back a moan—whether sadness or desire, I'm unsure.

An indeterminable flare sparks in his dove gray eyes. His lips form a perfect O. So kissable, I lift to my toes. His nostrils flare.

"Harris?"

The moment's bubble bursts at the sound of the woman's voice.

Harris pulls away as a scowl mars his handsome face. His lips pull into a sneer. Anger emanates from his body and hits me in the heart.

But I persist.

"Oh, Harris! I'm so glad I caught you. Please—"

My words end abruptly when he grabs my elbow and propels me to a corner away from the woman and the flow of others as they walk through the doors.

"You cannot be serious, Katrina *Jackson*! Why did you come here?" Harris snarls as he glares down his nose at me. When I open my mouth to respond, he raises his hand and continues. "You fucking *used* me. I will not believe a damn thing you say to me. Not. A. Damn. Word. In case it's not obvious to you, let me be very clear. That little farce of you and me? Done. Do not contact me or come near me and my family ever again. Count yourself lucky for Lachlan's leniency. I would have canceled your ass."

Without a backward glance, he pivots and stalks away from me. His long, muscular legs make quick work of the distance between me and the woman who waits for him. She flicks her curious gaze from me to Harris as he nears her. Her hand on his chest, then his hand on her waist breaks me.

I watch with tears streaming down my crimson cheeks as he guides her out the door to his Rolls Royce sedan at the curb. His driver opens the rear door for them.

The woman's glance of pity before she slips onto the seat followed by Harris' back as he joins her pierces my heart. It cleaves in two.

I cover my mouth and sob uncontrollably.

"All right, boys, get ready for loads of fun in the sun. No sob stories. No drama. No business. It's time to let loose and kick it up Laurent style!"

He emphasizes his declaration by lighting a Jackson Cigar and blowing smoke up towards the endless sky full of twinkling stars and a full moon.

It's the first night of our Guys' Getaway. Laurent selected to host the four-day gathering at STEELE Dorado —a luxurious enclave for royalty, international jet setters, and celebrities on Puerto Rico's northern coast. Along with our brothers, cousins Borya Alexeyev and Anton Alexeyev, and Patrick Rockett, we took over the largest private villa with twelve bedrooms and fifteen bathrooms on the beachfront property.

To start the fun with a bang, we came to Jackson Hole —the members-only, high-end hot spot for the über-wealthy in select STEELE resorts around the globe. The thumping bass of the music from the outdoor dance club vibrates in the tropical air around us. Bodies grind to the beat while Jackson Hole dancers gyrate on elevated Lucite platforms lit from within. The atmosphere proves as hedonistic as any LEVELS club. Sex on the beach, for real.

And I'm all for it.

"Hear, hear!" I respond as I strike a match and lift it to my cigar. The strength and flavor—spicy, woody, and earthy tones—of the tobacco fills me. A hint of the rich taste of Jackson Reserve Scotch I drink adds to the pleasure. A decadent sigh escapes my parted lips as the smoke curls around my face.

No sob stories. No drama. No business.

No thoughts of that redheaded Siren.

Exactly.

"Perfect time for a quick break with the guys before the rush of the holidays starts," Roger says.

"Yeah, Dad!" Lucien teases. "Gotta play Santa for the little lads and lasses. No more ho, ho, hoes for you!"

"Don't hate on the greatness of family life, Lucien. You're not immune, you know, brother," Malcolm says with a knowing smile.

Lucien narrows his eyes and hides a smirk with a sip of Scotch from his snifter.

Obviously, something is up in his love life. But... drama-free rule.

Some guys stay in our VIP area for a rum tasting—a more mellow way to enjoy the evening. Others head for the dance floor or bar. Before I make my move, I take another sip of Scotch as I survey the rest of the club.

Borya sandwiched between two brunette beauties—twins?—on the dance floor. The former MMA world champion turned personal trainer for Baz and running buddy of Malcolm impresses the women with his massive frame. He's a killer in the cage and on the floor. His partners toss their hair and wiggle their round asses in carnal delight.

The DJ plays a good mix, perfect to entice sweet little things to let loose. I could go for a little bump and grind with one—or maybe three of them as per the norm. A snicker emerges from my mouth as I swirl the Jackson Reserve Scotch over my palate. The flavor bursts across my tastebuds then warms my chest and belly, much like the delectable essence of an aroused woman.

Well…

One woman in particular…

"Fuck!" I mutter under my breath as an unbidden image of the Siren writhing from the ministrations of my mouth, tongue, and teeth on her pussy pops into my mind. Her cries of carnal bliss fill my ears as much as her sweet nectar coats my throat. Round ass cheeks clench in my hands as she cums undone for me again and again. And again. "Fuck me…"

I shift in my seat as my cock twitches uncomfortably in the confines of my leather pants. It threatens to jab a hole straight through the crotch.

Damn that Siren!

Three weeks passed, and I still can't get her—or fuck her—out of my head. No matter how hard or how much I try. I groan and shake my head to clear it.

Then I think of Haley's description of how women and men process a breakup.

I haven't banged loads of women—a few here and there. And certainly, much less than during my original playboy days. Despite my initial reaction to make up for lost time, not much has happened. My cock misses a certain redheaded Siren. Even if my bigger head wants to ignore the ache in my heart.

Didn't Baz say I'd fall hard?

Yeah… Well…

I puff on my cigar and close my eyes as the smoke floats from my mouth. Unknowingly, my hand rubs soothing circles on my chest.

"What's eating you, mate?"

As though a kid caught with their hand in the cookie jar —pun intended—I snatch mine from my chest and clench a frustrated fist. My eyes pop open to find Patrick's questioning green-eyed gaze on me.

Another Scotsman whose family's multibillion-dollar Rockett Construction Company he leads as CEO was for decades STEELE International, Inc.'s top competitor and sought to needle us at every turn. In recent years since he met Billie, who at the time was Lola's administrative assistant, he's not out to destroy us. Although we still go head-to-head on bids aggressively. These days it's business and not personal. Not to mention he and his brothers went to Saïd Business School with Lachlan and Lydie.

Before I answer the burly Scotsman, I take another sip of my Jackson Reserve Scotch.

Like an experienced negotiator, he waits patiently for my response. He blows cigar smoke as he watches me intently.

"It's not what's eating me. Rather, who *I'm* not eating," I respond as his eyebrows knit together.

Patrick's seen me with the Siren only recently. So, I'm sure he's confused.

I shrug and continue.

"Things weren't what they seemed with the bonny lass I was dating," I clarify. "I've tried my best to forget her between the thighs of other women. Although they prove distractions, she still invades too many of my thoughts. This trip should help. Well, I hope."

He nods and lifts his snifter.

"Failing means yer playin, mate!" Patrick proclaims with a grin and a wink.

Bloody Scots' sayings. I frown and shake my head.

His grin widens as his green eyes sparkle.

"Trying and failing, but at least you are trying," he explains. "Don't let the little lass get you down, Harris. However, if she's meant to be yours again and forever, nothing will keep you apart. Trust me, mate."

He nods sagely.

I tip my snifter to his glass.

We'll see.

Meanwhile, I pat him on the shoulder as I stand and head for the dance floor. Borya could use some help with the now four beauties surrounding him.

Nothing wrong with *failing*, eh?

* * *

"CLEAR A PATH ON YOUR LEFT, slowpoke! Coming through!"

Malcolm's shout fills my earpiece as I maneuver my glider high above the lush greenery surrounding Laguna Mata Redonda.

The brilliant sun glitters like diamonds off the lake's crystal blue surface. Ripples spread across the water from the wind blowing in from Punta Mameyes. People fishing on the lake glance up as the shadows from our hang gliders skim over their boats. A few of the fishing enthusiasts wave up at us.

I change my angle of attack and tip the nose of my glider down to increase my speed. There's enough space between my brother and me to avoid a collision. So I refuse to just give way to the ardent thrill seeker. I want to experience the adrenaline rush as much as Malcolm does.

His chuckles come through the earpiece in reaction to my defiance.

A glance over my shoulder as I shift in my harness shows he's further behind me than before. I smirk.

"Get in line behind the greatest, Malcolm, my boy!" I chortle.

"Quit your shenanigans and pay attention to what you're doing," Lucien cuts in. "Safety before bravado, lads!"

We continue until we lose the ridge lift and float towards the beach. As our boots touch the ground, we run along the sand to slow our landing. Each of us make it in unharmed, naturally. The ground crew assists us with the equipment, leaving us to head for the water after we strip out of our suits and footwear.

"Race to the pontoon!" Anton yells as he runs to the shoreline.

We whoop and holler as we follow him to the waves. Upon entering the warm water of the Caribbean Sea, it eases the tension from my body. Then increases as I propel forward through the current using powerful strokes. At the pontoon, I hoist myself from the sea and high five Anton who arrived first.

"Well done, bro!" He says with barely a hint of his Russian accent. After years of being in the United States and attending Harvard University undergrad and Business School with Malcolm, Anton's native accent only sounds when he's drinking vodka or excited.

The others join us to lie out beneath the sun's rays. We shoot the shit and talk about plans for the evening. It's our last day, so Laurent wants to go out with a bang. He won't give details, only saying we'll more than enjoy ourselves.

We return to the beach for lunch at the local shacks known for savory dishes of Puerto Rican favorites—the monster sandwich tripleta, bacalaitos fried salt cod fritters, and arroz con gandules with sofrito sauce.

Lachlan sits beside me at one of the tables we choose beneath the bountiful fronds of coconut palm trees. After we place our orders with a cute server, my brother-in-law turns to me.

"I know Laurent decreed our Guys' Getaway as *no sob stories, no drama, no business*. But I want to let you know the latest," Lachlan says.

I cock an eyebrow, curious about what he has to say and nod to encourage him to speak.

"Lydie came up with a brilliant plan. She forced the Stewarts' hands to sell 51% of Stewart Scotch to Jackson Corporation, so we have a majority stake in their family's business. On top of that, she folded Stewart Scotch within Jackson Corporation as the coup de grâce."

My mouth drops open.

The Shark took a massive bite out of their historic enemy. She crippled any chance of the Stewarts destroying the Jackson family and company for good.

"Hell yeah! Lydie dealt them a death blow, bro!" I exclaim. "Damn, she's no bloody joke."

"You can say that again, brother!" Lachlan says, as he chuckles and shakes his head. "*The Shark* had a more than satisfying meal.

"You should have seen their father Magnus' face when Lydie told him about that sodding wanker Chet's illicit deeds. Magnus railed on him while Bram sat triumphant. Undoubtedly, he assumed their father would select him as the heir. When Lydie told Magnus the terms of the deal, his face turned beet red, and his nostrils flared. He sputtered in Scottish Gaelic, unable to form words in English. He even clocked Chet upside the head.

Lydie proceeded to tell Magnus—since she ignored the brothers completely—the deal was nonnegotiable. Or we would ruin their company and family name for good. He signed the contracts post haste."

I raise my glass of water in honor of Lydie. Attagirl!

Lachlan's smile changes to a more serious expression.

Once again, I cock my eyebrow at him.

"I also let Chet know under no circumstances can he go after Kat or her family. Or we would strike back," Lachlan says, then pauses to gauge my reaction.

I sit in silence.

He continues with a nod.

"She damn sure fucked up, no doubt. But I will allow no one to harm a member of my family—including Kat, her mother, and her siblings. I read the apology letters Kat sent to everyone. She's pretty sincere and obviously in pain."

He pauses then goes on.

"I didn't see a letter for you, though. Care to share?" He asks.

My eyes drift back to the sea. The waves lap at the golden sand. A toddler squeals as the water kisses her chubby legs. A smile curls the corners of my mouth. Then I glance back at Lachlan and frown.

"She didn't send me an apology," I respond.

His eyes widen as his head jerks back in shock. He mutters a Scottish Gaelic curse under his breath.

"Instead, she showed up at the lobby of STEELE

London as I was leaving. I guess she wanted to apologize. But I wasn't interested in a word she said. I told her not to contact me or come near me and my family ever again," I say.

"Well, bloody hell," Lachlan mutters.

I grouse some more, and Lachlan shakes his head.

"I don't blame you for being pissed. Hell, I still am. But I believe her words. Let's see what actions she takes to back them up, Harris," he ends with a clap to my shoulder. "Now, Laurent's rule takes effect again. That is unless you have something to say."

Now it's his turn to cock an eyebrow as he scans my face.

I glance past him at the water as my thoughts drift. He gives me a moment to decide in silence. When I return my gaze to Lachlan, he raises his eyebrows questioningly.

I shrug.

"Who knows what tomorrow bring," I respond.

Lachlan nods, completely nonjudgmental.

"As for today, brother, let's end our Guys' Getaway with a rip-roaring time," I add, then call to the cute server for a pitcher—not a single glass—of mojitos.

I sure as hell need more than one drink.

KAT

"*B*abe... Babe... Kat, wake up... I miss you so much."

Can I be dreaming? Or do I really hear Harris' voice? The deep rumble of his baritone rolls over me. It ignites a fire to lick across my skin, straight to my needy core. Oh, God, please let it be true...

Slowly, I open my eyes and roll over onto my back. Leaning on my elbow, I stare in the direction of his voice. Even in the darkened room, I can distinguish Harris' sizable frame.

He stands at the foot of the bed. A swath of light from the moon crosses his face as the gauzy curtains flutter in the wind. His handsome face brightens as our eyes meet. Full, kissable lips part as he licks the bottom one with the tip of his tongue.

I close my eyes and envision that tongue and mouth on my suddenly engorged clit. A moan slips past the lips on

88

my face even as the lower ones swell with a desperate, aching need.

It's been way too long.

Eight excruciating weeks without the man I now realize I love. And want. Forever.

Thank God he's really here.

Harris' wicked chuckle rouses me from my pitiful musings. He glances down at my bare leg resting atop the sheets, then places one finger on the inside of my ankle. As he trails the tip along my instep, I moan aloud.

"You've been a naughty girl, Kitty Kat," he murmurs.

I gasp at the pressure he applies with his knuckle to the sole of my foot.

His dove gray eyes flick to my hooded emerald green orbs. He smirks.

"You tricked me. Naughty. Naughty. Girl."

He punctuates each word with a stroke of his knuckle.

The sensation on my erogenous zone morphs from pain to pleasure. My leg jerks as I mewl.

Harris grips both ankles and pulls me to the foot of the bed. I end up between his parted thighs.

My ass cheeks hang off the edge. The white silk sheets bunch about my waist. My exposed lower half draws his attention like a magnet. My hips shimmy of their own accord. His feral growl makes my pussy clench and flood with my juices. The musky scent of my arousal fills the space between us.

A predatory smile spreads across his face as his nostrils flare.

I swallow.

He grips my ankles in one sizable hand and hoists my hips from the mattress. I hang suspended with my shoulders pressed into the bed.

"Your attempt at an apology does not suffice in the least, Naughty. Naughty. Girl."

With his other hand, Harris swats my exposed pussy lips and clit.

WHAP. WHAP. WHAP.

I howl.

The sting radiates from my core to the tips of my toes and the top of my head. An electric current of erotic punishment zaps me.

"Do you understand how much trouble you are in, Naughty. Naughty. Girl?"

When I hesitate to answer, he spanks the sensitive juncture where my thighs meet my ass.

WHAP. WHAP. WHAP. WHAP.

My legs flail as I press my hands into the mattress to drag myself away from the punishing onslaught of spanks. To no avail. Trapped.

"You can dish the pain. But not take it, Naughty. Naughty. Girl? Too bad."

Harris sets a brutal pace for my punishment. Spanks land on my clit, pussy, sits bones, and thighs. Never landing on the same spot in a row. But not in a distinguishable pattern I can expect. No matter which way I flounder, I can't avoid the blows.

My howls increase as each second passes. The time uncountable. The pain memorable.

His silence as he punishes me allows my thoughts to drift back to the many ways I hurt him, Lachlan, and the rest of their family. I even recall the hurt on Lola's face as I told her about my parents' death in a car accident, just like hers.

Each lie I told accumulates to form a mountain of unstable rocks that threaten to landslide onto me as the spanking continues unabated.

Tears stream from my eyes to pool in my ears and drip onto the bed below. Chest-racking sobs pour from my mouth. So ashamed of my actions, I cover my heated face with my hands.

My pussy, ass, and thighs on fire, I submit.

Between howls and sobs, I beg Harris for his forgiveness.

He continues to spank me.

All tension drains from my body. Still held aloft, I sag. Spent completely. Tears continue to fall but in silence.

More time passes before the spanks change to caresses.

Soft rumblings glide over my skin as Harris soothes me. His murmurs draw more pleas of forgiveness from me. He settles on the bed and cradles me on his lap. I burrow my face into his neck as my entire body trembles. Sweat sheens on my skin, and my reddened ass ablaze.

The punishment a cathartic release.

"I forgive you, My Kitty Kat."

My heart skips a beat.

I raise my head to scan Harris' face. Can it be true?

His dove gray eyes glitter in the moonlight. They're filled with what I dare hope is love. Love for me. Even after all I did. Thank God.

His thumb brushes a tear from the corner of my eye. He slips the digit into my mouth.

"No more tears of sadness, My Kitty Kat," he murmurs before he slants his mouth over mine.

The kiss starts as a slow burn. Tendrils of warmth overtake the coldness that settled in my heart and soul. Our tongues dance an erotic tango. Flames lick through me. My toes curl as I meld my body to his muscular frame, crawling to surround him. The fire between us burns bright again.

"Need to be inside you…" Harris pants against my lips. He nips at me as he shifts position.

I lie on my back as he hovers above me. His mouth drops to my heavy breasts. He laves at the pebbled peaks. I yelp as his teeth sink into the sensitive flesh. His tongue flicks out to lap the pain away before he suckles first one, then the other distended nipple.

My head lolls. Cries of passion fall from my parted lips. I cup the nape of his neck to encourage his ministrations. Pressed flush, he hums in pleasure. The vibrations travel through me. I mewl.

Harris stands to yank his shirt over his head. He tosses it to the floor and grips the placket of his low-slung jeans. The metal buttons pop open to reveal the swollen, purple tip of his massive cock. Commando, his erection springs free.

My mouth waters at the sight of the pearly drop of pre-cum as it glints in the moonlight. I shudder at the memory of how his turgid girth and length burns my little pussy as he stretches me.

He pushes the jeans past his narrow hips. The muscles in his arms and thighs flex as he wrestles the unwanted material from his body. Standing tall, he fists his cock. The veins stand out in bas-relief. His heavy sac hangs below.

My tongue darts out to lick my lower lip.

Harris smirks and jerks his cock.

My pussy gushes.

His eyes lower to the apex of my thighs. A carnal smile tips the corners of his lush mouth at the sight of my glistening pussy lips. The juices slicken my legs. He growls.

In an instant, my hips lift in the air, and my shoulders press into the bed once again. I yelp in surprise and grasp the sheets to ground myself.

Harris holds me by both ankles. Legs spread wide in a vee. My core aligned with his cock. A snap of his hips, and he impales me on his dick.

I scream from the thick invasion. His tremendous girth fills me. The burn oh so good.

"FUCK!!!" He roars. Head back, muscles in his neck and arms corded. Harris stills but for a moment. Then...

"Take. Every. Inch. All of it!"

He pistons balls deep within me, punctuated by each word. My only reprieve when he pulls out to his bulbous tip. Held aloft, I have no choice but to take what he gives to me. And I do with absolute pleasure.

I writhe beneath him screeching like the cat in heat I am.

Fuck, he feels so damn good…

The slapping of skin on skin with the squelch of my pussy juices mixes with his grunts and groans and my cries. The erotic sounds arouse me like no other. They spur Harris on to fuck me into the bed. It groans in protest.

"Oh! Oh! Yeeessss… HARRIS!!!" I shout as a powerful orgasm rips through me.

A flash of white light sparks behind my eyelids, squeezed shut as ecstasy rolls over me. My inner walls tighten around his pulsating cock. He growls and pummels harder. Unstoppable. Relentless.

Booms blast and bright lights explode with each of the countless orgasms Harris forces from my ravaged core.

Sweat drips from his forehead to trail between my bouncing breasts as he leans over my torso. His dominant hands wrap under me to grasp my thighs as he changes the angle of his savage thrusts. His firm pecs drag over my taut nipples. Guttural groans and growls fill my ear as Harris chases his release.

As his cock swells impossibly larger, his body judders. Hot breath puffs across my sweat-drenched neck into my damp hair.

"Kaaat…"

His carnal cry and the copious amounts of his cum bathing my pussy trigger another epic climax.

I scream in pleasure as my eyes roll back and my back bows.

Harris collapses on top of me. The last vestiges of his release drip from my core, down my ass cheeks to the drenched sheets below.

"Happy now?" He murmurs in a raspy voice.

"So happy," I respond breathily as I squeeze him tight.

A streak of red shoots past the stars high in the sky.

A boom, then an explosion of red, orange, and yellow bursts.

"Happy… Happy… HAPPY NEW YEAR!!!"

I bolt upright in the bed sweating, breathing heavily, wildly looking around.

"HAPPY NEW YEAR!!!"

"HAPPY NEW YEAR!!!"

"HAPPY NEW YEAR!!!"

My hand swipes wet tendrils of my hair plastered to my face. My eyes dart from the chaise lounge on which I lay to the sky above where colorful fireworks explode. The over-sized pillow misshaped from me clutching it falls from on top of me to the tiled floor.

What the—???

I jerk to the left, seeking Harris. He's not here. I find myself alone.

Alone on the terrace of my hotel suite overlooking Sydney Harbor. I must have fallen asleep as I awaited the end of the old year. One I am more than happy to leave behind. I wanted to begin the New Year in the first big city to celebrate. A fresh start before my job in New York City.

There's no Harris here. No words of forgiveness and eternal love. And definitely no mind-blowing makeup sex.

With a frustrated yowl, I fall back against the chaise lounge. My hands cover my face as tears cascade down my flushed cheeks. Instead of my lover, cool air wraps around my sweat dampened skin. I shudder.

It was only a dream, after all.

The celebration below me only makes my misery more stark. Shouts of joy filter up from the crowds gathered to ring in the New Year. I envision couples kissing fervently. Their need to be with their loved one is strong. Promises for the future shared. Love declared.

My disappointing dream fades. Scattered on the breeze. The fiery passion a dull ache in my heart and deep in my core.

"Oh, Harris!" I cry in dismay.

The ringing of my mobile causes me to jump. With a dash of hope, I lunge for it. As I swipe it from the table, my gaze takes in the name on the screen.

Mum

Damn.

I mean, I'm glad to hear from her. But for a moment, I thought it would be Harris. Oh, well…

"Hi, Mum. Happy New Year!" I exclaim as I feign happiness. No need to upset her with my misery.

"Kat! Happy New Year! I set my alarm to call you. I wanted to be the first to wish you the best for the upcoming months. You deserve it, honey," my Mum says.

In the background, I hear Michael and Charlotte calling

out their best wishes to me. Our Mum's light-hearted laughter eases some of the sadness.

With a smile, I wish them Happy New Year, too. We chat some more before we hang up with my promise to call when it's their turn to celebrate. I set my alarm for just over ten hours.

As I hold the mobile, I consider calling Harris. Would he answer? What would he say? That is if he didn't change his number or block mine.

One last glance at the festivities and I head inside to the shower. As the water sluices over my body, I visualize a cleansing. The old me and ways swirl down the drain. I step out of the glass-enclosed marble shower revitalized. A New Year Promise ready to be declared.

"*Smiogaid suas, nighean,* Katrina Jackson! You will get your man back," I vow.

KAT

"Thank you for meeting with me, Haley. I truly appreciate it. I'm so sorry for all I've done and for how my actions impacted everyone. I hope that one day you will forgive me. I know it's a lot to ask. So I'll understand if you don't."

I remembered Lachlan's calendar noted he would be in New York City for January. He scheduled meetings with Jackson Corporation's executive team and important clients to kick off the year. His calendar also included references to time reserved for Haley and their family.

As soon as I arrived in the City, I contacted her. Surprisingly, on my first try, she agreed to have lunch with me.

Now her dove gray eyes—so like her brother's—pierce my soul. Her cool stare assesses me as I speak. No telltale expression gives away her thoughts.

I do my best not to squirm. As each second ticks by, I remind myself of my goal: get your man back.

The first step, convince his twin of my sincerity. They're super close. If I can get back in Haley's good graces, she may put me in contact with Harris. A positive word from Haley would make all the difference.

I pause to see if she will respond in some way to my subtle request.

She doesn't.

Holding back a dismayed sigh, I continue.

"I also want to let you know I accepted a job offer as the Development Director for a children's nonprofit organization on Fifth Avenue. So I'm living here permanently," I say, then offer a small smile with a shrug. "I've always wanted to live in New York City. Plus, it'll give me the chance to combine my MA Business Management degree with my love of volunteerism and the skills I learned during my administrative assistant positions."

Haley snorts.

A reaction at last, even if it's regarding the use of my skills and thus my past behavior. I can't really blame her, though.

I smile humbly.

The server places our dishes on the table and pours more wine. With a nod, he leaves us.

Haley leans forward. Her dove gray eyes darken to obsidian as they narrow on me.

"Listen, Kat, I did not accept your lunch invitation to

learn about your new job or life. I couldn't care less. What the fuck do you really want?" She asks pointedly.

Did I say she and Harris are close? Well, she's also a mama bear when it comes to her twin. And I just poked her. Bloody hell…

I take a gulp of wine and close my eyes for a silent prayer. When I glance at her again, she glares at me.

"Haley, I understand your anger with me. I deserve it. What I did was shitty. It would have been much better had I simply shared the knowledge about Iain with the Jacksons. However, years of struggles and self-hate blinded me to the right thing to do. I regret it. Not just because I was caught. But because as I got to know you and both of your families, I realized you're good people and don't judge me for my background. Not to mention what I initially thought was a smokescreen turned into true love."

She growls.

Quickly I go on.

"I never should have used Harris as I did. It was horrible and selfish," I say to calm Haley. I raise my hand and continue. "But I swear on my Mum's life I love Harris with all of my heart and soul. If I could erase the past, I would start with what I did to hurt him above all else."

I pause to drain my wineglass.

Haley takes a sip from hers and watches me over the rim intently. Once again, her face turns into an indecipherable mask. A cool veneer covers the simmering volcano just below the surface.

I tread carefully with my next words.

"What I want? I ask for your help to reconnect with Harris—"

"Are you *mad*?!?!" Haley erupts.

Wine sloshes from her glass as she slams it down on the table. I watch as the red liquid splatters onto the white linen cloth. The droplets remind me of bloody tears. Tears that soak my alabaster skin every night as I lie alone in bed. My thoughts on the man I love and how much I miss him.

Smiogaid suas, nighean, Katrina Jackson! You will get your man back. I recall my vow and raise my eyes to Haley.

"Yes. Madly in love with Harris," I respond unwaveringly.

Haley pushes back from the table. I rise and catch her arm. She drops her gaze to my hand and slowly lifts her eyes to mine. Her lip curls.

Before she can speak, I interrupt her.

"Haley, please! All I ask is for one chance to speak with Harris. If he tells me to bugger off, I will never bother him again. I promise! I tried to speak with him before I left the UK. But he was too angry to listen. I hope after two and a half months he'll hear me out. I cry every single day for him. Please, Haley," I beg as tears shimmer in my eyes.

She scans my face to determine my sincerity. The platinum daggers shooting from her eyes soften into glittery diamonds. She mutters to herself, then sits back down.

With a sigh of relief, I drop into my chair. My hand covers my face as tears fall.

"Here."

I peek through my fingers to find a white handkerchief

before me. A sign of peace? I pray so as I take the proffered cloth. After I dab my eyes and cheeks, I glance at Haley.

She sighs and signals the server. She asks him for a napkin to cover the spilled wine and for another bottle. Hurriedly, he and another server replace the tablecloth entirely and fill our glasses from a fresh bottle. They leave us with bows.

"Thank you—"

"Eat. You look like you could use a good meal. You've lost fifteen pounds easily, Kat," Haley cuts in. She shakes her head and mutters about women's reactions to breakups. "Afterwards, we'll talk," she adds aloud.

She's not kidding.

I haven't been able to eat much more than a few pieces of fruit or soup. The idea of food turned my stomach. I figured I lost weight since my clothes hang loosely. But for Haley to notice, I must have lost more than I thought.

I glance down at the Classic Cobb Salad before me. Knowing I may have a chance of seeing Harris, I dive in. The grilled chicken tastes divine. In moments, my bowl sits empty, and my belly is full.

"Hungry much?" Haley snickers.

My cheeks flush crimson as I shake my head. With a giggle, I swipe the last bit of tomato through the tasty vinaigrette and pop it into my mouth. Then I grin at Haley.

She laughs and nods.

"That good, huh?" She asks.

We order tea as the server clears the table. He returns with a pot and an assortment of fresh-baked cookies. The scent of brown sugar and chocolate makes my belly rumble. We indulge before Haley sits back and crosses her arms over her breasts.

"You do realize you fucked over my twin brother *and* my husband, don't you? Tried to ruin Jackson Corporation and Chet Stewart wanted STEELE International, Inc., too, right?" She asks, one elegantly arched eyebrow raised.

I blink at the 180-degree flip, then swallow.

"Yes, and I'm oh so sorry," I whisper as my head hangs in shame.

"Then you have balls to assume I would help you snag my twin," she says with a snort.

Bloody hell…

I squirm in my chair. I thought things were going in my favor. Obviously, I was way wrong.

A full minute passes.

"Gutsy. Okay, Kat. What's your plan?" She asks.

The breath I was holding burst forth in a rush. Light-headed, I clutch the table's edge in a white-knuckled grip.

"Yeah, I can make you or break you. Never, ever forget that feeling. Because if you fuck with my family again, I promise you by all things I hold dear, I will end you for good, Kat *Jackson*," Haley says. "Do you understand?"

I nod, then remember to answer verbally when she cocks her head.

"Y—Yes, Haley. I understand," I stammer, red-faced.

She eyes me for another minute before she reminds me to answer her question.

I tell her I just need an opportunity to sit and talk with

Harris. He hasn't answered my calls, text messages, or emails. If I could arrange for him to meet me, that would be great. But I'm fearful he may leave as soon as he sees me. With tears in my eyes, I ask if she can help me.

Haley glances away as she considers my emotional entreaty. Her mobile vibrates. She flips it over and glances at the screen. Her eyes flick to me.

"Uh, excuse me a moment," she says as she slides her chair back.

I reach out to stay her and shake my head.

"I'm going to the ladies' room," I say.

She nods and answers the call as I walk away.

It's either Lachlan or Harris. Otherwise, she wouldn't have reacted that way. My heart skips a beat at the thought of the caller being Harris.

Will she tell him I'm with her? Will she disclose my plan to him? What will he say?

Questions swirl in my mind as I make my way past the other diners. I wonder what Haley will do to get Harris to agree to meet with me. Or if she even does. I so hope he will hear me out.

As angry as he was, he must feel some kind of way for me. He certainly made me think so when we were together. All the passionate lovemaking we shared. The romantic trips around the world. The comfortable cuddles as we watched movies on Netflix.

I pray Harris and I can tap back into the good times and leave the past behind us.

As I return from the ladies' room, I make certain Haley

finished her phone call. I'd hate to interrupt. She smiles as I settle into my chair.

"I have to go now. But dinner tomorrow night at my penthouse duplex. I'll text the address to you," she says as she rises from her chair.

I jump up and hug her as I whisper words of thanks. She accepts my embrace, then steps back and leaves. I signal the server. Once I pay for lunch, I leave the restaurant with a giant smile on my face.

It was a close one. But step one is complete!

HARRIS

"*Y*ou appear rested, son. I take it Puerto Rico proved a trip full of relaxation?"

I return my father's embrace as he greets me.

We're having lunch at his request. My hope is for a catch up on life's happenings and not about the Kat *Jackson* fiasco. I scan his face as we settle into our chairs for a clue.

Morgan Steele, Alpha Dom billionaire who increased his family's fortune twice over while he reigned at STEELE International, Inc. for decades. Even post-retirement, the former CEO and Chairman of the Board remains active as Chairman Emeritus of the Board.

Most important of all roles as Patriarch of the Steele clan, he's extremely protective of his family. No one messes with a Steele or a Jackson and gets away with it. He has said little to me about the Kat *Jackson* fiasco. So, I'm certain he will reveal his perspective today.

Looking at my father mimics my reflection in a mirror thirty-seven years from now. A six-foot-four frame—he's three inches taller—still muscular from regular personal training sessions. Wavy salt and pepper hair kept short and neat. Clear platinum gray eyes. Well-dressed in a bespoke Brioni suit, custom dress shirt, silk tie with matching pocket square, and A. Testoni Oxfords. Morgan Steele is a distinguished older man who emanates power and wealth.

I strive to follow in his footsteps. Each of my siblings feel the same about our father. He's an excellent role model, and we value his opinion. So I wait anxiously for his words.

"Thanks, Dad. The Guys' Getaway gave me the opportunity to hang out with my boys and on the beach. You should join us for the next one," I respond with my signature cocky grin.

He chuckles and shakes his head.

"I do not believe you and the guys can keep up with me," he says. "However, I'll keep your invitation under consideration."

The server appears. Despite being younger than me—not to mention the platinum wedding band sitting prominently on his left ring finger—she gives my father an appreciative once over.

He ignores her sultry stare and places his order without glancing in her direction.

She gets the hint and turns to me.

I pin her with a reproachful look, and she drops the coy

smile instantly. Orders placed, she slinks away. I roll my eyes. My father smirks knowingly.

While we eat, we do the catch up on life's happenings. My parents plan to spend next week through the end of February on their megayacht *Serendipity* cruising the Mediterranean. After almost forty years of marriage, their love remains strong and unchallenged. Again, a feat my siblings and I wish to accomplish. Well, me, not right now.

"Tell me how you fare after the situation with Kat," my father commands as we drink coffee. His platinum gray eyes pin me with a gaze more intense than Roger's signature stare.

I swallow another sip as I form words to respond. With a shake of my head, I meet his gaze.

"Not so great, Dad," I say with a shrug honestly. "I feel guilty as fu—I mean—hell for being the one to bring Kat into our family's inner circle. To top it off, I harbored a hacker. Me, the co-head of STEELE Technology and Cyber Security, tech wiz, part of the Dynamic Duo."

I run my fingers through my hair and tug the longer strands. The thought of it all re-invokes anger and embarrassment. Damn Kat *Jackson*!

My father assesses me a moment. The server returns to refill our coffee. He waves her away like an annoying gnat as it buzzes around your head. She departs hastily.

"Harris, know not one of us faults you. Kat fooled everyone. Leave the blame at her feet, not at yours in any way," he says earnestly. "Your mother and I spoke. She wants you to know not to let this set you back. Remain open to love. It can surprise you whence it comes. Do you understand?"

I ponder his and my mother's words of advice. The weight on my heart lightens with the knowledge no one blames me truly. Not just blowing smoke up my ass to make me feel less of an idiot. Thank fuck!

"That makes me feel much better, Dad, thank you. I can't say when I'll be ready for love again. But I'll heed Mom's advice," I respond with a nod.

"Excellent. Now you get back to work. I have to pick up your mother from her spa day," my father says with a twinkle in his platinum gray eyes.

He rises from his chair, and I follow suit. I walk with him to his Rolls-Royce Corniche. The driver taps his hat while he opens the back door. My father embraces me before he slides inside.

With a wave, I watch the sedan pull away from the curb and merge with traffic on Fifth Avenue. As I walk back to The STEELE Tower, I contemplate my next move. Being with my father reminds me of the importance of family. It's time for Uncle Harris Babysitting.

"Oh, hi, *Harris.* What's up, brother of mine?"

I chuckle at Haley's greeting when she answers her mobile. I can picture her grinning with a mischievous glint in her eyes. My twin sense tingles.

"What are *you* up to, Hal?" I rejoin with a smirk.

"You called me, remember?" She asks instead of

answering my question. "I presume you must have something to share. So you tell me, *Har*."

I shake my head and chuckle. Fine.

"I haven't seen my niece and nephews in a few days. I need some *Tea Party and Transformers* time," I answer, using my name for playtime with the wee lass and lads. "Why don't you and Little Lord Fauntleroy go on a date night tomorrow? It is Saturday after all. A little LEVELS New York, perhaps? I'll babysit for you."

Haley's response comes after a moment of silence. Just as I'm about to ask her what's wrong, she speaks up.

"Why, that's perfect timing! Things always fall into place as they should when they should," she answers.

It's a bit of a mysterious comment. The tingling increases. But I opt to ignore it. Starr probably has Haley reading some New Age book, again.

"See you at seven," my twin says. "Gotta fly."

And she's gone.

What a weirdo…

I stare at the mobile screen, then out the floor-to-ceiling windows of my offices in The STEELE Tower high above Fifth Avenue and Fifty-seventh Street in the heart of Billionaires' Row. The striking, gray-tinted glass skyscraper for our headquarters and commercial, retail, and residential properties.

New York City stretches out before me with unobstructed views. Central Park to the north, the Hudson River to the west, the East River opposite, and the rest of Manhattan to the south from Midtown to Battery Park. On a beautiful, cloudless day like this afternoon, the panoramas can take one's breath away. I can spend hours watching the happenings of the bustling city. But not now.

My gaze returns to my laptop to prepare for a meeting with a recently gained client. I attained their corporate and the CEO's personal accounts while I was with that redheaded Siren. I told her she brought me luck since she kissed me before I had the initial meeting.

"Huh... Some luck she turned out to be. Get a grip, Harris Steele. You have work to focus on. Not that scammer," I chide myself aloud.

I pull up the analysis and presentation.

At the end of the day, I leave my suite of offices with a wave to my administrative assistant, who's wrapping up a phone call. I stride across the floor designated for STEELE Technology and Cyber Security's New York City headquarters. The layout and decor—as sleek as the Tower's exterior—features glass-enclosed offices on the perimeter with workstations clustered in the center, ebony wood floors, dove gray and white leather furniture, track light fixtures, Lucite tables, steel accents, and original artwork.

I make a point to chat with my staff as I make my way to the elevator. Our father taught my siblings and me to appreciate and to treat well those who work for us since they're our most-valuable asset. One reason STEELE International maintains a high employee retention rate.

As I near the reception area, I greet the two receptionists by name. They wish me a good weekend as they pack away their headsets. Like the three on the executive floor, the receptionists wear custom-tailored light gray dress suits and skin-tone heels that serve as uniforms and sit behind a spacious desk.

A member of the security team stands from his station as I approach. We talk about the latest Knicks' basketball game at Madison Square Garden while I wait for the family's private elevator. My palm to the plate by the doors calls it to the floor. The elevator links our residences on the fiftieth through fifty-seventh floors to our global headquarters on the nineteenth through twenty-ninth floors. Bonus? A less than five-minute commute to my office. Talk about a score!

I bid them a good night as I step onto the elevator.

I ride up to my full-floor penthouse on the fifty-first floor. It's above Haley and Lachlan's penthouse duplex on the forty-ninth and fiftieth floors. My other siblings' residences are above mine in age order up to our parents' duplex on the top floors. They gave each of us penthouses as graduation presents. Baz has a duplex. Haley created hers when she and Lachlan combined their residences after they married.

The elevator doors open to my entry foyer.

My mother decorated for me. She has extraordinary taste. So I trusted she'd make my bachelor's pad five-star. My only requirements were a home office with an adjacent secure room for my tech gadgets, a tricked-out game room, and an oversized sunken tub. A guy needs to relax after a long day at the office.

That thought stays with me as I make my way to my

primary bedroom suite. Before I left my office, I activated the water and the essential oils to fill the tub and set piano music to play. One of my home tech systems I make great use of on a daily basis.

I walk into my dressing room to strip out of my bespoke Saville Row double-breasted suit and custom dress shirt. The silk Hermès tie and platinum cuff links drop onto the center island. I toe off my A. Testoni Oxfords and Charvet dress socks. Fortunately, my house manager keeps things tidy for me.

The combined scent of lavender, chamomile, and sandalwood evokes an immediate sense of calm as I enter my all white marble bathroom. The warmth of the room heightens the relaxing scent. A deep inhalation and slow exhalation calm me. I give a nod to Starr, who hooked a brother up with the best essential oils available.

Slowly, I lower myself into the sunken tub large enough for four people. Not that I've had three women here. Nah. I leave my trysts at LEVELS. The only woman who's ever shared my bed outside of the clubs was that redheaded Siren.

Again, she pops into my mind unbidden.

I close my eyes and lean against the side of the tub with my head on a scented pillow. More thoughts of she who shall not be named fill my mind. I try to dodge them, to no avail.

"Oh, fuck it," I groan.

Instantly, her tempting image appears behind my closed eyelids. Her lustrous Titian hair cascades down her back.

The tips curl around her seashell pink pebbled nipples. They peek through her curtain of hair as she moves towards me from the opposite side of the tub. Voluptuous curves on full display. For my eyes only.

Each graceful step causes her mouth-watering tits to jiggle and her grip-worthy hips to sway. Her bare mons calls to me as though her glistening pussy lips hum a beguiling tune. Long, toned legs ease her into the water. She dips under, then resurfaces between my thighs.

Rivulets of water trail down her flawless skin, flush from the warm temperature. Droplets bead on the tips of her nipples.

I lean forward to lick a bead off.

She shivers despite the heat.

I want to make her entire body convulse with climaxes I cause.

My hands reach through the water to grasp her hips. I pull her closer to me as my head lowers to the other nipple. My tongue darts out to circle around the delectable bud. I draw it into my hot mouth and suckle. Hard.

The Siren throws her head back as a throaty moan slips past her parted lips. She gasps when I nip, then lave her nipple. I engulf as much of her luscious DD-cup tit in my mouth as possible. She writhes. Her fingers dive into my hair. She cradles my head. Her soft cries fill my ears as she lowers her cheek to rest atop my head.

"Oh, Harris," she mewls.

My ten-inch cock thumps against my abs. Like a water snake, it winds beneath the surface in search of its prey. In this case, it seeks the tight, wet snatch of the Siren. As though sensing its need, her soft hand wraps around its base and squeezes.

Her breast pops from my mouth on a groan.

She pumps my cock and swirls her thumb around the mushroom head.

"Fuuuck…" I breathe.

The Siren straddles me. Her knees on either side of my hips as she hovers her pussy over my cock, still fisted in her hand. When the tip breaches her lower lips, she slams her ass down. She cries out in wild abandon as my girth stretches her pussy.

She digs her nails into my shoulders to anchor herself as she circles her hips, then lifts to the tip and impales herself onto my cock again and again.

"You like how my big dick claims every inch of your little pussy. Don't you, Siren?" I growl.

She bobs her head as she pants. The movement makes her beautiful tits bounce even more.

I lean forward and suckle again.

The action sets her off for another round of riding me like a champion equestrian. I buck beneath her like a bronco. Each of her slams meets one of my upward thrusts. We find our erotic rhythm with ease accustomed to one another's bodies.

Water sloshes from the bathtub onto the marble floor. Our mutual cries of carnal delight overtake the soothing sounds of the piano. Sweat beads above the Siren's top lip. I lick it off.

We fuck like feral animals—a cat and a wolf—until we pass out nearly. Countless orgasms make her limp as I chase my release. I rise to my knees and flip her over to mount her from behind. The new angle hits her G-spot just right, and she howls as her body convulses with a final climax.

It triggers my balls to draw up and shoot my load deep into her well-used pussy. The energy drains from me with the last spurt of my jizz. I collapse atop her, then roll to sit with her held in my arms. I lower my face into the back of her neck and purr in contentment.

My eyes open leisurely.

I grunt and give my cock one more stroke to empty it fully.

"Damn that redheaded Siren for making me want her…" I groan wistfully.

"Good morning, Mr. Steele, Mr. Jackson. Welcome back to Goodman's Men's Store, sirs. I will let Dara and Cindy know you arrived. Would you care for a Mimosa or sparkling water?"

Laurent and I thank the greeter at the men's counterpart to Bergdorf Goodman—the centuries-old retailer for women's fashion. It's the global pinnacle of style, service, and modern luxury. We're in the specialty store across the street from its location on Fifth Avenue between Fifty-Seventh and Fifty-eighth Streets.

I walked over from The STEELE Tower. Laurent rode up in his Bentley Bentayga from his loft in TriBeCa. Some items we ordered arrived, along with new pieces from the latest collections.

Part of our playboy appeal is our sharp dressing. We look good for the ladies we charm.

Laurent and I stride through the store, heading to our

reserved rooms. Other shoppers and staff glance in our direction as we approach. The magnetism of two Alpha males who exude power and wealth attracts them. Whether it's our swagger or pheromones, women and some men stop and stare.

Laurent—who typically flashes a brilliant smile at his gawkers—doesn't notice them. His beauty, Yessenia, captured his heart. Oblivious, he goes on about a new tobacco leaf he's using for a special collection of Jackson Cigars.

I, too, disregard the others—even a cute little thing with tons of ebony curls around her golden caramel face that glows as she smiles at me. After last night's fantasy, it still set my mind on a certain redheaded Siren. A brown-eyed beauty fails to distract me.

With a sigh, I tune back in to Laurent as I sip my Mimosa.

We take the elevator to the second floor, where Dara and Cindy wait for us. After double air kisses, they chatter on about the latest fashion news as they lead us to the Personal Styling Services area.

Each woman is a good ten years older than us and married to successful businessmen. Neither woman has any interest in getting a ring from Laurent and me. Their professionalism and keen sense of style helped us to develop a decade-long relationship. Aside from a soaking tub, a man needs a good stylist.

We separate to individual rooms off a common area with a few raised platforms in front of full-length mirrors.

My room has two racks of clothes and accessories on the console. End tables with crystal lamps flank a gray velvet sofa with a matching ottoman. A tray with pastries and fruit and a pitcher of freshly squeezed orange juice with a glass rests on top of the ottoman.

I pop a grape in my mouth as I head to the curtained dressing room. I emerge in a gray silk robe and slippers.

"Shall we begin with the suits?" Dara asks with a smile. She inclines her head towards one rack. The crown of braids gives her a regal appearance. She claps her delicate hands as her toffee eyes sparkle when I agree.

"You will adore the fit of this Tom Ford number, especially with your muscular thighs," she says with a wink.

I chuckle and duck my head as my cheeks heat. Dara knows how to charm better than I do. No wonder her husband—who manages a super profitable hedge fund— showers her with lavish gifts, like the diamond cuffs on her slim wrists.

"Oh, don't be shy, sugar. You've known me far too long for that nonsense," she says with an airy laugh. "Here, take it with this shirt back to the dressing room. We'll add the accessories after you have it on."

"Yes, ma'am," I reply with a grin.

My grin widens when I stare at my reflection in the mirror. Dara sure knows how to pick 'em. And Mr. Tom Ford damn sure knows how to make a man look like a man. The cut and material are superb.

Dara claps when I step out of the dressing room. She

twirls her finger for me to show each angle. When I face her again, she gives me the thumbs up in approval.

"Now for the tie, pocket square, and socks," Dara says as she goes to the console. "Your tiger's eye and yellow gold cuff links will pair well with the suit."

When we first worked together, she came to my penthouse and had her assistant take photos of each accessory and piece of clothing I owned. As we add more to my wardrobe, she puts those images in the database app Haley created for her.

If the occasion calls for it, Dara puts together the list of items I need to pack. My house manager puts my luggage together. Then I reference my side of the app to coordinate the outfits. Looking fly on the fly. Bam!

Dara and I spend the next ninety minutes going through the collection she prepared for me. Laurent finishes with Cindy shortly after. They'll arrange to deliver the items to our residences. We bid them farewell with more kisses.

I send a text message to my administrative assistant to send a box of macarons from Ladurée Paris and a bottle of Dom Pérignon Rosé Vintage 2005 to Dara. They're her favorites. I'll send a handwritten thank you note to her by messenger later this afternoon.

"Ready to get your ass handed to you?" Laurent asks as we ride in the back of his Bentley Bentayga.

I snort.

"Yeah, right. I believe you meant to say the reverse," I retort. "It is *I* who will hand *you* your ass, dear cousin."

We're on our way to play squash, then have lunch at The Union Club of the City of New York on Park Avenue. The Steele men have been members of the one hundred-eighty plus year old, exclusive social club since its founding as the first of its kind in the City. Despite being notorious for denying membership to sons, they have always accepted us. A Steele as a founding member makes the decision an easy one.

When we pull up to the club, the doorman opens the SUV's door. Laurent grabs his leather duffle bag from the trunk, and we stride into the lobby. I salute the concierge, then continue to the main elevator for access to the men's locker room. We change into the required all-white clothing of a collared shirt, shorts, socks, and sneakers for our match.

With our racquets and goggles in hand, we head for the courts. Laurent continues to talk shit until I cream him by winning three out of the five games. He throws his towel at me as I crow. Deftly I catch it and toss it back at him. He rolls his eyes and exits the court as he mutters Scottish Gaelic curses under his breath.

In front of the viewing area, I stop and talk with other members. Laurent speaks with a man who owns a chain of high-end brasseries in New York, Chicago, and LA—a perfect match for Jackson Corporation's brands. The club offers many opportunities to network for both business and for pleasure. Many a deal gets made in these walls.

We return to the men's locker room. A quick shower to rinse off the sweat before we sit in the sauna to soothe our muscles. After a cleansing shower, we dress in our suits and ties—the de rigueur for The Union Club, even on a Saturday.

As I pass Laurent, I can't resist tousling his collar length sable brown hair after he fixed it just so. Loser. He retaliates by throwing an elbow into my flank. If we weren't at the Club, we'd wrestle until one of us gave in. Instead, he picks up his duffle bag, and we take the stairs up to the dining room.

The host greets me by name and Laurent since he frequents the Club with me regularly. We sit at the table reserved for the Steele men. From our prime spot in the center, we can observe the entire dining room.

A few members nod in greeting and others stop by the table. The server takes our order. I go for the French Onion Soup, a green salad, and Steak Frites. Laurent opts for the lentil soup, a salad, and Chicken Française. Plenty to replenish the stores used up by the intense squash match.

"So, what's the deal with your girl?" Laurent asks once we're alone.

I cock an eyebrow and give him the side-eye.

He chuckles as he raises his glass of San Pellegrino for a drink. His bottle green eyes dance with mirth.

"Don't play dumb with me, ol' chap. I hear she's on this side of the Pond," he says.

What the fuck???

My shock amuses him, and he throws his head back for a hearty laugh.

Surreptitiously, I kick his leg under the table. Fucker.

"Ow! Damn! Was that really necessary?" He grumbles as he rubs his shin. "Loosen up, cuz. Don't shoot the messenger."

I glare at him before I ask how he knows.

"Lachlan and Baz aren't the only ones with *guys*. I put a tail on the lass the moment we found out about her shenanigans. She's been pretty busy…" Laurent responds.

Okay. Do I want to know what that redheaded Siren has been up to for the last ten weeks? And by *busy* does Laurent mean with other men? Why the fuck do I care???

I go for the safe route.

"Did you tell Lachlan?" I ask.

Laurent cocks his head and returns my side-eye.

"Of course, I told the big boss. My last report placed her at a nonprofit organization for children. She's the new Development Director. Hopefully, she won't swindle them instead of raising funds," he says with a snort.

His comment rankles me. Then I chide myself for getting defensive. She deserves it.

I shrug, feigning nonchalance.

"Bully for her. Now tell me the latest with Yessenia since you're all in my business," I say.

His eyes light up at the mention of her name. Then he spends the next few minutes bringing me up to date. Ah, young love. It's wonderful for some.

Just not for me.

. . .

ON MY WAY DOWN!

I shoot the text message to Haley as I wait for our private elevator. The bags from FAO Schwarz sit at my feet. After lunch, I stopped by the toy store to pick up some surprises for my niece and nephew. Sure, Christmas just happened, and I gave them loads of goodies. But one can never have too many Barbies and puzzles.

I don't bother to wait for Haley's response. The elevator doors open, and I get in. My nostrils flare.

The faint scent of perfume floats in the air. Not just any perfume. Her perfume.

Can't be!

The elevator doors ping open. The scent follows me into the entry foyer outside of Haley and Lachlan's penthouse duplex.

I swear I better be mistaken. But Laurent's words come back to haunt me. She who shall not be named is in New York City. Lachlan knows. This is his residence. She's his distant cousin.

Before I can decide my next move, the double doors open. Haley peeks her head out.

"What are you waiting for?" She asks, then spies the bags in my hands. "Oh, Harris! You'll spoil them! Come on in."

Okay, perhaps I'm mistaken.

I breathe a sigh of relief. Or is it disappointment? Do not even go there, Harris Steele. I shake my head and follow Haley inside.

"Uncle Harris!" A chorus shouts my name.

Lilias, Leith, and Lewis rush towards me as fast as their little legs can carry them. At eighteen months, they've got walking down pat. They raise their arms for me to pick them up.

I put the bags down and scoop all three into a bear hug.

Sloppy kisses cover my face as chubby hands wave around. Laughter bubbles up, and my day just got better.

When I put them down, I crouch amongst them and show them their new toys. While they clamber about, dropping to all fours to get at their gifts, I rise and glance around for the five-month-old twins—Stirling and Struan.

Lachlan stands with them cradled in the crook of each arm.

I grin and make my way towards them. But I hesitate at the weird expression on his face. He flicks his gaze between me and Haley, who's still behind me. I look over my shoulder, and she plasters on a wide smile. When I turn back to Lachlan, he averts his gaze.

"Okay, clue me in. What's got you all awkward, Little Lord Fauntleroy?" I ask as I cross my arms over my chest.

That twin tingling peaks again.

I narrow my eyes at Haley as she steps around me to stand next to her husband. She drags her finger along the bridge of her nose as though pushing her glasses up. A tell she has when she's nervous. Although now she wears contacts, so it's even more obvious she's hiding something.

Then it comes together.

She's here.

Fuck. *Me.*

"Okay, Lachlan, what happened to *bros before h—*"

"You better not dare to finish that sentence, Harris Steele!!!"

"Oh, isn't this rich coming from Haley *Benedict Arnold* Jackson!!!"

"Harris, that's enough, bro!"

I stand just on the other side of the wall as Harris, Haley, and Lachlan argue. Over me being here. This is not how I imagined us reconnecting. The last thing I want is to cause strife amongst them. They're too close. It's just not right.

I bloody fucked up. Again.

Taking a deep breath and saying a silent prayer for peace, I round the corner. And come face to face with Harris.

My heart skips a beat. The breath leaves me in a rush. A

yearning so mighty tugs at my core, it cramps. I have to close my eyes to steady myself.

When I open them, he still stands with his arms folded across his chest. The biceps bulge beneath the long-sleeved t-shirt. Sweatpants can't hide his thick thighs as they flex from his wide-legged stance. Nor can I miss his impressive bulge even flaccid—in more ways than one.

But what really sets my heart and pussy aflutter is his handsome face. He's still so gorgeous—even angry. Maybe because he's so pissed it reminds me of my fantasy. Would he spank me?

I swallow thickly.

Harris must sense the lust swirling within me. A flash of equal carnal desire darkens his dove gray eyes to obsidian. They narrow as his nostrils flare and his jaw tightens. A vein raises at his temple. He's reining in his emotions, too.

In my periphery, I notice Haley with bags in her hands ushering The Trips out the front doors. Lachlan follows with their twins. They shut Harris and me in their flat. Alone.

"Listen, *Kat*—"

"Harris, I—"

We speak at the same time. Harris outraged and me plaintive. The sound of my voice softens his features. He closes his eyes and inhales deeply. As he exhales, his eyes focus on me. He gives a decisive nod.

"I presume you spoke with my twin and somehow persuaded her to set me up. If you passed her stronghold, then I might as well give you a chance to have your say," he tells me. He gestures behind me towards the lounge.

"Thank you," I whisper, then about-face on wobbly knees.

I get the distinct feeling Harris' eyes zoom in on my ass. A peek over my shoulder confirms my suspicions. I flick my gaze forward as a satisfied smile plays at the corners of my mouth.

More confident, I exaggerate the natural roll of my ass. The silk of my Diane von Furstenberg wrap dress swishes with the movement. The belt emphasizes my narrow waist and the flare of my hips. I chose a pair of Giuseppe Zanotti stilettos since Harris loves my long legs. Especially wrapped around his hips while my heels dig into his ass as he fucks me against a wall.

The visual hardens my nipples. A glance down reveals them pressed against the soft fabric. An obvious invitation for him to suckle the sensitive buds. Oh, please.

Gracefully, I lower on a sofa, cross my legs, and gaze up at him through the fringe of my eyelashes. My heart thuds in my chest. Will he sit beside me or opt for a chair?

Harris chooses the same sofa—albeit the opposite end. He folds his hands over his lap. But not before I notice his erection running along his inner thigh. The bulbous tip is blatant against the soft material of his sweatpants.

A vision of it breaching my wet folds floats into my mind. I bite back a moan as I shift position. I wore a black lace thong. Hopefully, I won't leave a wet spot on the back of my dress…

"Well?"

Harris' voice breaks through my reverie.

I blink and stare at him.

Here we go.

"Harris, you have every right to be angry with me. I was absolutely wrong. If I had a do-over, I would speak with the Jackson family about finding Iain's journals, his signet ring, and his sketchbooks. Ask them how we should proceed as a family. Then go from there," I say.

My gaze never waivers from his. I want him to see my sincerity. Know what I say comes from my heart. I want to atone.

The next part gives me pause. I worry the belt of my wrap dress between my fingers as I gaze down at my lap. After a deep breath, I continue.

"Part of that do-over would include meeting you organically. Allowing our connection to grow from a place of normal attraction," I say, then go on quickly. "Not that my attraction to you was—I mean *is*—not normal. The moment I saw you in the lobby of Jackson Town House, I experienced the most visceral reaction to any man I've ever met."

I pause and tilt my head to the side. Did I just hear a low growl? A possessive rumble from Harris' broad chest? Because I mentioned other men?

Oh, please let it be true!

He crosses his ankle over the opposite knee. He uses the action to avert his eyes from mine.

I scan his face anyway. But I can't decipher his sentiment. So I go on.

"My mind told me to use you as a way to enter the inner circle of your families"—his head jerks up, and he glares at me—"But my heart holds the truth. I want more from you. I need what only you give me. The security of a man who cares deeply for me, treats me as an equal, and makes me feel worthy. I want to be all things you want and need too."

I rise from my end of the sofa and sit beside him. As I take his hand between both of mine, I stare into his eyes.

"I apologize, Harris, with all my heart and soul. I pray you will forgive me. Even if you cannot give me another chance, know I love you truly," I say.

On a whim, I lean forward and slant my mouth over his full lips. One last kiss.

He stiffens at the contact.

But I refuse to miss the chance to taste him. The tip of my tongue sweeps across the seam of his lips—a sensual caress. They part. Without hesitation, I slip inside. My tongue finds his and teases it until it tangles with mine. I lean further into him.

He groans.

When he pulls me onto his lap, my hands seek his shoulders for balance. As he deepens our kiss, the fingertips of one hand dig into my butt cheek while the other clasps the back of my neck. He angles my head just so as he takes control.

The air whooshes from my lungs. The passion he shows leaves me breathless. But I don't stop kissing him.

My moans mingle with his groans as we seek to slake the hunger built over weeks of being without the other. The scent of his cologne mixed with the pheromones of this virile Alpha male drive me wild. My fingers dive into the longer strands of his hair. I grind my pussy lips on his thick cock as it tents his sweatpants.

Oh my God, Harris feels so bloody good!

I hump him like a teenager in the back of her boyfriend's car. Without a doubt, he'll have a wet spot on the front of his sweats. Do I care? Hell no!

A strangled cry pours from my mouth when the tip of his finger skims my pussy lips while the heel of his hand presses against my clit. I jerk in his arms. Head thrown back, eyes squeezed shut, the first non-self-induced orgasm in weeks rips through my aching core. My body convulses.

"My turn."

Harris' gruff voice filters through the haze of my carnal bliss. He slides me to my knees on the floor.

I stare up at him from between his thighs. His hooded gaze demands I give him his release, too. With pleasure.

Eagerly, my hands reach for the drawstring of his sweatpants. I skim my fingertips up and over his massive erection, still pushing into the soft cotton. His dick jumps at my touch. The control I have over him makes me smirk.

I tug at the bow to reveal my present. His length makes it necessary for him to lift his hips so I can lower the sweatpants past his erection. The material bunches at his knees. I duck beneath it to get closer to my prize.

Our eyes lock.

Without breaking the connection, both of my hands fist around his dick from the base to mid shaft. He's so large even stacked my hands don't reach his mushroom head. I save my mouth for that tasty morsel. I lap the bead of pre-cum, then swirl the tip of my tongue around the head. The flat of my tongue meets the top of my hand and licks up to the slit. I squeeze first one hand, then the other in an alternating rhythm.

"Fuuuck…" Harris groans. His hips circle and pump up. The control I thought I had ends with his hands buried in my hair. He guides my movements to the pace he prefers. "Take it. Take it all…"

My palms land on his muscular thighs. I open my throat and hum.

"FUUUCK!!!" Harris roars as he pulls my head down until my nose rests on his groin. My gag makes him groan.

His quads flex beneath my fingers as he gears up to fuck my throat. Deep and rough.

I take breaths through my nose when he allows me, as his tip rests just inside my mouth. Repeatedly, his hips snap, and I take his massive cock down my throat. My jaw hurts from the stretch. But I take it, all of it, as he commands. Happily.

"Just like that…" Harris grunts as his pace increases.

His thick girth swells and pulsates. An explosion of hot, creamy semen pours down my throat, straight into my belly. I hum in satisfaction. He roars in release.

When his grip loosens in my hair, I sit back on my

haunches. His dick pops from my mouth. I marvel at how it's still hard. It's the most beautiful dick I've ever seen. And the only one I want to know for the rest of my life. At least that's my hope.

I dab at the corners of my mouth and lick the remnants of his cum off my finger. I remember he told me *no drop wasted of your cream, Kitty Kat.* Will we share more passionate moments? Or was this a last hurrah?

Shyly, I gaze at Harris through my eyelashes.

He stares at me. Then he scoops me from the floor and places me on the sofa next to him. Not his lap, but not the door either. Quickly, he fixes his clothes. He swipes his palm over his face as he blows out a breath. His head falls back against the pillow.

Confidence gone, my nerves return. I adjust the belt on my dress and smooth the material. Anything to distract me from his silence.

Harris' mobile rings. He reaches into his pocket and smirks when he reads the screen.

"Yes, Haley?" He asks dryly. Instead of words, he answers with mmhmms, nothing I can use to figure out what they speak about. He flicks his gaze at me, then ends the call.

"Listen, Kat," he starts. My heart sinks. "I need some time to think things through. I don't want to rush into anything like before."

He stands up and glances at the door.

Oh, so here it comes.

I want to shout: You didn't need time to think before

you shoved your dick down my throat. Didn't hesitate then! Did you, Harris Steele?!

But I don't.

I got mine. He got his. We're even.

Besides, if I open my mouth, the tears will fall. Instead, I square my shoulders and lift my chin high. I give him a nod and move to the front doors.

Once again, he walks behind me. This time, I ignore the sensation of his eyes on my ass. A lass has to maintain a level of pride, you know.

He opens the double doors and steps back for me to exit ahead of him. His hand reaches around me to land on the plate to call for the elevator.

My eyes close as I inhale his scent one last time. It stays with me as I step onto the elevator. Our eyes meet until the doors close. I sag against the wall. My shaking hand covers my swollen lips. I will not allow one tear to fall until I'm safely hidden in the back seat of a cab.

I hold back tears as I hold my head high, walking through the posh lobby of The STEELE Tower. Not a glance left or right. I maintain direct focus on the front doors. A nod in response to the doorman's query to confirm I need a taxi almost causes a single droplet to slip from my eye. I tilt my head back and suck in a breath through my nose.

To avoid risking another slip, I dive into the back of a yellow cab with as much dignity as I can muster, given the level of hurt and embarrassment. The professional doorman utters not a word as he closes the door behind me. A rap on the roof signals the driver to pull away from the curb. And for the tears to fall freely.

By the time I arrive at my flat, tears drench my puffy face. I cry, not just for Harris' reaction—or lack thereof. But for all my pent-up frustration and the pain I caused others. When could I just catch a bloody break already???

The doorman helps me from the taxi. The greeting on his lips falters when he notices my distress. He asks if I need any assistance. Then quickly reaches for the front door when I shake my head a little too vigorously. He nods as I pass to enter the magnificent two-story lobby.

Another fabulous New York City property—One Fifth Avenue. The landmark prewar co-op a block north of Washington Square Park on the Gold Coast of Greenwich Village. With towers and multi-tiers as it reaches for the sky, the twenty-seven-story building rises above the nearby brownstones. Michael would appreciate its Art Deco design with bricks of varying colors to create depth. The thought brings a brief smile to my lips. I swipe an errant tear and avert my gaze from the concierge.

Once in an elevator, I press the button for the private tower floor on twenty-four. I refuse to glance in the mirror, certain my makeup has me resembling a raccoon. Not to mention my smeared lipstick...

I step out into the entry and unlock the double doors.

As always, the sight before me catches my breath. The incredible 360-degree views captivate me, especially at night. The lights of the Freedom Tower to the south, the ever-changing colors of the Empire State building to the south, New Jersey west of the Hudson River, and beyond the East River. All beckon to me on the other side of large picture windows.

Whenever I walk in, I also thank my lucky stars for my new friend, Vivian Murphy. Because of her largesse, I get to live in her luxury five-bedroom full-floor penthouse. We met my first day at work, and we hit it off immediately. She's the Marketing Director and was the last executive I met with before lunch. She took me to a cute cafe around the corner from the offices.

After I told Vivian I was staying in an Airbnb until I decided which neighborhood to live in—not to mention which I could afford—she offered to let me room with her. The spacious penthouse is where she grew up. Her parents moved to a villa in Tuscany when her father retired. Her older brothers moved out years before. As the baby of the family and the only girl, her parents gave the multimillion-dollar residence to her. Talk about lucky…

I peek to my right to check if Vivian is in her suite. She had a date earlier. The closed doors make me glad I won't have to face her. But bummed I don't have anyone to talk to about the night's fiasco or anything. With a sigh, I turn the other way to head for my bedroom on the other end of the flat.

As I round the kitchen, Vivian sits at the island with a glass of red wine and popcorn. She glances up. Her expression is as mournful as mine. No smile on her gorgeous ebony face. Only sadness in the pools of her toffee brown eyes.

"Awful night for you, too, huh?" Vivian asks. When I nod, she rises from the chair and fills another glass with wine. "Here, let's finish the bottle while we commiserate."

I take a healthy gulp of the wine. Its delicious flavor washes over my palate as its potency loosens my tongue. I confess everything.

Vivian sits silently until I finish with Harris escorting me to the elevator. As she watches me, I fear I made a mistake. Big mouth!

Then she nods thoughtfully and gulps the last of her wine. Without a word, she leaves the kitchen. I sit, nibbling my lower lip. Curses fill my head. She's going to kick me out. Damn!

"Time for the stronger stuff."

I jolt and spin around to find her holding a bottle of tequila.

"Margaritas and nachos coming up!" She says with a wink. "My lousy date doesn't compare to your story, Kat. So let's just skip it and get drunk. Deal?"

Tears of joy pour from my eyes. Vivian doesn't hate me or judge me.

"Deal!" I exclaim as I jump from the chair and embrace my friend.

Later in bed, I remind myself of my vow.

Smiogaid suas, nighean, Kat Jackson! You *will* get your man back. Like the most complicated piece of script in technology, I'll decode Harris Steele. All while I give him time.

KAT

"*listen, Kat, I need some time to think things through. I don't want to rush into anything like before.*"

Harris' words haunt me despite a full month's passing. My heart still aches as though he only just gave me the brush-off after he gave me the most incredible orgasm. And I paid him back in kind. At least I thought so. Enough to make him want me, not toss me aside. Or rather, out the door unceremoniously.

I stuck to my guns and didn't contact him in any way. Vivian reassured me it's best for him to have time to think of what happened between us and to want more. It's tough, but I keep busy.

Today, Viv and I have our Pilates duet session. Twice a week we come to the airy, sun-filled studio off Union Square. Viv swears by Mr. Pilates—as she refers to him. She's been a devotee since her teens when her mother introduced the fitness practice to her.

As Viv quoted Joseph Pilates, "Change happens through movement and movement heals."

After a few sessions, I must admit I feel much better. And the resulting strength to my core and uplift to my butt makes me better exponentially. So even though I'd rather have soreness from a bout in the bed with Harris, I thank you, Mr. Pilates!

I snicker to myself.

Viv shifts on her reformer to look at me questioningly.

I shake my head and grin like the Cheshire Cat. But the rosy blush on my alabaster cheeks gives me away. She snorts, knowing my thoughts focus on Harris. What else is new?

"Hi, Vivian and Kat! How are your bodies feeling this morning? Anything happened since your last session?"

I smile at Gina, our Pilates teacher. She's a bubbly twentysomething like us who's been teaching classical Pilates for ten years. She moves with the fluidity and strength of a dancer as she walks towards the reformers where our class will take place. Gina's long and lithe body speaks to her years of training and encourages me through The Hundred —or The Tortuous, as I call the exercise!

"Hi, Gina! Feeling great! We ran here, so I'm ready to go," Vivian responds with a thumbs-up. Ever the fitness enthusiast, she lives for heart-pumping activities. "What's the plan for today?"

Even though Viv is at the advance level, she does our duets at my beginner's order. She tells me it's just as vigorous since it makes her refocus on the basics. She uses her third weekly session as a private during which she works at her higher level.

I'm thankful for her companionship.

Gina grins and puts us through our paces from the sequence on the reformer to exercises on the chair. If The Hundred gets me, Going Up Front on the chair freaks me out. It takes total concentration and the use of the entire core to maintain balance. Add in the height changes, and it's a killer exercise. But I love it!

It spares me no time to think of Harris Steele.

Once our session ends, Vivian and I take showers and head out for our favorite post-Pilates brunch spot. It's a cute cafe known for its power smoothies located between Union Square East and Irving Place. We give our orders of smoothie shots and açaí bowls to the server who's as buff as the diners. Under other circumstances, his hazel eyes and square chin would make me swoon. But no one compares to Harris Steele.

And just like that, he's back in my mind…

I shake my head to clear it and tune in to Vivian.

"So, this guy I have a date with has a friend," she starts, then raises her hands when my eyebrows furrow. "Hear me out, Kat. I know you're still into Harris. But there's no harm in a bit of a distraction. Keep your flirtation skills sharp."

I tilt my head to the side and purse my lips.

Viv giggles.

"*Anyway*. My date asked if I knew someone who would

like to make it a double. What do you think?" She asks with pleading brown eyes.

I try to keep the stern look but soon relent.

"Okay, fine! I'll go. When is it?" I respond.

She whoops and shimmies in the booth.

"Excellent! I'll shoot him a text now," she says, then continues as her fingers fly across the screen of her mobile. "It's tomorrow night. Dinner at this new restaurant. For the opening. Should be fun! Let's go shopping after we eat. No sense in wearing something old for someone new."

She glances up and winks.

I giggle and drink the smoothie shot the server placed before me.

Why the bloody hell not?

* * *

"THAT COLOR LOOKS great on you. It's a striking combination with your lovely hair."

I stare up into the handsome face of my blind date. And even a blind person could see his masculine beauty. Well over six feet tall, chin length coal black hair, aquamarine blue eyes, muscular physique, Solomon is beyond swoon worthy. Even I can't ignore his magnetism.

Dammit to hell, Viv!

She and I just arrived at the bar of the new snazzy eatery in the Meatpacking District. The line was so dense, I didn't have time to read the name. The event organizers ushered us in after they checked our names off the list on their clipboards.

As we walked through the glass-plate doors, we made our way through other guests to the gleaming mahogany bar. A wall of glass with colorful bottles glittering beneath the strategically placed pot lights rises behind it. Bartenders shake and serve drinks to the well-heeled crowd gathered.

Vivian nudged me towards two just as impeccably dressed men.

"That's Brent with the blond hair," she whispered and giggled. "His friend is pretty good looking, too. Worth it now, huh?"

Now, as Solomon pins me with his electric gaze, I gape awestruck. I have to agree with Viv.

He smiles at my speechlessness. Not arrogant. Confident.

"Thank you," I squeak, then cough to hide my nerves.

"We have time for a drink before we sit. What would you like?" Solomon asks, as he signals the bartender.

I ask for a Manhattan. Why not go with the classic cocktail in the City it's named after?

He graces me with a devastating smile before he tells the bartender.

I try not to melt. Okay, I do. Just a tiny bit.

"Here you go," Solomon says as he hands the drink to me. His fingertips brush mine, and I jerk. He tightens his grip on the glass. "Whoa there."

"Must have been a shock. You know the ones you get from sliding around on carpet in socks. It happened to me all the time as a lass," I babble.

He smirks as he stares pointedly at the hardwood floor bare of carpet and raises his glass to mine.

"Here's to more electrical currents between us," he toasts.

Busted, I can't help but to giggle and shake my head before I take a sip.

"Tell me, what else did you get up to as a wee lass, Kat?" he says.

"Only if you promise to tell me some of your childhood hijinks," I respond with a grin.

Solomon holds up his pinky finger, and we swear on it as laughter flows between us easily.

As we trade stories, Brent leans over to let us know it's time to move to our table. Solomon helps me from the high chair. Again, a zing courses through me as his palm settles on my lower back. The possessive move reminds me of Harris.

I close my eyes as we wait for the hostess.

Get it together, Kat Jackson. Harris is undoubtedly not pining over you.

Pressure on my back returns me to the restaurant. I push the thought of Harris aside. This night I want to relax and enjoy myself with my friend and our dates. Besides, I haven't heard from Harris Steele in a month.

From beneath my eyelashes, I glance up at Solomon and

smile. His face lights up as his fingers stroke my lower back.

I'm glad Viv convinced me to buy the red crepe midi dress. The high neckline and pleated flared sleeves give it a chic look. While the v-cut back with a gold zipper to the split at the hem adds a touch of sexy. Paired with flesh-tone stilettos, my legs appear to go on for miles.

Solomon's touch skims along the zipper enticingly.

Hmmm.

We follow Viv and Brent to a table in the center of the room. Other diners watch as we pass. The women assess us. They take in my dress and Viv's black stretch-jersey mini dress she wears with Azzedine Alaia laser-cut knee-length boots. Then their gazes shift to our dates. Some stare openly while others peer discreetly. Admiration gleams in their eyes.

I straighten my spine. One thing I learned over the past few months, I'm just as worthy as these hoity-toity women. A description Payton loves to label me. With a grimace, I push my contentious brother from my mind, too.

"This place is fantastic!" Vivian exclaims with wide eyes. "How did you score an invitation, Brent?"

He sits taller in his chair and smooths his suit jacket, pleased by her comment.

I hide my smirk behind my glass of water. Vivian excels at the art of flirting.

"The chef is a buddy of mine. We met during a para-chuting excursion in the Himalayas years ago," Brent responds, as he adjusts his tie.

"Ooh! Parachuting? In the Himalayas? Do tell us more, Brent!" Vivian says as she places her hand on his biceps.

From the sparkle in her eyes, I know she's truly interested in his action-adventure side. In fact, it sounds incredible. I listen equally fascinated.

Not to be outdone, Solomon shares tales of his cycling on challenging terrains including mountain ranges around the world.

Throughout the meal, Viv and I listen to the two men. Our comments encourage them to reveal more about themselves. I don't mind since I prefer to keep private about my life until I get to know a guy better, anyway.

As the busser clears the table, Brent grins and stands with his hand outstretched to someone behind me.

"Hey, man! Dinner was superb. Congratulations on another fantastic restaurant. Not to mention scoring an invitation gave me cool points with our dates," he says. "Let me introduce you to Vivian Murphy and her friend Kat—"

"*Jackson.* Well, well, well. Nice to see you out and about in your new city… cousin."

Half turned in my chair to thank the chef, the smile on my face falls as my mouth drops open. Heat blasts my cheeks as I turn around completely.

Lucien Jackson owns this restaurant?!

"No kidding! Your cousin? And I thought I had the in," Brent chuckles as he claps Lucien on the shoulder.

Vivian connects the name to my sorry story. She recovers quicker than I do and jumps into the conversation.

"Lucien Jackson, so nice to meet *The Sexy Chef* at last. I'm a huge fan of your creations and of your show. Congratulations and here's to much more success for you!" She says as she tilts her wineglass at him. "And Brent, darling, you made it all happen. Cheers!"

"Absolutely!"

"Cin-cin!"

With ease, she defuses the situation and gives me time to pick my jaw off my lap. But unsure of how I should greet Lucien since I haven't seen him in months, I raise my wine glass and offer a slight a smile.

"*Slàinte Mhath*, Lucien" I offer to his *good health*.

He cocks an eyebrow as he stares at me just shy of a beat too long. Solomon and Brent don't notice as they sip their wine. As Vivian chats the guys up, she flicks her gaze between Lucien and me discreetly. But his chilly expression hits me directly to my chest like a fist. I wince and glance away.

Lucien leans down and double kisses my cheeks.

"Thank you," he says, then gazes at the others. "Everyone. Now, if you will excuse me."

He throws another meaningful stare at me before he pivots on his heels and strides away.

The breath I didn't realize I was holding slips from my mouth on a long sigh of relief. I gulp the rest of my wine and set the empty glass on the table.

My mind reels. Will he tell Harris? And mention me being on a *date*? What does Lucien think of me? Should I reach out to him? Try to explain?

Bloody hell…

The appearance of the server interrupts my brooding. He places the decadent Millionaire's Shortbread before each of us. The dessert made legendary by Mary Queen of Scots. Even its decadent layers of chewy caramel and thick chocolate on a buttery shortbread crust can't drag me from the depths of my funk.

"Mmm, as delicious as this seems, I must beg off. Kat and I have an early morning. Do you mind if we say good night?" Vivian comes to my rescue again.

The guys cave to her charming smile. Her beauty has Brent kissing her hand as he nods and asks her to do him the honor of dinner again.

She giggles and agrees.

Solomon smiles at me.

"I'd love to see you again too, Kat. Perhaps drinks and dinner tomorrow?" he says. "May I have your phone number?"

"Of course, that would be splendid, Solomon. Tomorrow it is," I respond, then recite my number as he enters it into his mobile.

As we make our way to the restaurant's entrance, the hairs on the back of my neck rise. I glance over my shoulder. Despite being surrounded by adoring women and some men at the bar, Lucien watches me intently.

I smile awkwardly.

He tilts his chin down with a brief smile in acknowledgement.

Well, at least he didn't throw me out or see me to the door. It's a start.

Yet I give a silent prayer Lucien doesn't ruin any chance I have with Harris.

The image of that redheaded Siren's luscious ass rolling and her hips swaying in that sinful dress remains forefront in my mind. Even after a month.

Her tight, greedy pussy squeezed my fingers like a vise. When she went off like a rocket, I swear I wanted to bury my aching cock balls deep in her wet heat.

But I wasn't that far gone. Hell nah! I didn't have a condom. No way would I fuck her bareback. I won't risk getting her pregnant for damn sure. Not just that Siren, but any woman.

I have a gazillion nieces and nephews. No need for me to jump on board the Daddy Train any time soon. I just got screwed with my first actual relationship—albeit a brief one. So, count me out. Not this player!

But I digress…

Four weeks, and that redheaded Siren emblazoned herself right back in my mind. I had to suppress the urge to hold her close to my heaving chest after she blew me—a damn satisfying job, I must say. She opened up to me, and I fucked her throat like I would have her pussy. Hot, wet, tight. Deep. Fuuuck!

Nothing and no one can distract my thoughts. I can't keep her out of my mind or my fantasies. I must've increased the muscles in my left forearm from the daily strenuous workouts I put it through. If I beat my cock one more time to the vision of her in the enthralling throes of ecstasy, it'll fall right the fuck off! Then I'd be dickless. Maybe that's not such a bad idea where she's concerned. Can't fuck her if I no longer have my jackhammer.

I spent plenty of time with my twin and brothers since they were all in the City for January. The time all of us work from STEELE International's global headquarters to set the new year's agendas. But now Haley flew to Aberdeen, Roger left for Paris, and Malcolm moved back to Southampton Village. I'll still get a chance to hang out with him and Baz since they work here.

However, Valentine's Day happens just over a week from now. All of them have plans with their boos, so I'm ass out. Again. Even Laurent ditched me. Not that I blame them one bit. I wouldn't say *hoes*, rather their loves take precedence over this brother.

Which brings me back to she who shall not be named.

Did that redheaded Siren really dig her claws under my skin enough for a trip back down that relationship road? Or do I just fuck her out of my system for good?

I ponder those questions as I sit in my kitchen eating an

omelet and home fries from Sarabeth's on Central Park South for breakfast. The gourmet chef's dream kitchen Lucien designed serves the purpose of heating up my takeout meals. The only appliance besides the microwave—or the oven if I'm feeling adventurous—that gets use is the Vitamix. I blend my protein smoothies with it every day.

Just like the rest of my full-floor penthouse, the kitchen is spacious, the size of a New York City two-bedroom apartment easily. With enough room for the six-seater banquette I sit at to eat. The sheer size of my residence reminds me of how very alone I am. No woman other than my female relatives has been here.

For a moment, I envision that redheaded Siren puttering about the kitchen…

The delicious aroma of a full Scottish breakfast wafts through the air as I return from my personal training session with Borya. I walk through the penthouse I share with My Kitty Kat drawn by the scent to the kitchen.

She stands at the stove butt naked except for a frilly apron tied around her narrow waist and sky-high stilettos. Her glorious Titian hair piled atop her head in a messy bun. One silky tendril snakes down her back to curl around her butt cheek.

I sneak up behind her and twirl the wayward strand around my finger, then tug it. She yelps in surprise, then moans as my mouth descends on her parted lips. She tastes like the bacon she's nibbling on. I eat her up.

She grinds her bare ass against my cock tenting my shorts. Her soft cries spur me on.

I lift her onto the oversized island. She gasps into my mouth as the cool marble touches her warm pussy lips. I still her squirming with a quick succession of spanks. She moans for more.

Naughty Girl.

My hands grip her hips to pull her to the edge of the island. Fingers flex to secure the hold. The thought of my marks on her alabaster skin hardens my cock to steel. Mine!

"Lose the apron," I command.

Hurriedly, she pulls the strings and tosses the hindrance to the floor. Her emerald green eyes glitter as she faces me again.

I press my lips to hers, then trail open-mouthed kisses along her jaw and down her neck to the mounds of her DDs. I suck as much of one into my mouth as possible. More than a mouthful, I stuff my face. My tongue swirls around until it reaches her rosy pink pebbled nipple. I suck it until she climaxes. A repeat to the other tit, and she begs me to fuck her.

But first, I need my fill of her cream.

I devour her pussy like a starved man. Legs thrown over my shoulders, ass cupped in my hands. She gushes, and I swallow all she gives to me. I wipe from my chin to my nose along her trembling inner thighs. A soft kiss to her swollen clit makes her wail.

With a snap of my hips, I bury my rod within the soaked depths of her core.

A strangled cry pours from her slack mouth.

I cover it with mine as I piston in and out of her tight pussy. Hungrily, it sucks me in each time I thrust forward. When she tightens her inner walls, a blinding light flashes before my eyes. I grunt.

"So good, Kitty Kat," I groan. "Cum for me one more time."

She digs her fingernails into my back and squeezes her ass cheeks. Her hips raise and match each of my brutal thrusts. Her pussy quivers along my length. She bites my shoulder as she screams my name.

I'm a goner.

Fire licks down my spine and up my legs. It meets at my lower back and shoots into my heavy balls as they swing like a pendulum. The force makes them draw up.

I band one arm around her waist and grip the edge of the island with my other hand to keep from crashing to the floor. I widen my stance and use my thighs and ass to propel up and forward. Rocking on my toes, I drill into her pussy.

The breath gets sucked from me when I blow a torrent of seed deep into her womb.

I fall across her torso, pushing her flat onto the island's surface as my legs give out. Our sweat-slick skin slides on the smooth marble. Its coolness does nothing to lessen the heat between us.

The frenetic beat of her heart matches mine. I bury my face in her neck as I try to catch my breath. She whispers words of love as her hands stroke my back. She soothes me.

Once I can stand, I lift her from the island and carry her to our bedroom as I call for the home tech system to fill the sunken tub. I set her on the white terrycloth pouf and strip out of my workout gear. Our eyes remain locked. Emerald fire lights in hers at the sight of my nakedness. I smirk.

"Behave, naughty lass," I admonish as I lift her and step down into the tub.

"But you like me naughty. Don't you, my love?" She purrs as she licks my cheek.

I chuckle and nod.

"That I do, Kitty Kat. That I do," I respond.

With a shake of my head, I glance down at the cold omelet and home fries. They're defiantly not as appealing as my fantasy breakfast. I roll my eyes and dump the food in the trash.

Mind made up, I snatch my mobile from the empty island and place the call.

KAT

"Good evening, Ms. Jackson. Mr. Solomon Givens arrived for you. Shall I send him to your floor?"

"Good evening. Kindly let him know I will meet him in the lobby in five minutes. Thank you," I respond to the concierge.

My breathing speeds up as I replace the intercom handset.

As promised, Solomon and I have plans for our second date tonight. This time without Viv and Brent. It's not the idea of being alone with Solomon that has my pulse skittering. Rather, the fact I'm attracted to him.

The way he listened intently to my more pleasant childhood stories and laughed with me eased into light touches and promise-filled aquamarine blue eyes makes him almost impossible to resist. Not only ridiculously handsome, but intelligent and funny, too. Solomon Givens is the total package who makes any woman want him. And I'm no exception.

Except…

The comparison to Harris happened all during the blind date.

Soulful dove gray eyes light up when he laughs.

His quick wit and easy banter.

The possessive and sensual touches of his sizable hands on my ass or as he strokes my cheek.

How he slipped past my defenses and made me love him.

Alas, that was then, and this is now. As much as I want to give him time, I'm not foolish enough to believe he's gone without the company of other women. He's virile—oh, so virile—and any woman wants him, too.

Does the thought of Harris with another twist my gut? Absolutely.

Do I blame him? Sadly, no.

I brought the loss of my lover on myself by being deceitful.

The only upside is our last interaction. He couldn't resist me no more than I could him. His body responded to mine just as fiercely as mine did to his carnal demands. The proof of his desire was apparent. Just the memory sets me ablaze again.

However, I will no longer hide in my room and cry myself to sleep. I'll go on another date with Solomon. But despite my attraction to him, I can't give more since Harris has my heart and my soul. I'll make it clear to Solomon tonight I'm not ready for a relationship.

With a wistful sigh, I check my reflection in the mirror. Satisfied my LBD, hair in a chignon, and natural makeup give off classic chic and not sexy kitten, I grab my coat and my purse. During the ride down on the lift, I think of how I'll let Solomon know my intentions. My hope is he'll understand. It's not as though he won't have trouble finding a woman who can give him more.

The doors ping open, and I step out into the lobby. As I approach a sitting area, my prediction proves true. A statuesque blonde in yoga pants that make her legs go on forever stands a bit too close to Solomon. She stares up at him, laughing about something. The shrill sound grates my nerves. But like I said, no loss for him if we don't date…

"Hi, Solomon," I say from behind him.

The woman flicks her gaze at me. Her hazel eyes rake over me from the crown of my head to the tip of my slingbacks. She all but snarls at the interruption.

I grin.

"Oh hi, Kat! You look lovely," Solomon says, then leans down to kiss my cheek.

The blonde purses her lips. But she doesn't move.

"Thank you. And you're as dashing as ever," I respond, smoothing the lapel of his cashmere overcoat and turn to the woman. "Hello."

She blinks in surprise I would address her. A spluttered response is all she can manage.

Solomon, however, doesn't hesitate.

"Kat, this is your neighbor," he starts, then turns to her. "I'm so sorry. Your name again?"

A flash of irritation skims across her pretty face. Recovering quickly, she extends her hand to me.

"Blanche Reeves," she says.

My grin broadens as I shake her hand and respond, "Kat Jackson. How nice to meet you."

Solomon glances between us, then nods.

"Right. Well, it was nice to meet you, Blanche. If you will excuse us," he says as he places a hand on my lower back.

She nods in return as her eyes shift to his possessive move.

"Yes, well, enjoy your evening," Blanche Reeves says, then slips around us to head for the elevators. She glances over her shoulder. A wistful expression replaces the irritation.

"Shall we?"

Solomon's words draw me back to him. I nod, and he guides me to the front doors, even as I hold back a giggle. Poor Blanche. If Solomon wants, I'll leave his number for her with the concierge.

A sleek navy blue Mercedes-Benz sits at the curb. The driver opens the back door when Solomon gestures towards the sedan.

"I hope you like Italian. I was able to—as Brent says— score a reservation at Carbone on Thompson Street. It's one of the hardest restaurants to get into. Not that I'm trying to one up my buddy," Solomon says with an easy laugh.

His eyes twinkle in the low light of the backseat. The glow of a streetlamp filters through the tinted window to illuminate his face. Laugh lines crinkle about his eyes as the corners of his full lips curl up.

Damn, he's gorgeous!

Good luck to you, Blanche Reeves, and to all the other women who'll have a chance with Solomon.

"Sounds delicious and well done! No pun intended," I respond with a grin.

He chuckles.

At the restaurant, we pass under the neon lights to enter a cozy dining area. A wooden ceiling, brick walls, and colorful tiled floor bring warmth from the cold of February. The host sits us amongst recognizable celebrities and models. We have more than a delicious meal of Dover Piccata and Lobster Fra Diavolo. During dessert and coffee, I recite the no relationship speech.

Solomon listens with an expression I can't decipher.

I tug the corner of my lip between my teeth as I wait for his response.

He reaches over and places his thumb beside my lip. Gently, he frees it with his thumb, then rubs the pad across my lower lip. His eyes study my face.

With a sigh, he sits back.

"Whomever stole your heart is one lucky son of a bitch. I hope he realizes how special you are. Even in the short time we've known each other, I can tell you're a gem, Kat

Jackson. I'll bow out. But know if he fucks up again, I'm here for you," Solomon says.

I lower my eyes from his intense gaze as my cheeks heat. Little does he know it's all *my* fault.

"Huh! Look who's here."

My head snaps up.

Laurent stands above me. He cocks his eyebrow as his head tilts. Bottle green eyes bore into the depths of my soul. He flicks his gaze at Solomon.

"Laurent Jackson. And you are, chap?" He asks with his hand extended.

Solomon glances at me, then stands. He grips Laurent's hand and responds, "Solomon Givens. I take it you're a relative of Kat's?"

Laurent gives a mirthless chuckle. His eyes dart back to me.

My face flushes crimson. My hands twist in my lap.

Not again! Bloody hell…

"You can say that, Solomon Givens. Kat and I are *cousins*," Laurent responds. He turns back to me. "You're doing well. New city. New man. Not bad—"

"Laurent, *Mi Amor*, I'm hungry."

So taken aback by Laurent's unexpected presence and stinging words, I didn't notice Yessenia behind him. However, her light brown eyes avoid mine. But she slides her hand around Laurent's biceps. The gesture encourages him to move away. After he throws a final scowl at me.

Thankfully, the server appears.

Solomon takes one look at my distraught face and asks

for the check as he gives her his Black American Express credit card. We wait in silence for her to return.

Inside the car, I press myself against the door to put as much space as possible between Solomon and me. I'm beyond embarrassed. He must regret the kind words he told me. Evidently so since he makes zero effort to speak with me. We sit in a tense silence as I watch the streets of Manhattan slip past us.

When we arrive at my building, I hasten from the Mercedes-Benz sedan as soon as my doorman opens it. Solomon follows. At the lift, I take a deep breath and turn to him.

"Thank you for a wonderful evening, Solomon. I'm so sorry it ended on a low note. I hope you'll forgive—"

He shakes his head. Coal black hair brushes his sculpted cheekbones.

"Everyone makes mistakes, Kat. Big or small. It's not what you *did* that matters as much as what you *do* to fix it," Solomon says. He cocks his head to the side at the sound of my whimper. Once again, he rubs his thumb over my lips. "Don't fret, little lass. You can still count on me."

He leans down and replaces his thumb with his lush lips. Surprised, I open my mouth. He slips his tongue inside and sweeps around to engage mine. I lean into his muscular body and let his tender kiss clear away my misery. If only for a moment.

Solomon steps back first. He pulls his lips into his mouth as though still tasting me. His hooded aquamarine blue eyes bore into my emerald green orbs, widened by surprise.

"Do not forget what I told you. I'm here for you, Kat," he says, then pivots and strides away.

The tears I held at bay fall silently down my cheeks.

* * *

"Why, good morning, lovey-dovey! How was your date last night with Solomon? Wait. Why the grim face? Did he do something wrong?"

Viv's joking tone changes to one of concern. She rises from the couch in the family room as I pass it on my way to the kitchen.

I got little sleep. Hopefully, a shot of caffeine will give me much-needed energy. Or is it too early for a pitcher of Viv's margaritas?

I shake my head as much to answer her questions as to answer my own. Get it together, Kat…

"No. But I could use a shoulder to cry on and the ear of a good friend to listen," I respond as I nod towards the kitchen. "A cup of coffee first."

Viv bounces to her feet.

"You know I'm here for you, Kat," she says as she loops her arm through mine.

A sob escapes my lips at her choice of words. They echo those of Solomon's from last night. Do I even deserve their friendship and consideration? I sigh as Viv squeezes my arm.

"We'll have a Russian coffee," she says. When I frown, she winks and adds, "A shot of vodka will do the trick."

I can't help but to giggle as she waggles her eyebrows.

"Sounds like just what I need," I say.

While Viv gets the bottle of Beluga, I start up the Breville. She had to show me how to operate the complicated espresso machine. All of its controls daunted me. Now, she calls me the resident barista.

We sit at the island. The scent of fresh coffee floats around us. I take a bite of the danish ring—Viv insisted we splurge. And I agree. What hips? Besides, Harris likes to grip them as he thrusts—AARGH!!!

"All righty then, Kat," Vivian says with an elegantly arched eyebrow raised.

My mouth opens and closes.

"I said that out loud? Didn't I?" I ask as my cheeks pinken.

She giggles and nods.

"Yeah, well, see, that's the problem!" I exclaim as I clutch my hair in both hands. "I can't stop thinking about you know who! As mouthwatering as Solomon is, I cannot get that other one out of my bloody head!"

Viv tsks and sips her coffee, ready for the tea.

I spill.

The entire evening from Blanche to Laurent, ending with Solomon's parting kiss and words tumble from my mouth. When I finish, I sit back and take a slug of my coffee. Still hot—since I brewed it to perfection—it burns my throat. As I choke, Viv pats me on the back and hands a napkin to me.

"Perhaps we should've gone straight with the vodka?" Viv queries. A grimace forms on her stunning face.

Once I recover, she goes on.

"Here's the thing, Kat. A breakup is never easy," she starts. "And when you add in family—especially as tight a bunch as the Steeles and Jacksons, from what you told me —plus the whole scandal... Well, you might as well forget it."

When I gasp and stare at her, Viv holds her hand up.

"Listen, I'm not saying forget it, forget it. Rather, it's a serious shitshow. Many people's feelings are involved. Not just yours and Harris'," she clarifies.

I stare bleakly at the island's white marble surface. The veining reminds me of those on Harris' long, thick dick. I shudder and shake my head.

"It's not insurmountable."

I hear Vivian continue.

"Just don't expect everyone to jump up and give you hugs and kisses right away. Maybe some will. Who's to say? But the most important thing to do. That is, if you truly want another go with Harris. You have to make amends with him. When his family sees he's accepted you back in his life. They will come around out of their love for him. Get it?"

She sits back and pops a piece of danish in her mouth.

I mull over her words.

What she says is absolutely on point. I can't expect to breeze back into their lives no more than I can into Harris'.

At least not yet. I know I said I'd give him time. But maybe if I reach out to him—even just to say hi and ask how he's doing—he'll be receptive. A way to make amends.

I face Viv and smile.

"You're right. I'll call him and—"

My mobile rings. The vibrations make it skitter along the smooth marble.

I glance at the screen. My eyes nearly fall out of my head as I stare in shock.

"OMG!!! Harris!" Viv exclaims as she peers around me. "Kat! Answer it already! It's a sign!"

HARRIS

"*H*ello, I can't see your wrist. Would you like to play later?"

I glance up at the redhead before me as I sit at the long, reclaimed-wood-covered bar for LEVEL 4 Restaurant. Although she has a banging body, she's not *that* redheaded Siren.

Yesterday, I gave in and called her. It was either keep fantasizing about her or fucking her. I choose to fuck her out of my system.

One week.

She doesn't know my intentions. Yet.

I invited her to dinner at LEVELS New York. If she's down for it—which judging by her response to our impromptu tease and please, I'd bet a resounding yes—we'll start tonight. No point in delaying.

Intent on the upper hand, I arrived early. Now this beauty wants my attention.

"Nothing on my wrist," I respond as I lift my arm and push my suit jacket and cuff up as far as the links allow.

LEVELS New York's top priority is the safety of its members, their guests, and applicants. Management enforces strict protocols everyone must follow. From nondisclosure agreements to names not given unless provided by the person to super tight ongoing background checks and other security measures.

Another measure to avoid unwanted interactions amongst club participants is the requirement for partnered subs to wear collars given to them by their Dom; partnered Doms wear gold enamel bracelets; available subs wear red; available Doms wear white; voyeurs wear black. Those not seeking another wear nothing.

That redheaded Siren is on her way. Hence no bracelet for me tonight.

This one pouts as her eyes linger on my mouth.

"Could I entice you to choose a white bracelet to top me or black so you can watch me cum for you?" She purrs as she licks her berry-stained lips with the tip of her tongue.

I wait for my cock to stir in appreciation for her wanton behavior. But no dice.

"No," I answer, then offer her a winning smile when the corners of her mouth droop. "I'm more than positive you'll find a worthy partner tonight. Have a drink on me while you wait."

Her beautiful face glows as she names her cocktail —no pun.

After the bartender hands the glass to her, she pats me

on the chest and leans in to whisper thank you. She tells me I'm a keeper before she sashays to the other end of the bar.

I watch the sway of her hips beneath the silk of her mini dress. With a sigh, I turn to face the elevators.

Past the bustling crowd of the crème de la crème of society who mingle as they sip their top-shelf drinks, I spy *that* redheaded Siren. Her Titian hair makes it easy to spot her amongst the blondes and brunettes.

When our eyes connect, emerald greens scorch my dove grays. Her alabaster cheeks deepen to crimson as her nostrils flare. With narrowed eyes, she spins on her heels and stomps towards the elevators.

Hmmm… Not quite the start to the evening I planned for us.

I hop off the leather and black metal stool and weave past the clusters of matching high-top tables. Despite the open-plan layout of the room, I get caught up by members who want the chance to speak to or play with a Steele. I smile and incline my head as a brief greeting, but rush towards the entry. I'm not here to chit chat or seduce tonight—at least not with them.

"Kat," I call out as she steps onto an elevator. I lunge forward to place my hand between the doors. "Come out of there."

They open, and I take her by the elbow. Without a word, I guide her along the path between the two areas of the bar towards the LEVEL 4 Restaurant's maître d' station.

She huffs and jerks. But I ignore her feistiness. While my cock responds as though I rolled a 7 in craps. It's a win-win situation.

The hostess welcomes me by name and sits us in a corner booth. As she leaves, she loosens the ties on the curtains. Immediately, the sounds and the view of the dining room disappear. The redheaded Siren and I cocooned in our own world. I prefer the privacy the booth provides. No one will overhear our conversation.

Her eyes dart around as she realizes we're in a close space. She sits less than an arm's distance from me on the u-shaped banquette. The scent of her alluring perfume fills the air surrounding us.

I fight to stop myself from closing my eyes and inhaling deeply. Instead, I watch her.

Eventually, her emerald green eyes reach my face. The blaze returns at my smug expression. She places her palms on the table and rises.

"Sit. Down. Kat."

She jerks in response to my sharp tone. But lowers her luscious ass back to the leather seat. She folds her arms across her chest in an attempt at defiance.

The move only serves to push her DDs higher. Their nipples poke the silk of her cream blouse. She paired it with a leather pencil skirt, fishnet stockings, and fuck-me stilettos.

The sex kitten came prepared to taunt me.

Well, let's play, Kitty Kat.

"Why did you come if you planned to run away?" I ask with a cocked eyebrow.

Her mouth gapes.

The memory of my dick widening her throat jumps to the forefront of my thoughts. It twitches in my pants. Down, big boy.

I wait for her response. Who speaks first loses and all.

"I did not plan to run away. Nor did I plan to see you eye fucking another woman after you bought her a drink, Harris!" She all but yells. Eyes flash. Cheeks heat.

Jealous? Oh, shit! The Siren doesn't want competition. Hmmm… Interesting. Point for Harris Steele.

"So your response is to rub it in by smirking?" She snarls. "Well, then I made a huge mistake coming here and will *leave*—not run away."

As before, I catch her elbow.

"Ah, ah, ah, Kat," I say as I shake my head. "You do not get to be pissed at me. After the shit you pulled, you're mistaken about who should be angry."

She flinches and her cheeks burn as though my words physically slapped her. The steam dissipates, and she sags against the back of the banquette. Her teeth tug at her bottom lip as her gaze lowers to the table in front of her.

I'm surprised by a pang of remorse. Then I clear my throat.

"Listen, Kat. I didn't invite you here to rehash the past. What you did was beyond fucked up. You've owned it. Time to move on," I say.

She gasps and raises her eyes shiny from unshed tears

to me. The hopeful expression on her face makes my gut twist.

For a second, I'm tempted to not tell her my plan. Just have dinner and end it all forever. But then…

"Oh, Harris, thank you! I want so badly for us to have a positive relationship. Even if it's not a sexual one. I just want to know you don't hate me," she says. The last of her words trail off as her gaze drops back to the table.

Whoa there, little lass! Who said anything about no sex??? We're at LEVELS New York—a den for fucking, for fuck's sake.

"One, I do not hate you, Kat," I say. Her softened eyes rise to peer at me from beneath the thick fringe of her eyelashes. My gut twists again, but I plow ahead.

"Two, the relationship part of your statement directly ties to the point of me bringing you to LEVELS New York," I add, and pause to ensure I have her full attention.

She blinks as she considers the meaning of my words.

"Okay, what about it?" She asks, a tinge of pink returns to her cheeks.

I sit back and pour her then myself a glass of Jackson Cabernet Sauvignon. Ahead of our arrival, I ordered our dinner and wine. Of course, we'll dine on exquisite meals prepared by chefs trained by Lucien. The staff left the bottle open to allow the wine time to breathe. When I hang the green tassel from the curtain tie-back hook, the server will bring the food.

Did I say privacy or what?

I lift my wineglass to my lips. My eyes never leave hers.

I incline my head at her glass. The shakiness of her hand gets noted. She's nervous. Good.

After I take a healthy sip, I set the wineglass back on the table. I twirl the stem between my fingers as I watch the legs drip along the bowl of the glass. As the tension mounts, I wait for her to place her glass down.

Then I lift my gaze. Pinned, her eyes widen and her cheeks flush from pink to berry like her succulent lips.

My cock stirs.

I sit back against the banquette and adjust my dick, no longer content to remain confined. Soon, I think as I stroke its turgid length.

What this redheaded Siren does to me. She has no clue.

But I digress.

"Time has done nothing to ease my hunger for you. True to your nickname, you are a Siren. That night's brief encounter did not slake my need. I remain unsatisfied," I say.

The crimson color now infuses her chest and neck. Nipples peaked. Lips parted. Eyes blown. She watches me as she holds her breath.

Just as I thought.

I pinch the tip of my swollen cock to stop the pre-cum from dampening the leg of my trousers. Then swallow a moan when the tip of her little pink tongue flicks out as though tasting the air ripe with the scent of her arousal and my pheromones.

With my other hand, I reach into the inner pocket of my suit jacket.

"Here is a one-week guest pass to LEVELS New York. For you," I say as I slide it along the tabletop. I stop it smack dab in the middle between us.

Her hooded eyes drop to stare at the envelope. Katrina Jackson handwritten in swirly calligraphy dances across the cream parchment. She bites the corner of her lower lip.

Damn! My cock jumps beneath my palm.

Again, I wait for her to make the next move. The winner of negotiations often emerges triumphantly because they don't give away too much before the other party rejoins.

A minute passes.

Her chest rises and falls with ragged breaths.

"What does that mean for me?" She asks with her eyes glued to the invitation. Her shoulders rigid, as though bracing her hands from picking it up.

I wait until she looks at me before I respond.

"It means you and I have one week to fuck each other out of our systems."

She gasps as her eyes pop from their sockets like Roger Rabbit seeing Jessica for the first time. If I weren't so horny, I'd laugh out loud.

"Wh—What?" The redheaded Siren stammers.

I lean forward. Our noses mere inches apart. She swallows but doesn't pull away.

"You and me fucking until neither of us can sit, stand, or walk. Every. Single. Night. Starting tonight. Should you agree, that is," I respond.

Our warm breath mingles. The dark fruity and spicy

essence of the wine wafts between us. Her arousal even more obvious than before my salacious explanation. I ache to savor more.

Say yes, Siren. Say yes, Siren. I chant like a mantra in my mind.

The sound of her swallow makes my lips quirk.

Almost there, little lass.

"After the week ends? Then what?" She asks breathlessly. Her eyes never leave mine. The pupils so dilated only a rim of emerald green remains.

I inch closer.

"I cannot predict the future. Can you, Kat?" I parry.

Her golden-tinged red eyelashes flutter as her eyes roll back in her head. A puff of air slips from between her lips. She inhales through her nose deeply.

Does she want a taste, too? I wonder.

Neither of us moves. Locked in position. Not daring to be the first to answer.

But I have the advantage. She owes me. And I'm rascal enough to take advantage.

Beads of sweat break out above her top lip. Just as pre-cum collects at my engorged tip.

Make the move, Siren, I command in my mind.

One minute.

Two minutes.

Three—

Her eyes fly open. She nods.

My breath rushes from me. But it's not enough.

"Words, Kat. I will have your words," I murmur, too lightheaded from holding air in my lungs.

"Y—Y—Yes, Harris," she stammers.

"Good, little lass," I say before my mouth crashes over hers.

We come together. Teeth and tongues collide. Hot breath stokes the smoldering embers into a roaring inferno. No longer denied, it rages unabated. The flames lick along my shaft to the point of pain.

I groan into her mouth. She responds with a throaty moan of her own as her body trembles against me.

Kaaaaat, I think to myself. Fuck, I've missed this woman. She satisfies me like no other. Before or after.

But she can never know how much I need her.

I pull back and wipe my mouth with the back of my hand. I watch her face. Eyes closed, body leaning towards mine like a magnet to steel. Her eyes open languorously. Unfocused, they land on my face.

Seeing me adjust my clothes, she sits up straight and brings her fingertips to her kiss-swollen mouth. The gesture makes me want to kiss her all over again. She's fucking delectable. Better than anything Lucien can create.

Speaking of which…

I part the curtains and slip the green tassel on the tie-back hook.

The redheaded Siren needs to eat before I fuck her senseless.

HARRIS

"So, what do we do now?"

Oh, yeah, just what I want to hear. Belly full. Balls fuller. Ready to empty both of them with rounds of backbreaking sex. Expend calories and seed.

I reach over and take her chin between my thumb and forefinger. As I stare into her eyes, her lip trembles.

"Relax, Kat. This is not the first time we've been intimate with one another. Nothing has changed. Well, as far as what you can expect—toe-curling, mind-blowing orgasms by the dozens," I say with a smirk.

The corners of her mouth quirk up and the heaviness in her shoulders releases. Her hand reaches up to cover mine on her face.

I notice it's steadier this time. Her nerves passed.

Good.

"Okay," she whispers.

Her reaction tugs at my heart. But I remove my hand

and slide from the booth. With my eyes on hers, I extend my hand to her. She doesn't hesitate. Her hand slips into mine, and I help her from the banquette.

Once she's standing wedged between me and the table, I lean down and place my lips on hers. Our bodies align. I don't hold back the press of my erection against her lower belly. Instead, I grind against her. She moans and sways against me, matching my rhythm as she rises to her toes. My cock notches at her pussy seam.

My arm bands around her waist to pull us flush. My other hand dives into her hair to tilt her head just so as I deepen our kiss. She whimpers against my mouth when I tug at the silky strands.

"Harris," she whispers as her breath catches.

"Let's go," I respond thickly.

The temptation to carry her over my shoulder through the restaurant and down in the elevator to my private suite flares within me. But I don't want her embarrassed by my caveman conduct. I'll save it for the bedroom.

I part the curtain and usher her ahead of me. Not just being a gentleman, but because I want to watch her ass roll beneath the supple leather of her skirt. Lifted by those heels, it sways with each of her steps. Long legs stressed by the black seam up the backs of each one.

A low growl pours from deep within my chest.

Captain Caveman alert!

I look neither left nor right as I follow the redheaded Siren past the other tables and out to the bar. I barely respond to the hostess as she bids us a good evening. Little does she realize just how *good* of an evening I plan to have with the Siren.

We make it to the elevators with no interruptions. Once inside, I place my keycard against the panel to select the second floor. It features twelve private suites for members to continue their pleasure apart from the BDSM levels of Peepshow and the Cellar.

I watch the Siren out the corner of my eye.

She stares up at the dial showing the floor. We've played at LEVELS London, so she's familiar with the layout. Each club mimics the other except for the point of interest or landmark visible from the Sky Lounge on Level 7.

Where London has the Tower of London, New York—located in the Meatpacking District—offers a stunning, 360-degree view of Manhattan and across the Hudson River to New Jersey's shoreline. The Siren and I won't have time to revel in the scenery. We'll be too busy fucking in my suite, on Level 2 or below ground.

Who needs panoramic views when I have the best view in the house of a naked Siren spread before me?

I chuckle as I hold the door open for her to walk into the hallway.

The foyer—sparsely decorated and dimly lit—sets the mood for carnality. The hypnotic thrumming of sensuous music piped in through hidden speakers add to the intensity and expectation of the sexual activities that happen behind the twelve closed doors. On this level, plush silk wool carpet covers the floor to mask the sounds of eager footsteps.

I place my palm at the base of the Siren's spine to guide her down the quiet, equally dim hallway to my corner suite. At the door, I place my palm on the plaque to disengage the lock. No need to fumble for keys. Lucien and Malcolm thought of every convenience. Haley and I implemented the best technology for security.

I usher the Siren to enter the suite ahead of me. Although she's seen the inside of one in London, her hooded eyes glance around at my decked-out suite compared to others. Since New York's club serves as my home base, I maintain a suite here for my personal use only.

With a fresh perspective, I study my suite through her eyes: set in the middle of the room is a massive, custom rose wood, king-size bed with four posters and a rose gold lattice canopy rings hang; ruby red silk sheets, duvet, and various sized pillows with a white cashmere blanket draped over the foot; from the rose wood tray ceiling, along with the Swarovski crystal chandelier and recessed lights, hang hooks; the walls and ceiling panels covered in red silk damask; the floor carpeted in deep ruby silk on silk; drawers of an antique armoire filled with anal plugs, clamps, cords, cuffs, vibrators, and more; a spanking bench and a Sybian saddle stand on the wall opposite the armoire; below windows treated to not allow visibility from the outside sits a chaise with rose gold rings; one door next to the armoire leads to the all white, Carrara marble bathroom that has a walk-in shower for four, an oversized soaking tub, double vanities, and a separate water closet for the bidet and toilet; behind the other door lies my dressing room filled with suits, casual wear, and footwear.

It pleases me to see the Siren awed by the suite's majesty —especially the toys. I smirk when her lust-filled gaze lingers on the Sybian saddle. Her breath quickens at the sight of the dildo standing tall in the middle of it. If I had the remote in hand, I would start it just to hear her gasp.

We'll add a ride on it to the list of erotic activities. Not tonight, though. Tonight, I have to have her fast and rough. It's been way too long since I indulged in her carnal delights.

I walk up behind her and lower my head to her ear. A warm breath makes her silky strands skim the side of her face and neck.

She shudders as her fists clench.

"Strip," I command in a throaty growl.

The gasp I ached to hear slips past her parted lips. Her entire body convulses. Hands unclench and fist again.

"Now," I add.

She mewls.

I step back and stand with my feet planted apart. My fingers pinch and stroke my hungry cock beneath my trousers.

Her eyes widen when she spins and sees my erotic actions. She swallows audibly. But her hands lift to the buttons on her blouse. At first distracted by my pulsating cock, she fumbles with the tiny buttons. She growls in frustration and nearly rips the placket apart.

I bite my lower lip to hold back a chuckle.

The Siren proves eager.

A growl of my own rumbles in my chest when the sheer mesh of her cream-colored bra reveals the curve of her DDs tipped by pebbled nipples. So hard they threaten to poke holes through the skimpy material. A delicate bow rests between the mounds. Sinful and sweet. Yum.

The vision combined with the friction caused by my fingers and the heel of my hand damn near unleashes a torrent of jizz. I close my eyes and squeeze the mushroom head to seal the slit momentarily. Once I regroup, I open my eyes narrowly. Just a peek reveals the Siren shimmying out of the tight leather pencil skirt. The blouse discarded to the floor in a heap.

Her tits bounce as the fullness of the tops spills from the demi-cup bra. They flash in and out from behind the curtain of her lustrous Titian hair. The color even more glorious amidst the ruby reds of my suite. How perfect.

She steps from the skirt pooled at her feet. One long leg after the other frees her. She stands. A matching G-string conceals nothing of her bare mons. The slit of her pussy in plain view. Above the scrap of sheer material, a matching garter belt wraps around her narrow waist. The straps skim along her thighs to hold the tops of the black fishnet stockings in place. My mouth waters as my gaze follows the lines to the black fuck-me stilettos.

Her hands hesitate at the garter belt clips.

"Shall I continue?" She asks in a raspy voice.

"Yes. Remove everything," I respond. "I want you completely naked."

The clips in the front open, followed by those in the back. Fishnets slide down her toned thighs. Bent over, she rolls them down her legs before she slips her shoes off. Five inches shorter, she barely reaches my shoulder.

With a gleam in her emerald green eyes, she unfastens the garter belt. It dangles from her index finger, drawing my eyes to it. I watch as it drops to the floor atop her blouse. My gaze returns to her flushed face.

She pursers her lips as she cups her tits—too large for her hands, just right for mine. Her head lolls to the side when she tweaks the rosy buds of her nipples. She licks her lower lip.

I mimic the act.

The supposed sweet bow pops apart. Her ample tits bob freely, heavy from her arousal. Another tweak to her nipples and she loops her fingers into the G-string. They drop to the floor. She kicks them aside.

The Siren emerges in all of her magnificence.

I swallow thickly, then command her in a gruff voice to strip me.

She sashays forward. Eyes locked with mine. Confidence returned, she makes quick work of divesting me of the unnecessary encumbrances to our fucking.

Her tongue skims her lips in a complete circle as she holds my turgid length in her palms. The moisture gathered reminds me it's time to bury my cock deep in her wet pussy.

I grip her hips and toss her onto the bed.

Arms and legs windmill as she flies through the air. Tits jounce on impact. Eyes widen, then narrow as she watches me stalk towards her. Mesmerized, her mouth hangs ajar. Ready to be filled.

My cock thumps against my eight pack with each step. Heavy balls swing like a pendulum.

I climb onto the bed, straight between her thighs, open in welcome. The slick of her arousal coats them. Her scent musky. She bleats when I lower my head, part the engorged, glistening lips, and blow a stream of warm air over her sensitive flesh.

The insides of her knees bind my head as her hips buck from the swipe of my tongue along her seam. She may be wet. But I need her drenched and pliant for my massive return.

My hands shift position to cup her ass from beneath her thighs to lock her in place. I sate my hunger for her cream. Licks, nips, and plunges draw multiple orgasms from her before I rise to plank above her.

The Siren lies limp. A sheen of sweat covers her skin dotted by goosebumps. The crimson flush reaches from her hairline to the tips of her darkened rosy nipples. Pupils dilated, she stares up at me in a daze. Pure carnal bliss.

I drop my mouth to a peaked nipple and suckle. Hard.

She gasps as her eyes refocus.

Exactly. Stay with me until I'm just as satisfied.

I lower to my forearms. Wedged between our bodies, my cock presses into her soft belly. I groan against her tit when she spreads her thighs and hooks her ankles beneath my ass. She bends her knees and lifts her hips.

"Harris, please…" The Siren pants.

"Please what?" I ask. Our eyes meet over her pillowy mounds. I cock an eyebrow.

Her blush deepens.

"Please fuck me!" She cries out as she writhes in agony.

I grab a condom from the secret drawer in the headboard. Then I fist my covered cock, align it with her soaking pussy, and snap my hips. The forward surge sheaths me to the root within her core in one motion.

"Fuuuck, Harris!!!" She wails.

"Ask and you shall receive," I grit out as her pussy walls clamp around my cock.

She's so tight, there's no doubt. No other man has laid with the Siren. MINE!

The thought jars me.

What the hell, Harris?!

I push that unwanted line of thinking right out of my mind. This is for one thing and one thing only. Fuck this redheaded Siren out of my system in one week. Period. End of discussion.

Her sigh and the shift of her hips bring me back to reality.

I focus on my mission: mind-blowing sex again and again. All night long until neither of us can move a muscle.

My body responds in kind.

I withdraw to my tip, then slam back in. She slides up

the bed from the force of my thrust. Her arms reach above her to grapple at the headboard with her hands.

Good idea, Siren…

Rising to my knees with her legs still hooked under my ass, I collect her wrists, then bind them in suede-lined restraints. A total of four connect to each corner of the bed. The bit allows turning in every direction.

She tugs to determine the length. Realization not enough to wrap her arms around me, The Siren drops her head back with a huff.

I smirk, then slip from her sweet pussy and jump from the bed. I stride to the armoire and remove just what I need.

Back at the bed, I attach her ankles to the spreader bar. As I gaze down at her, I stroke my weeping cock. It's as keen as I am to plow back inside of her creamy pussy. She's ripe and oh so ready.

"Harris," the Siren whines as she tugs at her restraints and wiggles her hips. "Please, please fuck me."

I grip the backs of her thighs and flip her to lie on her belly. She squeals when I pull her up onto her knees. My hand presses between her shoulder blades and slides along her spine. Head down, ass up, and spread wide, I take a moment to appreciate the bounty before me.

Both holes clench when I spank one ass cheek, followed by the other. She moans, and I groan at the sight of my handprints blooming pink on her milky skin. A few more spanks, and I grip her hips to mount her from behind like a stallion.

She bucks and lets loose a string of curses in Scottish Gaelic.

I alternate brutal thrusts in with long, slow strokes out. Shifting angles to hit every inch of her pussy. She feels so good my head falls backwards as my eyes roll towards the heavens. Divine indeed.

Her pussy flutters along my length, coaxing my release. I hold out. Not ready to give in yet. I rise to crouch behind her and drill down while I play with her engorged clit. After I demand three more orgasms from her quivering core, I brace myself for an epic climax.

It grabs a hold of me and doesn't let go until I blow my load in the condom with a feral roar. My legs give out, and I collapse on top of the Siren with one arm banded around her waist and the other on the mattress beside her tousled head.

Once I catch my breath—and my vision returns—I release her from the restraints and the spreader bar. I massage her limbs to soothe the sore muscles. When she curls into a ball on her side, I head to the en suite bathroom. There, I remove the condom and toss it in the basket before I clean myself.

Back in the bedroom, I take care of the Siren. She protests halfheartedly at being roused from her sex-induced slumber. But I persist. She'll thank me later for not being sticky with her juices and our sweat.

That is, until I get her dirty all over again. And I cannot wait.

"OMG!!! Harris! Kat! Answer it already! It's a sign!"

My mind processes Vivian's words like a hippo trudging through a vat of mud. The sight of Harris' name on the mobile screen slows every brain cell in my head. Only my eyes function.

"Hey! Snap out of it!" Vivian cries out as she snatches the mobile up and waves it inches from my face. "Don't miss his call or your chance, Kat."

That gets the synapses firing.

My muscles flex as I swipe the mobile from Viv and punch the green accept button. The mobile rises to my ear.

Heart pounding against my ribs I answer, "Hello."

A slight pause, then a gush of air followed by silence.

I pull the mobile away to glance at the screen. The call is still active. With a frown I raise it to my ear.

"Hello, Harris?" I ask.

This time, I hear him clear his throat. Relieved, I give Vivian the thumbs-up. She bobs her head, toffee eyes wide with excitement.

Her infectious grin makes me smile.

"Hello, Kat," Harris says in a gruff voice.

Did he just wake up, or is he nervous like me? I don't have much time to ponder when his next words rock my core—literally.

"Let us meet at LEVELS New York tonight at eight," he states.

I jolt as memories of us at LEVELS London jump to the forefront of my mind. The erotic images of us and of others in the throes of passion at the hedonistic sex club will be forever burned into my brain. And I loved every minute of it.

If Harris wants us to meet at the New York flagship, he must want to… play?

My nipples harden beneath my tank top as my empty pussy clenches with need. Heat spreads across my cheeks. I all but moan aloud.

"Kat?"

Harris calling my name—not in the way I want at the moment—awakens me from my daydream.

I shake my head to dislodge the sensual imagery and clear my throat.

"Aah, yes. Yes, Harris, I'll be there," I respond breathlessly.

Bloody hell, Kat, could you be any more obvious? Huge eye roll.

After he tells me he'll be at the bar of the restaurant, he ends the call.

I stare at the mobile's screen. Did that really just happen? I pinch myself to make sure I'm actually awake. The bite of pain confirms Harris did call me.

"Well? What did he say?" Vivian asks sitting on the edge of her chair.

Slowly, I bring my gaze to hers. I bite the corner of my lower lip and widen my eyes as my eyebrows raise to my hairline and my shoulders lift.

She laughs at my silly face of shock and nudges me.

"Spill it, Kat!" She demands.

"We're meeting tonight at LEVELS New York!" I shout as I leap from my chair and spin in a circle. I clutch my mobile to my chest as I giggle giddily.

Harris and I are going to have sex! Less than twelve hours from now. HOORAY!!!

I do a Scottish jig.

"Fantastic!" Viv shouts as she fist pumps the air.

I grab her hands and pull her to her feet so she can join me in my happy dance. We jump about and shimmy our hips until we collapse on the floor. Our giggles fill the air.

"Now what's LEVELS New York? Is it a new restaurant?" Viv asks.

In my excitement, I blurted out the club's name. I never told her about *that* side of my love affair with Harris. My cheeks heat again. I won't lie to my friend.

"Um… It's an exclusive members only BDSM/dance

club founded by his brother Malcolm and Lucien," I answer.

Her jaw drops.

I nod and shrug.

"Holy shit, girl! Look at you! I never would have guessed Kat Jackson is into bondage and all that kinky stuff," Vivian says. She stares at me through squinty eyes. "Can your boy hook a sister up?"

We double over in laughter once again.

I CHECK the seams of my fishnet stockings in the reflective doors of the lift at LEVELS New York. Vivian helped me to pick out an outfit she says doesn't scream fuck me. Just whispers it seductively. I giggle at her description for my silk blouse, leather pencil skirt, and stilettos.

Getting in and out of the taxi didn't mess up the straight line of the seams, so I turn around just as the doors ping open.

Stepping out my gaze wanders around the space. They converted a warehouse in the Meatpacking District for the club. I admire the way they incorporated the old brick and ductwork with expensive pieces made of leather, metal, and wood. It makes the space warm, dark, and erotic.

I smile at the thought of the night ahead as I make my way towards the bar.

Then the smile melts from my face like hot wax on a sub's tit.

A woman stands between Harris' legs. Heads bent

together they talk. I stare in shock as he orders a drink for her and watches as she struts away.

Rage boils in my gut and races outward to fuel my anger.

How dare Harris invite me here under false pretenses?!

He must feel the fire shooting towards him as he turns from the woman to face me. I *level him* with a glare and march to the lifts.

Damn if I just missed one. I slap the call button as hard as I would his face. Another set of doors open, and I hurry inside.

"Kat."

I jab the close button repeatedly.

Just before the doors come together completely his hand reaches in. Blasted!

"Come out of there."

I swat at his hand as he reaches for my elbow. He ignores the blows and removes me from my escape route. I don't go easy and pull away only for him to tighten his grip. He marches me to a booth in the restaurant where the hostess releases the curtains sealing Harris and me inside.

He sits there smug.

To hell with this, I think as I rise. The dominance of his command to sit makes me shiver. But I hide my reaction to him by crossing my arms with a glare.

I almost laugh when he accuses me of running away. Ha! I chose to remove myself from a vile situation. Namely him flirting with another woman knowing I would see them.

After I tell him just that, he thwarts another of my escapes.

His next accusation of me being the one out of line since I wronged him guts me. He's got me there. I slump in my seat defeated. When he says we can move on, I perk right back up and thank him profusely.

Then more than my spirit perks up. My entire body stands at full attention, more than ready for what Harris has to offer.

"Here is a one-week guest pass to LEVELS New York. For you," he says.

I stare at the fancy envelope and nibble the corner of my lower lip. I can't get enough air into my lungs and damn near pant. My fingers ache to grab the invitation and rip it open to find out more.

"What does that mean for me?" I whisper still engrossed by the offer on the table.

Harris doesn't respond. I glance up at him.

"It means you and I have one week to fuck each other out of our systems."

And boy is Harris a man of his word. After hours of *fucking*, my sore body, wrecked pussy, and blown mind—not to mention back—need time to recuperate. A groan escapes my lips swollen from his kisses and dick as I roll to my back at the sound of the shower.

I awoke as the sun's rays peek through the curtains. The light falls on the chaise to remind me we're in his play suite at LEVELS. He even blanked my memory…

Closing my eyes again, I mentally scan my body from

head to toe. The delicious sensation of Harris' giant dick plundering my pussy lingers as does his wicked tongue on my nipples. The faint red marks on my wrists and ankles make my pulse quicken. Being bound and helpless puts a blush on my face and my cream gush.

Reflexively, my knees squeeze together. I whimper as a tremor runs through my core. Fingers dance across my belly and lower. Only a thought and I'm keyed up for more.

Moisture eases the glide of my finger past puffy lips. The tip of my finger brushes my clit. I cry out and arc from the tangled sheets.

"Harris…" I croak.

"Yes?"

My eyes fly open as I whip my head towards the sound of his voice. So engrossed in my fantasies, I didn't notice the water stopped in the shower or his re-entry into the bedroom.

A towel slung low on his narrow hips can't hide his ginormous dick. It grows right before my eyes. Like a puppet on a string, it lifts the white terrycloth inch by ten inches until it sticks straight out. And points towards me.

I lick my lips.

"What do you need from me, Siren?" He rumbles deep in his powerful chest.

Another groan slips from my mouth as a second finger joins the first to penetrate my slick pussy. Words prove impossible as my eyes squeeze shut in ecstasy. I yelp.

"Ah, ah, ah, naughty lass," Harris says as he yanks my

wrist leaving my pussy bereft. "Only I will give you pleasure this week."

His reminder he only gave us a week should sting. But I'm too far gone to notice its harsh bite. Instead, I whimper and beg him to fuck me.

He swipes his fingertip along my seam to collect natural lube, then slips the digit inside of my needy core. Its thickness as it dips in and out of my channel makes me hiss.

"You're too sore for my finger. My cock will make it worse," Harris says as he withdraws completely.

He brings his finger to his full lips as his tongue darts out to lick it clean of my cream. Dove gray eyes darken to obsidian as lust takes over his vision. A satisfied masculine moan pours from his mouth.

"Breakfast time. First you, then me," he says with a smirk as his towel falls from his hips and he lowers his head between my straining thighs.

I agree wholeheartedly.

"What are you doing?"

I glance over my shoulder at Harris as he rises up onto his elbow.

We haven't left his suite all day. Hours of fucking interspersed with nourishment from meals brought to us by restaurant staff occupied our time. Not that I have a complaint. No, ma'am.

He's so bloody sexy. Even more so with his hair tousled from my fingers, lips made swollen from our fervent kisses, and ripped as fuck physique put to the test by our vigorous carnal bouts. I could drown in the pools of his dove gray eyes. Lose myself in Harris Steele forever.

Then I remember it's fleeting. Only seven stupid days. Well, six now. I agreed to Harris' suggestion because of Vivian's words. *If you truly want another go with Harris. You have to make amends with him.* And damn if I don't want to just make amends. I want to have him in my life as my lover and my friend. Maybe even more if he'll let us get that far. But then I only have six more days to persuade him...

I avert my gaze from his questioning one as tears well up in my eyes. I can't help the flush on my pale skin. But he doesn't have to see my sadness.

With my mobile in hand, I stand from the bed and walk to the bathroom.

"Responding to a text message from a friend," I answer. Thankfully, my voice doesn't waiver.

I shut the door before he can say anymore and lean against it. Head tipped back to staunch the flow of tears, I pray for strength and for Harris to relent.

He's been free with his emotions. Well, as far as making his carnal needs known. So at least he's not closed off from me completely. I think it surprised him when I was jealous of that woman from the bar. But would it upset him if another man angled for my attention?

I may never know since six days is all I have at the moment. And no, I can't predict the bloody future, Harris Steele.

With a shake of my head, I opt to take a shower. Cleanse my body and soul of all signs of negativity. Only positive hopes and dreams for me.

The warm water cascades from a rain shower head and massages me from six others positioned in the walls. I lather up in a gel scented with lavender, chamomile, and sandalwood. It reminds me of the essential oils Harris uses when we soak in the bathtub. Duh… This is his suite so this must be his special blend.

I inhale deeply to imprint the scent of Harris on my mind. Eyes closed, I hold the sponge beneath my nose and sigh.

"Miss me so soon?"

I gasp and spin around. The quick movement on the wet marble floor causes me to stumble.

Harris grasps my waist. He stares down at me. A flicker of longing passes over his features. As quickly as it came, it disappears as though the steam from the shower's warmth cloaked it in its mist. He clears his throat.

"Be careful, Siren," he admonishes. "We're only just getting started for the day with the time we have left."

My eyes drop to his chest as I nod unable to form words without sobbing.

HARRIS

Three days of endless fucking, and I still want more from that redheaded Siren. Just the thought of her luscious curves, breathless moans, and tight, wet snatch hardens my cock painfully. No matter what I ask of her, she does it without hesitation.

I've had her on her knees deep throating her mouth.

Strapped and spanked on the bench.

Buried to the hilt in her ass in the tub.

Like the other Ms. Jackson sings, "Any Time, Any Place." I make *Kat Jackson* hit high notes every. Single. Time. Plucking her keys ruthlessly.

The bummer being tomorrow—Monday looms. The countless hours of the weekend will give way to work. Maybe it'll be good to have some space from her sexual thrall.

NAH!!!

"What's so funny?"

I chuckle some more and cock an eyebrow at the Siren.

"Do you really want to know?" I question.

She tugs that plump lower lip between her teeth as she considers her answer. I want to bite it. Better yet have my cock balanced on it.

"From the expression on your face, I guess it has something to do with another round?" She responds with a smirk of her own.

I pounce and flip her onto her back beneath me. Her giggles make my heart sing.

Dammit, Harris! Enough with the sappiness already. Remain focused.

But the intoxicating aroma of her arousal mixed with my scent on her skin calls to my inner caveman. I want to mark, claim, and fill her with my seed. Mine!

This time, I don't push the errant thought away. Instead, I bury my face in the side of her neck and inhale deeply. The warmth of my exhalation causes goosebumps to erupt on her flushed skin. I suck it into my mouth, worrying it to leave a mark.

She mewls and wraps her arms around my shoulders. Fingertips trail along my back and flanks in a lazy pattern. A hum in the back of her throat emerges as a contented purr.

"Oh, Harris," she breathes.

Pebbled nipples poke against my chest as she arches into me. She parts her thighs to cradle my pelvis. I shift to widen them further as I nestle against her wet warmth.

It's moments such as this one that take me back to the

months we were a couple. No drama. Just My Kitty Kat and me.

Why, Kat? You should have been honest! I yell in my head.

I nip her sensitive flesh harder than I meant to, and she cries out. Not in erotic bliss. Dammit! Way to let your emotions mess you up. Again. I admonish myself.

Crooning to her, I lick the spot while I rock my dick against her pussy to soothe her. She settles. But my heart races.

"Um, Harris?"

"Yes?" I respond with my eyes still closed.

The room is dark. So I hear more than see the Siren shift to a seated position beside me on the bed. The lamp on the nightstand by her bursts to life. I throw my arm over my eyes and groan.

"Oh, sorry," she says but doesn't turn the lamp off.

I squint up at her.

She pulled the sheet over her tits. But it can't hide her erect buds. Titian hair tangled about her head. Cheeks and lips stained like raspberries. Absolutely fuckable.

My cock twitches.

I stifle a groan.

"It's late, and I need to get home. You know work tomorrow and everything," the Siren says, eyes skittering around the suite. "I, uh, need to go. Now."

That lights a fire under my sexually sated ass—well, for

this minute. I sit up and study her face. She meets my gaze, then averts her eyes.

"What?" She asks. Fingers twist in the sheet draped over her lap. "Why are you looking at me like that, Harris? Do I have something on my face or something?"

She reaches up and swipes at her mouth and chin.

I smirk at the memory of my jizz dribbling from her lips as she struggled to swallow.

She blushes and rolls her eyes, knowing where my carnal thoughts went. Then huffs and slides to the edge of the bed, taking the sheet with her.

"Hold on, Kat," I tell her as I catch her forearm. She continues to stand and my hand slips to hers. Our fingers intertwine. Out of habit, I rub the pad of my thumb across the back of her hand.

She looks down at the intimate contact. Her lips part.

I yank my hand away. But cover the move by running my fingers through my hair. Fuck! That was close. Not at all on the plan. I already chided myself for kissing her. She proves impossible to resist, ever still.

"Well, uh, about that," I grapple for words. Then blurt it out. "It may be a work week. But you owe me four more days."

Her head snaps back as though I slapped her. Even her cheeks flush crimson from the pseudo-contact.

I rush on.

"Obviously we can't stay in my suite every hour as we did this weekend. You will meet me here at 6 each night.

Pack a bag and bring it with you tomorrow because you will spend the night. Every night. Do you understand?"

Now emerald fire punches me in the face. I wince inwardly. She glares at me and stands akimbo—no longer concerned with her nakedness as the sheet slips to the floor.

"How bloody dare you, Harris Steele?! I am not some tart you can make demands of! Be here at 6… Spend the night… Warm my bloody bed!" She roars.

Kitty Kat morphed into a lion.

Hot damn!

My cock responds by taking this moment of all moments to stand tall. Her blazing eyes scathe over me.

"Oh, and now you're hard, Harris?! What would you like me to do, huh? Get on my knees and suck you off. Oh, I know… Bend over the footboard while you barrel into my from behind until the wood leaves marks on my hip bones!" She shouts as her arms flail about.

I sit stupefied.

She pins me with another glare. Ample tits heave as she breathes through flared nostrils and out of her mouth.

Completely speechless.

"Oh, nothing to say? Well, then fine… And fuck you!" She shouts and spins on her heels to race towards the bathroom.

The slamming door and rattling of the crystal chandelier rouse me.

I jump from the bed and march after her. My forward

motion halts when the door doesn't open. She locked it! Dammit!

"Open the door, Kat," I say as calmly as I can muster. No sense in poking the bear or, in this case the enraged lion.

"Sod off, you prat!" She yells through the still closed door.

"No!" I shout back. "Listen here, Kat! You agreed to this week! I didn't force you to fuck me, did I? And you damn sure enjoyed each second of it based on your moans and screams of my name!"

The door opens, and she jabs me in the chest with each word, pushing me back towards the center of the room.

"You. Bloody. Prat! I *agreed* to it. But that does not give you the right to speak to me like I'm. A. TART!" She screams up at me, then spins and runs back to the bathroom.

The door slams again and the lock clicks loudly in the now silent room.

I race after her. But it's too late.

"Open this gotdamn door, Kat!!!" I yell as I bang on it with my fist. I curse the fact it's made of hardwood. Especially when my shoulder screams in protest when I use it to ram the door. It doesn't budge.

"KAT!!!" I scream.

Soundproofed suites—another standard design. So no one will hear our argument. Thank fuck.

I slam both palms on the door in frustration.

How the hell did this go so left so damn fast?!

One minute we're wrapped around each other. The next we're at each other's throats—and not in a good way.

I throw my head back and roar.

Minutes pass while the sound of the shower is the only thing I hear on the other side of the door. Oh, so she thinks she's getting cleaned up and will waltz her ass out of here? I. Don't. Think. So.

I snatch her blouse and leather skirt from the closet and stuff them under the bed. Then I drop onto the mattress and watch the bathroom door.

The water stops.

Five minutes go by. The door cracks open. Then wider when Kat pokes her head out and peeks around the silent room. She narrows her eyes when she spies me. Undoubtedly, she assumed I left. Wrong!

The door shuts again, then reopens fully. She struts out wrapped in a bath sheet that reaches her shapely calves. Back ramrod straight. Head held high. She ignores me and waltzes into the walk-in closet.

Hangers clang along the rod.

Not in there, sweetheart. I chuckle to myself.

She storms out and points her finger at me.

"Where did you put my clothes, Harris?" She demands. Her head explodes when I cross my arms over my chest and lean against the footboard. Yeah, that footboard. "Give me my clothes back, damn you!!!"

She runs across the room and collides with me. I fall onto my back with an oomph. Her fists pummel my chest as tears fall from her eyes. I can't understand what the hell she's saying, but her tears undo me.

I grab her wrists and flip us over. She screams bloody murder. I have to press my weight into her to keep her from bucking me off. My palms slide up to cover hers. I intertwine our fingers again and squeeze.

The action stops her flailing.

She stares up at me. Red eyed and red faced.

My mouth crashes down on hers. She whimpers.

My tongue breaches between her parted lips, seeking her tongue to dance with mine. She moans, and all tension dissipates. She lies limp beneath me—except for the circling of her hips.

"Kat, baby," I groan against her mouth.

"Harris…" she sighs amorously.

No more words needed.

This time we don't fuck. We make love, again and again.

I ROSE before Kat and watched as she slept. Swollen lips parted, soft snores whistled past her teeth. One hand rested beneath her cheek while the other reached for the spot where I laid. When I left the bed, I slipped her head from my chest and tucked the blankets back around her. The vision of her contentment plays before my eyes as I sit at my desk in The STEELE Tower.

Before I left, I put a note on my pillow.

The choice is hers.

Throughout the day, I refuse to check for a missed call,

text message, or email from Kat. Nor do I reach out to her. The note said it all.

Thankfully, I have a full day of project status meetings, one-on-ones with my leadership team, a client lunch, and several conference calls. No time to mope about Kat. Or how we ended things.

The way she went ballistic shook me. So many pent-up emotions it overloaded her system. And made me rethink things. She may have fucked up. But I can't continue to let it eat at me. Each of us deserves more in life than so much anger and resentment.

It's not healthy.

My alarm goes off at five-thirty. I have half an hour to get from midtown to LEVELS New York. Alonzo Masa— my driver—knows to meet me out front of The Tower promptly. It's the rush hour traffic that may hamper my arrival by six.

I shut down my laptop and pack it in my Loewe messenger bag. I resist the urge to check my mobile and head for the private elevator. As I pass through the floor of STEELE Technology and Cyber Security, I bid my administrative assistant and other staff members good night.

Downstairs, I slide onto the backseat of my Black Badge Rolls-Royce Cullinan with a nod at my driver, who holds the door open. He knows where to go, so I sit back and watch the bustling streets during the evening commute.

I check my watch when we get stuck behind a delivery truck in Chelsea. Damn 5:55. I don't bother to bug my driver for a faster route. He knows the ins and the outs of the City. He'll find the way. I shoot a text message to Kat without looking for one from her.

Finally, the SUV pulls up to LEVELS. It's ten past six. Great. I don't wait for my driver to get out and open the door. I grab my messenger bag and hop out. Nods to the security team at the entrance and I rush inside. The greeters smile and welcome me as I head to the elevators.

I open the message app on my mobile. Nothing from Kat. Dammit!

But I go up to the bar for LEVELS 4 Restaurant, anyway. I'm a man of my word, after all. It's too early for a large crowd. So it's easy to see Kat isn't in the bar or in the restaurant when I glance around the dining room.

Fuck. Me.

Feeling more disappointed than I care to admit, I trudge back to the bar and order a Jackson Blend Scotch. I nurse my drink while I plot my next move.

"Rough day?" The bartender asks while he cuts lemon slices. Then raises one. "Time to make lemonade?"

I chuckle despite my tight chest.

"Yeah, you could say that, man," I respond.

"May I have one, too?"

"*May I have one, too?*"

My heart thumps in my chest.

Kat!

I swing around.

She stands there with a wry smile on her gorgeous face. Emerald eyes sparkle with mirth as she stares back at me.

"Well, what does a girl have to do to get her drink around here?" She asks with an arched eyebrow. Her gaze never leaves mine. But the bartender rushes to place a Waterford Crystal snifter of the Scotch next to mine on the bar.

"Here you are, miss," he says.

She flicks her gaze at the glass, then back to me.

"I meant a glass of lemonade because I had a shitty day that needs turning around. Starting with waking up in an empty bed," she says straight-faced.

The bartender sputters, but I throw my head back and laugh.

She can't hold the serious expression and giggles.

"But… We can start with this fine Scotch," Kat quips as she tosses back a healthy swig.

My girl can hold her liquor, I chuckle. Then blink at my reference to Kat as my girl. That's still to be determined.

She sits in the chair next to mine. Her head dips.

I follow her gaze to the floor, where a duffle bag rests by her feet. My face nearly splits in two. Slow down there, fella, I reprimand myself. We still need to talk.

"Good to see you came prepared, Kat," I say with a nod as I sip my Scotch.

"Yes, I did," she says. The tip of her finger skims around the rim of the glass as she stares into its golden brown depths, then she brings her gaze to mine. "Did you, Harris?"

I nod.

"Of course. Let's finish our drinks, then go to the table," I tell her, then reconsider the phrasing. "Sounds good?"

The corner of her lip quirks up and she nods.

"Sounds good," Kat responds.

We make small talk about our days.

The development work she does at the children's nonprofit organization seems to suit her. It's a great way to combine her education and passion for less-fortunate kids as she was when she grew up. When she speaks about it and the children, her emerald green gaze glows, and her words tumble from her mouth. It's apparent she revels in it.

Kat tells me about her colleague and friend she rooms with. As a native New Yorker and an heir to a company with a real estate development division, I'm familiar with One Fifth Avenue. Her friend Vivian must come from a wealthy family. Especially with a full-floor penthouse in the tower. Those residences are far from inexpensive in the eight-figure range and highly sought after. A safe and respectable place for Kat to live.

I must admit, she's doing well with a new life in New York City. It makes me wonder if she's dated anyone. I know she hasn't been with a man sexually since me. A stroke to my ego. But that doesn't mean she doesn't have any suitors. Not that I believe she would pursue a relationship with me again and have someone on the side.

The questions make me realize I still have trust issues with Kat. Perhaps after our talk tonight, we can ease my concerns. With that thought in mind, I ask her if she's ready for dinner. She nods and stands. When she reaches for her bag, I take it from her and hand it to the bartender, asking him to call a staff member to put it in my suite. He nods and picks up the house phone.

I place my hand on the small of Kat's back and guide her to the host.

It's like déjà vu. She must sense it too since she glances over at me as the host releases the curtains. I smile at her. She returns my smile with a confident one of her own.

"Harris, I want to—"

"Kat, I hope you can—"

We cut each other off. She giggles, and I chuckle. I gesture for her to speak first. She sits taller on the banquette.

"Harris, I want to apologize for my outburst. You're right. I did agree to seven days with you as a means to fuck each other out of our systems. I will hold true to my commitment. That is if you want to continue," Kat says.

"I do. But first, I hope you can forgive me for the phrasing I used. In hindsight, I realize it was wrong. I was wrong. Even though you agreed to the week doesn't equate to you being a tart in any sense of the word. You are far from it, Kat. Do you forgive me?" I respond.

She nods.

I cock an eyebrow.

She smiles and answers verbally.

Thank fuck that's out of the way, I think as I drink some water.

"Shall we wait until after we eat or now? Your letter mentioned us having a conversation to clear the air," Kat asks.

"Let's talk now so we can enjoy our dinner. If things go as I hope, we'll need the nourishment for what I have planned afterwards..." I reply with a smirk.

She laughs and agrees.

When I said we'd talk, I meant for me to tell her my thoughts on what she did and how it impacted me, not just my family. She's apologized to everyone—including me—multiple times. Now it's a matter of what happens next.

I can't promise a ring for a walk down the aisle. However, I do know these last three and a half months have not been the same as the three months we spent together. I actually felt the loss of Kat.

All of it could have been a ruse. But she didn't fake our intimate interactions and not just the sexual ones. The times I sensed her watching me, unaware I saw her expressions of longing and of tenderness. Now that I think about it, even remorse saddened her face on some of those occasions.

There's no excuse for what she did. Period.

But who am I to not forgive?

"Kat, I know you apologized and attempt to make up for your... actions. The donation to Aberdeen Children's Center further proves you strive to redeem yourself," I say aloud after my internal musings.

"I really am so sorry and want to make amends," she interjects as she leans forward.

"Good," I respond, then continue. "However, I want you to understand the depth of the pain you caused to me personally and professionally. Not to mention the embarrassment of being the one to bring you into my family's personal world."

Kat sucks in a breath. Her gaze lowers to her lap as she sits back.

"I'm so sorry, Harris," she whispers. "I wish I could take

it all back. Even the part of meeting you if it would erase your pain… So stupid of me… Bloody hell…"

Her hands cover her face as a sob slips from her mouth.

My heart wants to comfort her. But my mind says no. I hold back. She needs to understand truly. Feel a bit of what I went through. I give it time to sink in.

"Personally, I opened up to you unlike I ever have with other women"—I continue as Kat winces—"I remained exclusive to you. The closest to a relationship ever. Dalliances, yes. Commitment, no."

I take a sip of water and study her reaction over the rim of the glass.

She sits with her shoulders slumped and a forlorn expression on her crimson face. She holds my stare.

"Professionally, Jackson Corporation is a client of STEELE Technology and Cyber Security. I was unaware of your… activity despite the systems in place. Lydie told me she allowed you a higher level of clearance, so no alerts occurred. But still. I was in bed with the enemy. Had it been a different company, they would have viewed me as an accomplice. Considerable damage to my reputation and to my name—my family's name. Not. Good."

Kat's eyes widen as she inhales sharply.

Yeah, cupcake, you didn't think of that, did you? I muse to myself.

"As for my family—both Steele and Jackson—they don't blame me," I say, then incline my head towards her. "They blame you—"

"Harris! I—"

"No, no," I cut her off. "Whether they forgive you is a different story. They do. As do I. But your actions are not forgotten easily—if at all—by any of us.

"So you see, Kat, I'm in a bind. Yes, I still want to finish our week. But I can make no promises of the future. One day at a time. And I will not tolerate any more deception from you. Or it's game over. Forever."

I sit back, finished with my speech. Now, it's up to her. The ball is in her court.

Kat gives me a pleading look. Wide eyes filled with unshed tears. Mouth agape. She opens it further to speak. But dry mouthed, she can't utter a sound. A sip of water clears her throat, and she tries again.

"Harris, I understand. What I did was terrible. I regret the pain and damage it caused. Thank you and your family for your forgiveness. I will do my very best to make up for my erroneous actions," she says.

Her hand lifts to touch the top of mine resting on the table between us. She watches as she intertwines our fingers. I watch her. She swallows, then brings her eyes to mine.

"I still want to finish our week, too. Even though you can't make promises of the future, I hope you are open to giving me—us—a second chance," she says and squeezes my fingers. "I, too, have never let a man into my life the way I have with you. And I know you feel as strongly about me as I do for you."

Impressed with her return shot, I nod.

"Well then, let's see how this goes," I respond.

Kat's gorgeous face lights up as a serene smile spreads from her lips to her eyes. When she leans over, I accept her kiss. She licks the seam of my lip until I open for her. Our tongues touch, and she moans.

I cup the back of her head, threading my fingers in the silky strands. Deepening the kiss, I plunder her mouth with a fervent passion. Her whimpers drive me to the breaking point.

"I want you now, Siren," I growl.

Quickly, she scampers onto my lap, hitching up her skirt to the waist. I push the table back and cup her ass. My palms hold the bare globes as my fingers dig into the softness of her ass. Meanwhile, her fingers free my cock, growing harder by the millisecond.

She doesn't hesitate to impale herself on my girth. She hisses from the burn and stretch as I bottom out deep within her pussy. We groan in unison.

I tighten my grip to lift her to my tip. She slides her hands beneath my suit jacket to dig her fingernails into my shoulders through my dress shirt. I flex the muscles of my thighs and ass to thrust up as I yank her down. Each pistoning thrust entices her juices to flow. I muffle her screams of passion with another toe-curling kiss.

Time has no meaning as we lose ourselves in each other. The only things that matter are Kat's ragged breaths and moans as she climaxes around my cock. She's never felt better. So tight, slippery, and warm it's not long before my release hits me like a freight train at maximum speed.

My heavy balls draw up to unleash a geyser. Her pussy

walls milk my cock of every drop to the point of pain. But I don't stop my lazy thrusts.

Kat trembles in my arms. I rub her back soothingly as I nuzzle the side of her neck. Sated, she sighs. My ego gets a boost.

As my mind returns from nirvana, I notice an unusual amount of stickiness in my lap. I know Kat climaxed multiple times. But it feels like more.

I shift her to the side of my lap. My semi-hard dick slips from her pussy.

Fuck. Me.

No condom.

"Fuuuck…" I groan as my head slams back against the banquette. My eyes squeeze shut. Never have I gone without a condom. Damn!

Kat moves from me completely. The rustling of her clothes follows. A damp napkin strokes my cum-slicked cock.

"It's okay, Harris. I get a birth control shot regularly and can give you my bloodwork from three months ago. Um, after we broke up, I got tested. Not that I expected anything. No need to worry. If you want proof, I can have my gynecologist send a note to you," she says as she gives me aftercare.

Role reversal or what?

I open my eyes.

Her head bowed over her task, she doesn't notice me watching her. The glow of erotic bliss flushes her face and neck. Bee-stung lips still swollen from our ardent kisses.

Her nipples poke into her silk dress. The scent of sex surrounds us, trapped behind the curtain.

My dick pulses in her hand as she holds it up to bathe my balls and my groin. Her tongue pokes out to lick her bottom lip. Then she tugs it between her teeth. She squirms on the seat. Her arousal returns.

As does mine.

But first...

I cup her cheek to raise her gaze.

"Kat, I apologize for my irresponsible behavior. I should have had better control and stopped to put on a condom. Do you forgive me?" I ask.

She closes her eyes and presses her cheek into my hand. When she looks at me again, it's with such a tender expression, my breath escapes in a rush.

What this redheaded Siren does to me. She has no clue.

"Of course, I forgive you Harris. I was just as caught up and forgot," she says, then lowers her eyelashes. The long, golden red tips sweep the tops of her cheeks. "We could go without a condom. If you want."

My dick thumps.

She bites back a giggle.

"Well, I guess you have your answer," I say with a chuckle. "But in all seriousness, I will have my doctor send my last test results to you. I'd appreciate yours from your doctor, too, along with the confirmation of current birth control."

Nodding, her face flushes a deeper red, knowing she has to regain my trust. But if she wants a second chance at us, that's one of the necessary steps. And the basis of any genuine relationship.

I thank her for taking care of me and tuck my junk away before I hang the green tassel on the curtain tie-back. Time for that nourishment. The night's still young.

KAT

"**I** go out of town for a few days, and you shack up with your ex-boyfriend in a sex club? Gurrrl! New York, where dreams really do come true!"

Vivian throws her head back and laughs uproariously.

Some diners in our favorite sandwich and soup shop near the office turn in our direction. They smile at Viv, who dabs her eyes with a napkin. I can't help but to join in.

"So a call turns into an invitation, then a pledge for a week of nonstop *shagging,* as you Brits call it?" She asks as her toffee brown eyes twinkle.

I nod, giggling.

"And was it good? All you wanted and more?" She continues with a smile.

"Incredible *shagging!*" I respond with a wink.

"Well, way to go, Kat! You're on the path to a second chance with your lover boy," she chortles but raises an eyebrow at my shrug. "Okay, what happened?"

I tell her about Harris and the future. She assures me his reaction is only normal, especially given the circumstances. The reminder hurts. But she tells me to get over it. If Harris can let it go, I can't be the one to play the victim. Viv's candor is what I need. I tell her so and ask about her trip.

We spend the rest of our lunch catching up and her plans for a Girls' Valentine's Day Extravaganza. She and some of her other single friends plan to go to dinner with dancing afterwards. It sounds like fun.

Since the week with Harris ends right before Valentine's Day and he doesn't do the future, I tell Viv to count me in for the Extravaganza. A girl can't sit at home alone and mope all night. Plus, I really like her friends. They've embraced me into their circle. So Valentine's Day is something to look forward to and not ignore.

As ever, the clotheshorse, Viv suggests we go shopping for new outfits. I remind her it'll have to be during lunch tomorrow since Harris occupies my evenings. My response starts her to giggling again.

We leave the restaurant with our arms linked, laughing all the way back to the office. On our floor, we part ways.

I filled my afternoon with proposals and grant writing. Not the sexiest part of my responsibilities. But necessary to get funding to get the children what they need and to keep the organization's programming and back office going. As the head of development, I take my job seriously. And I love it!

"Hi, Foster, anything happened since I left?" I ask my administrative assistant as I walk up to my office.

"Oh, nothing special. Unless, of course, one considers a gigantic bouquet of long-stemmed red roses average…" he responds with a straight face. He laughs and points to my closed office door. "I put them on your desk, and I didn't peek at the card. Handwritten, though. Lovely script."

Harris!

My heart skips a beat. I thank him and hurry inside my office. The bouquet sits in the middle of the desk. The heady aroma of the fragrant roses fills my nostrils. I inhale and smile. Some of the flower petals stand tall with open buds while others closed tight in the stunning bouquet.

I lift the card with my name written in an elegant calligraphy—exactly like the invitation. A grin wider than the Cheshire Cat's covers my face. How romantic!

Then it drops as I frown at the signature.

xoxo Solomon

Crap! It's not Harris at all… Solomon sent the bouquet.

I scan the message: he wishes me a happy Valentine's Day and an invitation for dinner.

With a disappointed sigh, I drop to my desk chair. The sight of the beautiful red roses makes my stomach hurt. The scent makes me queasy. Instead, I swivel to face the windows overlooking Fifth Avenue behind me.

I analyze my feelings of distress.

I assumed Harris sent them as an apology or as a thank you for continuing the week.

The fact it wasn't him hurts since he didn't think to send the flowers for the assumptions I made.

I wonder if he'll ever see me as more than a *shag*, especially since I want more from him.

Is it worth going through at all?

Then I remember another point Vivian made at lunch: cut out the victim role.

Spot on.

I shake my head to dislodge the ridiculous thoughts in my mind and refocus. Spinning around, I remove my mobile from my handbag.

"Hi, Kat!"

I smile—not as big as the Cheshire Cat, but warmly—when Solomon answers my phone call.

"Why hi, to you, Solomon. The roses are simply amazing. So thoughtful. Thank you," I say, meaning it sincerely.

He doesn't deserve to partake in my pity party. What he should have is a woman who can go to dinner with him on Valentine's Day. And that woman isn't me.

"You're welcome. Glad you like them. And dinner?" He asks. "I don't mean to be presumptuous. But I guess you may not have plans with the tosser who broke your heart?"

I flinch. Ouch!

"Thank you for the dinner invitation. However, I have plans and regrettably must pass," I respond, bypassing the *tosser* part. I hope he does, too.

A beat goes by before Solomon responds.

"I understand. Perhaps another time, Kat," he says.

"Solomon, I don't want to mislead you—"

"Nonsense. I'm an adult and can handle a rebuff," he says with a chuckle. "You can't blame a guy for pursuing a beautiful woman. Can you?"

I smile. He's good.

"You flatter me, Solomon," I respond.

"Should things change, you know how to reach me, Kat," he says.

"Thank you for understanding, Solomon. Take care," I reply.

"You, too, Kat," he says and ends the call.

I turn back to my desk and the lovely bouquet. He'll make another woman thrilled.

Smiling, I call Foster and ask him to have the roses delivered to the shelter. Their beauty will brighten Valentine's Day for someone less fortunate than me.

The reminder alert for writing my first proposal chimes. Time to get to work. All thoughts of exes turned sort of lover and amorous interests clear out.

"Hey, Kat."

Hours later, I glance up to find Vivian standing in the door of my office. She has on her coat and carries her Chanel handbag and matching laptop case. Exaggeratedly, she looks at her gold Cartier Panthère watch, then up at me.

"Don't you have someplace to be in… oh say… twenty minutes?" She asks.

Shit!

I look at the time on my laptop screen. 5:40. The alarm

didn't go off. Why? I check but I set it for 5 a.m. not for 5 p.m. *Bloody hell!*

Vivian giggles as I save my work, shut down my system, and run around my office frantically. If I'm late, Harris will punish me like he did the other night.

I stop mid stride as a thought occurs to me. A smile blooms on my face like the heat on my ass did when he spanked me bound to the bench for my transgression. I shudder at the memory as my nipples bead and my pussy clenches.

"I do *not* want to know what you're thinking right now, Kat Jackson," Viv says as she covers her ears and sings tra-la-la.

"I never kiss and tell. Or rather, spank and speak!" I quip and strut past her.

She bumps my hip with hers and laughs.

"You're a total mess, Kat," she replies merrily.

When we step outside, the back door to a Rolls-Royce SUV opens. A long trouser-clad leg comes out, followed by the top of an ebony-haired head. Standing at his full height, Harris grins at me. Dove gray eyes shine like molten platinum.

"I was in the area and figured we could ride together," he says as he meets me halfway, then leans down to kiss my lips softly.

His eyes flick to Vivian, and he blasts her with the full wattage of his sexy as sin smile.

"You must be Vivian. I'm Harris. Nice to meet you," he says as he extends his hand.

She's momentarily stunned by his masculine beauty and stares bug-eyed at him. I nudge her side, and she blinks, then closes her mouth. She gives her head a shake and giggles as she offers him her hand.

"Yes, I am and it's nice to meet you too, Harris," Vivian says with a broad smile. She turns to me. "Well, my car is over there. I'll see you in the morning."

She hugs me and whispers, "Damn, girl! Even better looking in person."

When she steps back, she eyes Harris again and grins as her shoulders shake with glee. She nods at him and heads to her chauffeur-driven Mercedes-Maybach sedan. We watch as he opens the back door, and she slips inside with a wave over her shoulder.

"Nice friend and car," Harris says as he takes my laptop case from me in one hand and my elbow in the other. "If she's single, I have plenty of buddies who'd love to date her. If Laurent wasn't with Yessenia, he'd be the first I told."

I grin at his compliments and tell him I'll let her know. Viv will be so excited!

Settling into the back of his SUV, I think how Harris may not have given me a beautiful bouquet of long-stemmed red roses. But he did surprise me with a ride. And he wants to match my friend with one of his buddies. His gestures are a more meaningful gift to me than the roses. I smile happily at him as he sits beside me.

"What?" He asks.

I touch his cheek.

"Thanks for picking me up. I lost track of time with

grant writing, and by mistake, I set my alarm for 5:30 in the morning. So this is perfect," I respond.

Harris stares at me for a moment. His eyes scan my face.

My smile falters a bit at the intensity of his gaze.

Then he nods and says, "You're welcome."

The awkward moment passes when he asks me about the grants I'm reaching out to for our latest programing. As we ride down to LEVELS New York, we talk about our days. The conversation resembles those we had during our prior relationship. It makes my heart swell with hope.

By the time we get out, I'm giddy with happiness.

We make our usual stop at the restaurant for dinner, then go to his private suite for dessert. But this time, a black lace corset with a black sheer G-string and black sky-high marabou mules lie on the bed. Two black enamel bracelets rest on a white silk cloth beside the lingerie.

I stop right inside the doorway of the suite as my eyes snap to Harris. He smirks and walks past me further into the room. Without a backward glance, he saunters into his walk-in closet. I stare back at the sexy lingerie on the bed—Lola's Coterie, I'm sure.

I skim my fingertips over the intricate pattern of the lace and the boning on the corset. I lift it up to admire the detailing. On the back, double-face silk ribbons lace up in front of a black silk panel. I set the corset aside. The G-string leaves nothing to the imagination. Good thing I maintain Brazilians.

"Ready to play or what?"

I jolt at Harris' question.

He stands behind me dressed in head to toe black. A sheer shirt with loose sleeves unbuttoned to reveal his sculpted chest and the top six of his impressive eight-pack abs. Buttery soft leather pants mold to his ample package, thick, muscular thighs, and firm ass. Heavy boots round out his bad boy air.

Who wants a good boy? Not me.

"Most definitely. Thank you for the lingerie," I purr. "Just give me a few minutes, and I'll need your help with the laces."

I scoop up the pieces in one hand and the shoes in the other. Then I sashay to the en suite bathroom. Once inside, I pin my hair in a sexy bedhead updo, take a three-minute shower, apply lotion, and don the lingerie. More mascara, bold red lipstick, and a walk through a spritz of my perfume, and I slip into the marabou mules.

Harris' eyes bulge when I step into the bedroom. His hooded gaze wraps me in a sensual caress from the top of my head to the tips of my red-polished toenails. A rumbled growl rises from his chest as he stands and prowls towards me. The wolf is out tonight.

Slowly, I pivot to ensure he catches every angle of my body.

"Will you tighten my laces? Then I'll be ready," I purr as I wiggle my shoulders and shift my hips. Then I yelp when his sizable hand connects with one bare ass cheek.

"That's for being late, Siren," Harris growls.

"H—How? You picked me up," I stammer.

He chuckles wickedly.

"And we arrived at Six. Fifteen. Naughty. Lass."

He emphasizes each word with spanks that make me rise to the balls of my fee and gasp.

Wobbly, I grip both sides of the bathroom's doorframe and cry out. But secretly, I trill from the erotic punishment.

Using my hold as leverage, Harris pulls on the corset's laces and ties them. I hate he does it so well. Briefly I wonder who else he helped into the seductive lingerie. The question flies from my mind when another spank catches the bottom curve of my ass. It jiggles from the contact.

Again, Harris chuckles wickedly, then puts his hands on my hips and spins me around to face him. I peek at him from beneath the fringe of my eyelashes and bit the corner of my bottom lip. I know it'll make him wild with lust.

He drops his head to the top of one breast and sucks the soft flesh into his mouth. He worries it until satisfied he leaves a mark on my alabaster skin.

I glance down and see it for myself.

"Now, you're ready, Siren," Harris says smugly as he inclines his head at his handi—rather mouth work. "Off to Peepshow we go. Tonight, we watch. And if you're good, I'll let you cum…"

Goosebumps break out on my heated skin as I shudder in erotic delight.

"Good afternoon, Mr. Steele. Mr. Lucien and Mr. Laurent Jackson have not arrived yet. Would you prefer to wait for them at the bar or at your table?"

I opt for the table and thank the host. He leads me down the ramp to Jackson Pub's primary seating area. He stops at the Jackson's reserved table in the center of the room. In clear view of the entrance and by the other guests.

I nod at or shake hands with some of them as I pass their tables. The restaurant bustles with the lunchtime eaters. Every table full and the bar busy despite reservations being scarce. The din of conversations and silverware on plates fills the air along with the aroma of tantalizing dishes.

Lucien, Laurent, and I are having lunch at one of the two restaurants. Both run by Lucien and his team in

Jackson Building—their New York City headquarters on Park Avenue between Fifty-second and Fifty-third Streets. Jackson Pub is a mecca for closing big business deals or for killing them since many of the world's most powerful lunch here daily.

I take a seat at our table and the menu from the host. As I scan today's specials, the server appears. Like the food, the service is impeccable. Lucien would have it in no other way.

"Would you care for a drink, sir?"

"Only bottled water for now. I'll wait for the Jacksons to arrive," I respond.

"If you have any questions regarding the menu, kindly let me know," he says as he fills my glass. He bows his head and walks to the server's waiting area where others stand.

Lucien likes for them to be visible in one spot where the guests can signal to them. He hates for guests to search for them or not have their glasses refilled or plates cleared promptly. *The Sexy Chef* is a hardass—albeit a talented, multiple Michelin starred one.

After I decide on a green salad and the Wagyu Beef with Matsutake Mushrooms, I scroll through my emails. But my mind drifts back to last night. Particularly to moment Kat stroked my cheek and thanked me for picking her up from work.

The tenderness in her eyes so full of joy struck me straight in the chest. Dazed, I could only stare at her. I scanned her face for any sign of a ruse. But she wasn't pretending, as her radiant smile stalled until I spoke.

I covered the awkwardness by asking her about her day.

Once again, her eyes lit up. This time for the happiness her job brings her. She rattled on about the grants and proposals and how they'll help support the children and the nonprofit. I thought how useful she could be at STEELE Foundation.

If things were different, I'm sure my Mom would love to have Kat work with her at our family's foundation that builds and manages attractive, affordable housing for urban, lower-income families. The name plays on the house foundation being strong and supportive like steel. Even though each of us and our cousins support it with our personal funds, Kat could help to manage external contributions.

Then she'd be like Lola, Leonie, and Starr, who partner with STEELE International. For their businesses, as in Lola and Starr's cases, and with a division Leonie runs. Kat could join on our philanthropic arm.

Okay, Harris, you're jumping the gun here, man, I chide myself. Instead, I reflect on the mouthwatering vision of Kat in the Lola's Coterie corset and G-string set I gave her. Totally fuckable. And I did.

My cock stirs in my trousers at the memory of Kat squirming on my lap as she became more and more aroused. We watched an edging demonstration on the primary stage at Peepshow. The woman naked except for the Shibari rope that twined around her body, immobilizing her completely. Leaving her unable to avoid the erotic torture of her Domme.

Over and over, the Domme played her sub's pussy like a fine instrument, only to disallow her orgasms. The poor girl had tears in her eyes by the end of the demonstration. But climaxed so hard her entire body shook as she hung suspended from the ceiling. The chains clanged from the force. Her high-pitched wails bounced around the entire room as her pussy gushed repeatedly.

Her Domme was more than happy to lap up her honey.

My leather pants bore witness to Kat's orgasm as I finally allowed her to cum with the sub. My fingers fucked her spasming pussy until she begged me to stop. Suddenly, she licked my fingers clean. Like a good little Kitty Kat.

My head jerks at the reference. I haven't called her by that nickname in months. Damn, Harris, going soft, playa?

"What's got you frowning?"

"Yeah, you look like you lost your best friend. Oh, no, can't be because I'm still here!"

Chuckles break out as I get clapped on the back.

Lucien and Laurent take their seats, laughing. Fuckers.

I give them a wry look.

"Whatever, some people do have important shit on their minds, you know, unlike you two clowns," I grumble. I shift in my seat to signal the waiter. I'll take that drink now.

"Oooh... Touchy. Yikes!" Laurent digs in.

Lucien smirks before he glances around his kingdom with an assessing eye.

"Good afternoon, Chef Lucien, sir," the server says reverently.

I hide the roll of my eyes behind the raised menu. Laurent snickers and kicks my shin under the table. I angle my menu to show him another eye roll.

Lucien ignores us and speaks with the server. After he takes our drink orders, Lucien glares at us.

"Listen, you little brats, you may be here for lunch. But this is still business for me. So cut off your antics around my staff," he snarls. *The Sexy Chef* is not pleased with our behavior.

Laurent and I exchange glances. Next, we burst out in laughter.

Lucien growls.

"Okay. Okay, cuz! Sorry. All right?" I say with my palms raised. "We're wrong, and you're right."

"Hear, hear!" Laurent concurs with his water glass held aloft in a mock salute.

The server returns with our glasses of Jackson Reserve Scotch. He leaves after we give our food selections.

It's been a while since we last saw one another in person. So, we have a lot to catch up on. Our conversation turns to work highlights—Lucien's up for a prestigious award as per the norm—and sports. We have dates set aside at the STEELE International luxury suite high above the basketball court at Madison Square Garden. The first after everyone gets back from their Valentine's Day getaways.

Which reminds me my week with Kat ends tomorrow, right before the holiday. I'm not ready to stop our time together. We won't stay at LEVELS New York every night. But I'm not opposed to us making a go at a second chance.

I consider my options—

"Earth to Harris!"

"Seriously, cuz, you're out of it today. What the bloody hell is going on in that head of yours?"

Laurent and Lucien's comments draw me from my musings. They frown at me as they await my response.

I'm not quite ready to disclose Kat and I have spent the last week together and especially not at LEVELS New York. Although Lucien may have an idea since he co-owns it. But then, strict confidentiality rules take precedence over ownership unless it involves an issue with members. So my tryst should be safe. For now.

"Sorry about that. I have some stuff going on, so I'm a bit distracted. What did you say?" I respond earnestly.

Lucien studies me for a moment.

Fuck! Does he know, after all? I wonder.

He shrugs.

"Okay, we'll quit riding you. But I do have a question," he responds. He pauses until I nod for him to continue. "What's up with you and Kat?"

Definitely a fuck…

"What do you mean?" I hedge. I won't lie. But I won't show my hand either.

Lucien narrows his eyes at me. The emerald green so like Kat's I feel a tad guilty for not being forthright.

"The other night I saw her. The night of my new restaurant opening. You know, the one you missed…" he says pointedly.

He piques my interest. So I ignore everything but him seeing Kat. Was she alone? Or was she with someone? Maybe only with her friend, Vivian.

"She was there with her friend, a stunningly beautiful woman with skin that reminds me of a decadent ganache…" Lucien waxes on poetically about Vivian.

I nod in agreement. Then he mentions they were on a double date. Damn!

Laurent sits forward.

"Hold on. Yessenia and I saw Kat the other night, too. She was at Carbone with some guy," he says, then goes on. "What did he look like? This guy has black hair and blue eyes. Muscular build around our heights."

Lucien responds it must be the same guy and how they appeared cozy. He remarks how it went from a double date to a single over night.

While they go on and on playing the Hardy Boys solving a great mystery, I fist my hands in my lap to prevent myself from punching something. Jealousy rips through every cell in my body. Who is this fucker? Did she lie to me about not having been with anyone since me? Those dates had to have happened right before we reconnected. Damn!

The server comes over to ask if we want dessert or a digestif.

I tell the guys I need to go—which I do. Like right now.

They stare at me quizzically. But before Laurent can

speak, his mobile vibrates. He checks the screen, then says he has to take the call while he rises from the table. A brunette saunters over and places a hand on Lucien's shoulder.

I use their distractions to make haste. I have a stop to make before I head back to The STEELE Tower.

My driver pulls the Cullinan in front of the building for the children's nonprofit office. I jump from the back seat and stride through the doors. Security calls up to Kat, then directs me to the elevator to access her floor.

Her surprised face morphs into one of concern when she greets me in the vestibule.

"What's the matter? Are you all right? Your family?" She asks in rapid succession.

I shake my head and tell her let's go to her office. She nods and leads the way. As we walk, she casts worried side-long glances at me. But I stare straight ahead. She instructs her administrative assistant to hold all of her calls, then steps into her office. I close the door behind us.

"Harris, tell me," she says as her eyes scan my face.

"Are you seeing someone else?" I ask without preamble. It takes effort to keep my voice level.

Her head snaps back as though slapped. She frowns, then opens her mouth to speak. Shakes her head, then tries again.

I cut her off, grasping her chin between my thumb and forefinger. Holding her head in place so she can't avoid my eyes, I lean close. Her warm breath fans across my face.

"Do not lie to me, Kat Jackson," I warn gruffly.

She attempts to shake her head. But I hold her firm. Her hands lift to my forearm. Fingers wrap around my coat sleeve, slipping along the soft cashmere.

"No, Harris. I'm not seeing someone else. Only you!" She says, staring straight in the eye. "And I promised not to lie to you again."

We stare at one another. I gauge the veracity of her words. She assesses my reaction. I break first.

"Then who did Lucien and Laurent see you with on back-to-back dates?" I growl.

My inner caveman pushed to his limits can barely contain himself.

Realization dawns in her eyes as they brighten to a jade green. She snatches her chin from my fingers.

"Oh, so that's what this is all about? They ran and told you what they saw?" She lashes out as her eyes blaze.

The answer is obvious, so I remain silent.

Wrong move.

Kat narrows her eyes at me and pokes me in the chest. Even through the layers of my coat and suit, the tip jabs me.

"You cannot possibly be pissed because I went on *two* dates with someone when it took you weeks to contact me after we… after we made out at Lachlan and Haley's flat!" Kat snarls.

When I don't answer, she flares her nostrils and continues—jabs and all.

"Can you honestly tell me you didn't fuck other women while we were apart?" She throws out.

Now, I avert my eyes, and she growls.

She stalks away from me to the door. Pausing with her hand on the knob, she glares at me over her shoulder.

"That's not fair of you, Harris. I don't hold it against you, you were with others. So you don't get to be pissed with me for going on *two* dates. Now, I have work to do," Kat says and opens the door.

In three strides, I'm in front of her and push the door closed. I crowd her personal space, boxing her in with my hands on either side of her head and her back against the door.

Her hands come up to push at my chest. But her pupils dilate as her cheeks flush with her instant arousal.

I bend my knees so we're on eye level. Her breath comes out in pants. I slam my mouth over her parted lips. She nips my bottom one, and I respond in kind. The kiss is brutal and demanding as we battle for dominance.

I win.

Then I damn near rip the placket of my trousers as I use one hand to release my cock while the other squeezes her hip bone. She squeals into my mouth. I swallow it down and lift her up. She yanks her dress, then the skimpy lace of her panties gets pushed aside.

I grunt when she fists my cock and lines it up with her pussy. I raise her higher to give clearance, then thrust up as I pull her down. Her back slams against the door. She hisses as much from the forceful invasion as from her collision with the solid wood.

Fortunately, it holds as I pound into her again and

again. Sweat beads down my back from the heat our bodies create and the clothes I wear. Kat cries out into our kiss as she clenches her pussy around my cock. Mini orgasms build to a major one. When it hits her, she cums like a tidal wave. It triggers my release, and I roar into her mouth.

"MINE!"

I mark her pussy with my seed, satisfying the caveman in me.

She twitches from the aftermath as I carry her to the desk chair. I disengage our intimate connection to set her down on it. Our combined essence drips to the floor. I stare at it, pleased, then pull my handkerchief from my suit jacket pocket. I moisten it with water from the bottle on her desk and clean first her, then myself.

Less dazed, Kat rearranges her dress. When she babbles about cleaning up in the bathroom, I put her panties back in place, securing my seed and scent inside of her. She arches her eyebrow but doesn't argue.

I rise from a crouch and kiss her breathless.

"I'll pick you up at five-thirty," I say, then leave her stunned and slouched in the chair.

KAT

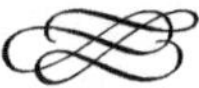

"Harris! What are we doing at an *airport*? Wait a minute. Is that your private jet??? It's only Friday. I have to get to work!"

My mouth hangs open as I gape out the window of his SUV at the Gulfstream G650ER gleaming in the morning sun. The jet waits on the tarmac with its door open and the boarding stairs lead from it to the ground invitingly.

But this is one invitation I cannot accept.

When Harris stepped out of his Rolls-Royce as I walked through the doors of my flat's building, He happily surprised me. Picked up from work two nights in a row, then the next morning? Awesome!

He sauntered over to me and brushed his lips over mine as he murmured a good morning.

I melted.

Inside the SUV, I prattled on, really about nothing in particular. I was just so hyped by Harris' boyfriend-like behavior. He indulged me with a smile on his handsome face. I talked so much I didn't notice we weren't in front of my office building when the SUV stopped. Alonzo—his driver—opened the door.

I stood beside the Hudson River. A helicopter waited with a crew member by the open door. My head swiveled to Harris, who rounded the back of the SUV. He strode with confidence and took my elbow. But I held back and asked why we were there instead of on Fifth Avenue.

He wanted to take me on a morning flight around Manhattan to experience it from the air…

Ha!

Now, he hits me with a lopsided grin. I would swoon at the absolute sexiness of this man if I wasn't ready to strangle him!

I throw my hands up in the air and yowl in frustration at his silence. Then I knock on the partition separating us from his driver. He rolls it down and glances over his shoulder, first at Harris, then at me.

"Yes, Ms. Jackson?" Alonzo asks.

"Would you be so kind as to drive me to my office on Fifth Avenue?" I respond.

His chocolate brown gaze shifts to Harris.

"You know, never mind. I'll call an Uber," I say, then reach for my attaché and handbag on the floor.

The partition rolls up, and Harris places his hand on mine to stop me.

"Kat, it's okay. I spoke with the organization's director, and she gave you time off until the Monday after this one.

She'll handle any pertinent meetings you have with the help of your team," he says.

I close my eyes and shake my head in disbelief.

"Seriously?! You took control of *my* work? To what end? And she just agreed with no incentive?" I ask, keeping my eyes squeezed shut. Maybe I can push this whole thing out of my mind.

Harris sighs.

"That's a bit of an extreme description of the situation, Kat. I wanted to surprise you with a memorable trip… for Valentine's Day. That's all," he responds.

I soften at his words. How romantic!

"Oh, Harris—"

"The director was more than pleased with the million-dollar donation I made," he continues as I speak.

My head jerks back, and I snatch my hand away from his hold. What the bloody hell?! He *paid* for me?! Like a tart. Again?!?!?!

"W—What's the matter? Why do you look like you want to kill me?" He asks, taken aback by my dagger-like glare.

He's so oblivious to the way one could interpret his actions. I can't get mad. He's also trying, and I appreciate it a lot.

So, I close my eyes and inhale deeply through my nose and exhale out my mouth for a count of ten to avoid a massive explosion. A mantra for peace and tranquility Starr taught to me whispers from my lips.

"Kat?" Harris calls.

I reopen my eyes to his concerned face.

"I apologize for my outburst," I start and wait for his acceptance before I continue. "Thank you for doing so much to take me away for Valentine's Day. How thoughtful of you.

It's the donation part that really gets to me. I know you don't see it as anything wrong and more than likely consider it charitable—extremely so, in my opinion, under different circumstances.

But to me it seems as though you bought me. And it invoked the memory of the other night. I hope you can see it from my perspective."

Harris opens his mouth, then closes it. His eyes scan my face. He gives a shake of his head and groans as he slaps his forehead with his palm. He returns his remorseful gaze to me.

"Damn, Kat, I see it now. But as I said that night, there's not a chance I think of you in that way. At. All. Yes, I'm an Alpha male who needs control. But not outside of the bedroom. We're not in an M/s or a D/s relationship with total power exchange. Even then, the sub has the final say. However, that's not my thing, and I don't believe it's yours either.

But if you want to go to work, I'll understand. We'll go now. What do *you* want to do?"

I glance down at our hands laced together. He rubs his thumb over mine in a soothing manner. I smile.

How can I be a bitchy grump with a sexy AF man who went through all of this to surprise me with a trip for Valentine's Day? I can't.

I weigh my options... So I guess I'll miss the Girls' Valentine's Day Extravaganza!

Giggling, I clamber onto Harris' lap and hold his face in my hands. I cover it with kisses, whispering naughty words of all the ways I plan to thank him from now until we return to New York City.

He squeezes my ass and growls.

His dick thumps beneath me, and I grind down on it wantonly as I nip his plump lower lip. Circling my hips, I lower my mouth to his neck. Now, I leave my mark on his flesh. He groans and flexes his fingers to dig deeper into my butt cheeks.

"If you keep this up, we won't make it to the jet," he says as he lifts me from his lap onto the seat. "Once we're in the air, you best finish what you started, Siren."

Harris waggles his eyebrows at me.

I bite my lower lip and nod with hooded eyes.

"Yes, Harris," I purr.

He smirks and opens his door. I do the same and hop out of the SUV. He takes my hand to lead me to the awaiting jet.

He won't tell me our destination, only that we have eleven hours to add points to our Mile High Club travel bank. By the time we land, we could take a nonstop trip around the world...

"KEEP your eyes shut until I say open them. Or else."

I giggle as Harris unties the red silk blindfold from

behind my head. But I heed his warning, even though I wouldn't mind his form of punishment. He put the blindfold on before we stepped off his private jet.

The clues I gathered tropical heat, the scent of hibiscus and gardenias, and waves lapping at the shoreline as my toes dig into sand lead me to believe we're on an island. The distance of eleven hours from New York City can put us anywhere.

"Okay, open your eyes!" Harris says enthusiastically.

I blink against the bright sunlight. It takes a beat for my eyes to adjust. Then I gasp.

Ahead of me a stretch of crystal-clear, shallow water separated by a low sandbank from the vast turquoise blue ocean takes my breath away. The contrast of the black sand to the white-tipped aqua hues of the water is majestic.

I clap my hand over my mouth in awe.

"Beautiful, isn't it?" Harris murmurs in my ear as he wraps his arms around me from behind. "Do you like?"

"Oh, yes, Harris," I breathe.

"Hmmm… I like how you say my name, Siren," he says, nipping my earlobe. "Come, there's much more to see."

He squeezes my hip bones, and I moan. He turns us around to bring me face-to-face with a magnificent private villa that sprawls beside the lagoon. The lush foliage reminds me of pictures I've seen of Hawaii.

"Where are we? Hawaii, right?" I ask excitedly. I've always wanted to go to the volcanic islands. The black sand beach gives it away.

Harris chuckles and nods.

"You guessed correctly—Maui specifically. Now, what should your prize be?" He responds, tapping his chin with the tip of his index finger, eyes skyward. "Skinny dipping in the lagoon? A late naked lunch of local delights? Couples massages beneath a gauzy canopy on the beach? You choose."

I turn and wrap my arms around his neck as I rise to my tippy toes.

"Each one while I'm naked?" I giggle, kissing his lips.

"This is a no-clothes-allowed week," he answers, lapping at my throat. "You didn't see any luggage, did you?"

I tilt my head to give him better access for his seductive kisses. Can this get any better?

"You choose, Harris," I purr as I grind my belly against his rigid dick. "Whatever you desire."

His warm breath skitters across my skin as he responds, "Hmmm, be careful what you offer to a cad like me, Siren."

"Don't tease me…" I moan.

Harris steps back. Immediately, I feel his loss and ache for him. I pout. He chuckles, a sound as dark and promising as the sand beneath our feet. A promise I beg for him to keep.

He takes my hand and leads me to the Balinese-inspired masterpiece for a tour. The luxury ten-thousand-square-foot compound sits on twenty secluded acres. Its four pavilions nestle amongst lush gardens, fruit trees, and serene ponds. An infinity edge pool with spa stretches to the horizon in the center. Each pavilion connects to the other by breezeways and footbridges.

We enter the main two-story pavilion with an expansive gourmet kitchen, dining area, living room, office, state-of-the-art media room, wet bar, full bathroom, plus one king-size bedroom with en suite bathroom. Harris comments we won't need the fancy fitness studio.

We bypass two sumptuous guest suite pavilions, each with a king suite and an en suite bathroom, private indoor/outdoor showers, wet bars, and lanais.

Instead, Harris takes me to the massive primary pavilion with a king suite, lounge area, wet bar, and a spa bathroom with an indoor/outdoor shower, dressing room, and a walk-in closet. Three lanais, each with distinctive views of the lagoon and the Pacific Ocean beyond.

"First course of action, we strip," Harris says as we stand on the lanai facing the sparkling water. "They train the staff in the utmost discretion. They only come on the property when summoned."

When I pull a face, Harris stops taking off his dress shirt and walks barefoot towards me. His pecs and abs flex as the material blows in the soft breeze. His happy trail draws my gaze to his unbuttoned fly. The trousers slung low on his narrow hips.

Piping hot sex on a stick.

And I want a bite.

But the idea of strangers seeing me nude. Uh… no.

He rubs my arms and stares into my eyes.

"I promise you the staff is offsite in a caretaker's house. This is a STEELE BLACK property—one of our über-luxury villas that caters to the top echelons of society.

People who protect their privacy fiercely. But if you don't want to, I won't pressure you," he says, then winks. "I, however, will be in the buff all week long."

He swivels his hips exaggeratedly until I giggle and push him away. Why not live a little?

Harris whoops when I do an impromptu striptease. Fully undressed, I stand before him. He tugs his lower lip between perfect teeth. His heated gaze rolls over me like a lava flow. Hot enough to turn my body into a pile of ash.

I shiver despite the warm breeze.

"More beautiful than the view," he rasps. "It's time to get you wet."

He slips his hand in mine and walks along a path. Petals from the flagrant flowers I smelled earlier collect on the stones. Each step coaxes more of their aroma into the air to float around us. They create a heady sensation, and I close my eyes for a deep whiff.

The path leads us back to the black sand beach.

I glance around to absorb its grandeur. Then squeal when Harris scoops me from my feet and runs into the waves. I hold to his neck tightly when he dunks beneath the surface. We rise laughing.

With a twist of my slippery body, I break free of his grasp and cast a seductive eye over my shoulder at him. He catches it and reaches out for me. Like a mermaid, I undulate my legs and swim for the sandbank.

I reach the black sand before Harris—undoubtedly, he let me out swim him. Then open my arms wide, throw my head back to the sky, and spin in a slow circle. The sun licks my skin, and I know I won't have long before its pale hue reddens. But for now, I enjoy myself. Sunblock later.

Harris spins with me and shouts to the cerulean heavens.

It's so freeing to just be. Not a care in the world. And with the man I love.

Oh, so happy and grateful, I join in his shouts.

"I WISH the week didn't have to end. It went way too fast..." I pout as Harris and I stretch out on a sunbed, watching the fiery sunset.

He rolls onto his elbow and traces circles radiating from my belly button to my breasts.

My nipples pucker, and he leans over to suckle one while he tweaks the other. It's a gentle touch, like he's been for the last few days. He's still passionate. But not as feral in his need.

I worry he's finished *fucking me out of his system.* A shudder runs through me at the horrible thought of this being the end.

"Cold or aroused?" Harris asks with his chin resting below my breasts.

His dove gray eyes peer into my emerald green ones.

I shake my head.

His gaze dips to my jiggling tits, and a lazy smile spreads across his face. He turns his head and nips at the bottom curve of one. I cry out softly.

"Not cold," I purr as I push the lingering thought to the side.

"Mmmm…" Harris murmurs. "Let me see what I can do to satisfy you, Siren."

He slips between my thighs. When his mouth engulfs my sex, I mewl and arch my back. He's relentless in his ministrations. By the time he sits back on his haunches, I'm boneless. Mind blank.

Harris chuckles.

"Well, actually, I planned for us to spend the weekend in Beverly Hills. We'll leave early in the morning. So we'll have Friday through Monday. Returning to New York in time to have you at the office by eight-thirty," he says.

I jump up and throw my arms around his neck. He falls back on his butt, laughing.

"This is the BEST Valentine's Day I've ever had! Thank you, my love!" I exclaim.

Harris's laughter stops as he stiffens.

Bloody hell! I did not just call him *my love* out loud!

But I refuse to let my oopsie ruin the marvelous time we've had and will have over the weekend. So I pretend as though I don't notice the change in his body language. Instead, I distract him with a trail of open-mouthed kisses from his stubbled jaw, over the planes of his muscular chest and abs, and to his erect dick.

This time when he stiffens, it's from me swallowing his length down my throat in one go. I work his cock like my favorite sucker. The tip of my tongue swirls around the mushroom tip, flicking a bead of pre-cum from its slit.

Tilting my head, I use the flat of my tongue to lick from root to tip. Then I take all of him back down my throat. It expands to accommodate his sizable girth and length.

I repeat until his thighs quiver and his hands fist my hair. Then I sit back and let him fuck my face through the explosion of his orgasm. I hollow out my cheeks to suck every drop of his cum, not spilling one bit.

Harris collapses to his side, then back, chest heaving, eyes squeezed shut.

A satisfied smirk plays on my lips as I think of what Vivian told me: use what you got to get what you want.

And make no mistake, I want Harris Steele. Now and forever.

HARRIS

It freaked me out when Kat called me *my love*. I use a lot of four-letter words every damn day. But I wasn't ready to say *that* one, not out loud. At least, just not yet.

Where I thought last week was for fucking Kat out of my system. This week confirmed it's not quite over for us. Aside from the incredible sexual chemistry and mutual satisfaction, the out of the bedroom time is great too.

Kat's natural wit and her care for children add to her appeal. Not to mention how she's trying really hard to prove to me she deserves a second chance. We deserve another go.

The weekend in Beverly Hills was a last-minute add-on. The Maui villa had another party arriving on Saturday. I couldn't very well cancel it even if I wanted to. Not a good look for STEELE International to boot out a Crown Prince and his family for their two-month-long holiday.

So ever the brainiac, I thought quick on my feet and extended our trip to my penthouse in West Hollywood on the Sunset Strip.

It's a sleek bachelor's pad with a private full rooftop terrace that once belonged to Malcolm. Then Starr came around, and bam! The end of his Alpha Dom playboy days. Fortunately for me, I benefitted from his—well, not a loss per se—new status.

He had it so well decked out, I didn't need to change a thing. I come out at least once a month for a week and work out of STEELE Los Angeles. Then party at LEVELS Beverly Hills, Jackson's Couch, or some other hot spot. Except it's been a while since I was in Aberdeen and London, then the Holidays followed by time in New York City.

I figure it'll be an excellent test to go out with Kat like we used to for a night of fun. See if being outside of the bubbles we lived in at LEVELS New York and in Maui feels the same. I hate to admit it, but I want to see if Kat was genuine for real.

We've spent enough time in a LEVELS. So we'll skip the club here, although it's one of my favorites. Instead, have dinner at the exclusive and exquisite Urasawa—my go-to sushi restaurant—then dance at a new spot a buddy told me about. It's in West Hollywood, fifteen minutes from my penthouse. We won't have far to go to get back. Not that it matters since I have a STEELE Los Angeles driver to take Kat and me around for the weekend.

After we arrived, I took her shopping on Rodeo Drive

since, no shit, she really didn't have any clothes in Maui. Save for two floral-printed silk kimonos and the dress she wore for work. A maid had it dry cleaned for Kat to wear for the flight over.

She was psyched to hit all the stores. Naturally, we went to the STEELE Galleria Rodeo Drive. Kat picked out a few lingerie pieces from the Lola's Coterie boutique there. I persuaded her to get a sexy negligee-inspired mini dress to wear tonight.

The scene in *Pretty Woman* of Julia Roberts' character shopping here flashed through my head. But I didn't want to get knocked out by Kat, so I kept my mouth shut.

We had lunch at Maude, then returned to the penthouse.

Tuckered out from a busy day of travel, shopping, and fine dining, Kat opted to take a nap before we go out tonight. I left her to rest in my bed and came up to the terrace. It gave me space to think over things and figure next steps.

Once again, I decide to take it a day at a time. Next week I travel for business and won't have a chance to see Kat until I return. Time apart may put a different perspective on the development of a relationship between us. I hate to use a cliché, but I'll see if absence makes the heart grow fonder and all that wussy jazz.

Then I'll tell my family—starting with Haley—what's going on. I won't keep them in the dark, especially my twin. It's not like I'm being deceitful now. They're all still away for Valentine's Day and won't get back until next week. Meanwhile, I'll be in South America.

I give my brain a rest and close my eyes for a catnap—no pun intended…

Wet warmth surrounds my cock. Its fat head brushes the palate as my length slides towards My Kitty Kat's throat. I stroke the top of her cheek where a tear slips from her eyes as she stares up at me from where she kneels.

"Open your throat for me, Kitty Kat," I murmur. "Relax and let me in."

She squeezes my thigh three times—her hand signal of understanding when her mouth is otherwise occupied or gagged.

I nod in recognition and ease another inch into her mouth.

She hums in the back of her throat. The vibrations dance along my length to tease me. I stare down at her with hooded eyes. She feels incredible.

Halfway there, I pull back to my tip to give her jaw a rest. She takes a breath through her mouth, then licks the slit. I shudder and slide back in, deeper still.

Soon we pick up a pattern she can handle and gives me pleasure. I put my hands behind my back and only use my hips to fuck her mouth slowly. My head lolls back. A groan slips through my slack mouth. I swivel my hips.

My Kitty Kat moans.

I can tell her fingers play with her clit when her right shoulder bumps against my thigh. My hooded gaze drops to watch My Kitty Kat pleasure herself while she deep throats me. The sight of her naked on her knees, pussy juices slick on her spread thighs, hand moving rapidly, all while she stares back at me with my cock stretching her mouth finishes me.

I grip her long, silky Titian strands in both hands to hold her head in place. My ass clenches, ready to surge ahead. I pulse on her tongue as I push as far down her throat as she can handle. A gag and I go off like a rocket. My eyes roll back in my head as a primal roar punches the air.

My Kitty Kat moans and convulses. She joins me with a climax of her own, belly full of my seed.

Hands still in her hair, I drop to my knees in front of her and cover her swollen mouth with mine. She clings to me and mewls.

Breathless, I have to leave her mouth and bury my face in her neck as the aftershocks continue to roll through me. I pull her onto my lap, unable to remain on my knees. She curls into me like a contented Kitty Kat.

"I love you, Harris," she whispers.

"I love you, Kat," I respond.

She gasps.

"You do?"

"H—Harris? Did you hear me?"

My eyes open slowly. Kat comes into focus. Her wide eyes move rapidly over my face. I frown.

Was I dreaming? Damn, I must've been because she's wearing the Lola's Coterie mini dress, not naked on her knees.

I swipe my hand over my face and sit up from the double chaise.

"What time is it?" I ask, voice hoarse with sleep.

Kat doesn't answer, so I glance back at her. I cock an eyebrow questioningly. She shakes her head and sighs.

"It's a quarter past seven," she responds quietly.

Then she rises from sitting beside me. She smooths the front of her mini dress and turns for the interior door leading to the stairs and the penthouse below.

"You should take a shower," she says over her shoulder and wipes the corner of her mouth with her pinky finger.

A cool breeze skims across my crotch. I glance down and my eyes bug out.

My semi-flaccid cock glistens with saliva as it rests against my open jeans. I jerk my head towards Kat. But she's already closing the door behind her. I look back at my dick.

"Was I fucking dreaming or what?" I ask aloud, baffled.

Then it hits me.

Kat must have given me a blow job while I slept. Okay, nice. I feel bad since I didn't get her off, too. I tuck my cock inside and re-button my jeans.

Wait a minute. Did Kat tell me she loves me? Did I tell her *I love her*???

Fuck. Me.

No wonder she looked so shocked and bolted.

I fall back on the double chaise lounge. A string of four-letter words pours from my mouth.

So a sleeping man getting his dick sucked tells no lies…

Damn.

What do I do now???

I could pretend as though I don't know what happened. Or be a man—as The Godfather says—and talk to Kat.

Well, since I'm a grown ass man…

I find Kat sitting in a chair by the window in the darkened living room. The panoramic view of the Sunset Strip lights up the nighttime sky behind her. It bathes Kat with an ethereal glow.

Even though she faces the window, I can tell by her slumped posture she's thinking of what happened.

And she's defeated.

Way to go, Harris Steele, I chide myself.

My goal is to break a woman. But that's when we're in bed and I want her to come undone for me. Climax to ecstasy.

Kat is not floating in carnal bliss. She's drowning in a sea of sadness. And it's my fault.

So deep in thought. She doesn't notice my approach until I crouch before her. She jolts.

I take her hand and watch as I intertwine our fingers, then squeeze.

"Hey," I say after I bring my gaze up to her face.

Kat stares at our hands, then averts her eyes. She lifts a corner of her mouth and whispers, "Hey."

Wanting her eyes on me so I can read her expression, I cup her cheek to turn her head around. But she keeps her eyes downcast.

"Look at me, Kat," I say, then wait until she raises her gaze to meet mine. "I thought I was dreaming. It didn't hit me until after you left the terrace, what happened—what we said—was real."

She blinks to hold back tears. But keeps her focus on me.

"I won't deny what I said. I can't. What holds me back from saying it while awake is fear of what you say and do aren't genuine. Call it PTSD. But I need to be one-hundred and ten percent certain you're not pretending," I admit.

"Harris, I—"

I put a fingertip on her lips.

"My heart feels. But my mind needs to know. We're a lot further along now than before. So there's a plus in our win column. Let's leave it at that and take each day as it comes. Okay?" I say.

Her eyes scan my face, and I remain open to her. I won't lie and I won't hide. Satisfied with what she sees, Kat squeezes my hand and smiles softly.

"Okay," she says with more confidence than a minute ago.

I nod as I rise.

"Give me fifteen minutes. A certain redheaded Siren enchanted me while I slept. So I need to shower and get dressed," I say wryly.

"Oh, is that what you call a blow job, Harris?" Kat asks as she giggles. Her emerald green eyes glow brighter than the Sunset Strip.

My Kitty Kat makes my heart soar.

Damn, I'm fucked. For real.

. . .

"Hello, Harris. Good to see you. It's been a while."

I return Hiro Urasawa's smile as he greets me in his eponymous Beverly Hills restaurant. He's right since I dine in the ten-person shrine to sushi each time I'm in town. I will never get enough of his masterful creations. They're the best in the world.

"Good to see you, too, Hiro. I'm happy to be back," I tell him, then turn to Kat. "Allow me to introduce you to Kat Jackson. Kat, this is Hiro Urasawa the Great."

He chuckles at my introduction and bows deeply to Kat. She smiles and returns his gesture of respect. I help her into a seat while Hiro returns to his next masterpiece.

"He's incredible. I feel privileged to be here," Kat says as we watch Hiro, his movements as precise as a neurosurgeon.

I agree, and we sit in a comfortable silence as he prepares the dishes for this evening's meal. The other eight guests also watch on in reverence.

A server places an assortment of appetizers before us. Kat selects edamame, and I bite into a tantalizing beef dumpling. The flavor bursts over my tongue. I groan, it's so good. Kat hums in harmony.

I selected a cold-matured sake to accompany our appetizers. Kat tells me it's the best she's ever had and licks the corner of her lip to catch a stray drop. Even though she's not being a siren, my cock still twitches, envisioning her tongue on my slit, lapping a bead of pre-cum.

Not now. No sexual thoughts. This is a date night.

I shift my gaze back to Hiro in the center or the

rectangular wooden bar around which the patrons sit on two sides. The light from above shines on the various ingredients he uses. My mouth waters, then curves into a grin when dinner is served.

THE MUSIC PUMPS from the speakers as My Kitty Kat and I grind on the dance floor. My hands grip her ass to mold her to my body. Her arms drape over my shoulders as she shimmies. Our foreheads touch with our eyes locked on the other.

Even though people moving similarly crowd the dance floor, it's as though they don't exist. Only the rhythm of the music penetrates our bubble.

When the song changes, My Kitty Kat spins around and throws her arms in the air. She bends her knees to glide up and down the front of my body. Her sensual moves make my already painfully hard cock weep and beg to enter her enticing body—mouth, pussy, or ass.

I grip her hips, bend my knees to align her ass with my cock, and sway us back and forth. She bends over and grabs her ankles, shaking her sweet thing. I damn near cum in my leather pants.

Instead, I step back and smack that ass.

She rises onto her toes but doesn't stop her gyrations. Her body begs me for more. And I oblige.

I alternate a pump of my hips with a spank to a different ass cheek. When the next song blends into the last, I tug her up by her throat with one hand and slip the other around her hip. Her back pressed to my front and held in place, my finger slides beneath the hem of her mini dress. It finds her juices coating the tops of her inner thighs.

She moans, and I groan into her ear.

"So wet for me, Siren?" I ask thickly.

"Only for you, Harris," she says against my cheek.

I growl and plunge my finger into her dripping pussy. My finger flexes and curls as the heel of my hand grinds against her engorged clit. It pulsates as her inner walls flutter. I add another finger.

She arcs her back on a moan. My mouth covers hers. No need for others to get even a hint of what I do to My Kitty Kat. For my eyes and my ears only.

She cums with a muffled scream. Her whole body trembles. I band my arm around her waist to keep her from collapsing to the floor. She rides out her orgasm on my fingers as they slide in and out gently.

"Time to go," I croon in her ear.

She nods.

Back at my penthouse, we shower, then fall into bed. In moments, she's asleep curled into my side with her head resting on my chest and one leg thrown over mine. Staring at the ceiling, I trace a fingertip along the curve of her hip.

The night replays in my mind. I must say we had a really good date. As my eyes close, I wonder what it would be like to fall asleep with My Kitty Kat in my arms not just for a few days. But always.

"So… How was your surprise Valentine's Day trip to Maui with that sexy man of yours, Kat?"

Vivian grins at me as we leave the conference room after the Monday morning executive status meeting.

As Harris promised, he dropped me off at my office building at a half-past eight. He flies out later this morning for Buenos Aires on business. He's there for the entire week.

I pouted, and he kissed me senseless at the revolving doors. He cared little people were flowing around our passionate embrace. With a wink, he was gone. And my heart leaped out of my chest to follow him like a kitten with separation anxiety.

Words cannot describe our time away together. Maui was a spectacular paradise. Harris fulfilled an absolute dream of mine. After I got over myself with the initial anger at his actions, I couldn't be more grateful. But the brilliant beauty of Hawaii pales in the light of the' natural glow emanating from Harris' eyes as he watches me.

I know he isn't ready to give in to his love for me fully. But the spark is there. It's grown from the embers left in his heart. Soon, it will ignite to engulf us in a fireball of undeniable love.

"That good, huh?"

Vivian's words and giggles bring me back from thoughts of Harris to the office. As the images of the black sand beach and the bright lights of the Sunset Strip fade away, I glance around the corridor. Not a palm tree in sight. I sigh.

"Viv, you have no idea. Once my anger dissipated… Wait a minute, you knew, too?!" I ask taken aback.

Her toffee eyes gleam like amber as she bites her lower lip to stifle her laughter.

"Of course! Who do you think gave him the idea to donate to make up for taking you away for so long as you've only been here for a short while? You raise funds, so you being away still brought in money. A win-win situation," Vivian says with a wink.

I throw my head back and laugh. All of my craziness and Harris hadn't thought about making a donation to pay for my time. Now, it's confirmed I overreacted. Duh. Duh. Duh.

Viv quirks an eyebrow at me.

I loop my arm through hers and tell her all about it as we walk back to our respective offices. Then I promise to fill her in on the rest over lunch—my treat. I'll make it up to Harris when I see him again. My heart lurches. He's not back for DAYS…

The rest of the morning went by quickly. The director and I met to discuss the happenings while I was away. She was more than pleased with Harris' donation. She joked he could take me away each month if he'd contribute each time, and we'd more than make our yearly goal.

I had to laugh along with her. Viv put a whole new spin on his donation. It makes me feel so much better and erases any lingering negativity.

Vivian calls to let me know she'll meet me at the lifts. I'm shocked to find it's already half past noon. Jet lag has me at breakfast still. I wrap up an email and grab my coat and handbag. As I slip my mobile into the outer pocket, it chimes with a text message.

I grin like the Cheshire Cat.

Harris!

Hi, Kitty Kat. Getting ready to take off. I'll call you tonight. H.

My fingers fly across the mobile screen as I type back.

Safe travels. TTYL KK ;)

I wait a moment to check for a response before I drop my mobile back in the outer pocket. But no three dots appear by the time I make it to the lifts. Bummer.

It's a chilly day, so Viv and I head to our favorite sandwich and soup shop a few blocks from the office. We join the throngs of people on Fifth Avenue. Tourists mingle with workers and residents on the bustling sidewalk. The scent of roasted chestnuts beckons from a vendor on the corner. Store windows changed from the red roses, bows, and ribbons for Valentine's Day to the latest summer fashions.

I tighten the belt of my warm wool coat as I shake my head. Only days ago, I was swimming in the lagoon naked. Harris' sleek muscular frame beside me. Now, the blasted cold of New York City in February. And here retailers display mannequins in colorful bikinis and sarongs in the windows!

If only I could roll back time…

During lunch, Vivian can't stop oohing and aahing over all things Harris Steele. Especially when I tell her he offered to tell his buddies who'd love to take her on a date. Then she claps her hands and shimmies in her seat. She's been so good to me, I'm happy to return the many favors.

The following five days blend into each other. Throughout the busy workdays and long, lonely nights, my mind wanders to the lazy days and passionate nights with Harris. He calls, and we've pleasured ourselves via Face-Time. But nothing beats the real thing, including the BOB —Battery Operated Boyfriend—Harris sent for me to use while he watched hungrily.

By the time Friday rolls around, I'm keyed up and can't wait to see him tonight. He surprised me again with an invitation for dinner at his penthouse in The STEELE Tower. I greedily accepted wanting the food he ordered from one of Lucien's restaurants and for the taste of my man on my tongue.

After work, I rush home to shower and to change into a

slinky black dress with a sheer mesh bra and matching thong. To complete my sex kitten look, I pile my hair into a messy bun, tie a black silk ribbon into a bow around my neck, and slip into sky-high black stilettos. Before I leave, I add shell pink lip gloss and walk through a spritz of my perfume.

"Whoohoo! Sexy Bae Alert!" Vivian says as she wolf whistles upon seeing me emerge from my room. "Somebody's getting her freak on tonight! *Rawr*, as Missy Elliot says."

She falls back on the sofa, cracking up about her own joke.

I laugh and wave.

"Have fun for me, Kat!" She calls out as I round the corner, headed for the coat closet and lift.

My mobile rings as the doors open in the lobby. I grin at Harris' name on the screen.

"Hi, Harris," I say breathlessly, in keeping with my sex kitten persona. "I'm walking towards the lobby door now."

"Hey, Kitty Kat, I'm stuck in traffic. So I won't be able to pick you up. I sent a STEELE driver with a silver Mercedes-Benz S 580 for you. He's out front. Do you see him?" Harris tells me.

I pull back a disappointed sigh and nod at the doorman as I pass. The STEELE driver stands beside the sedan and opens the back door when he sees me. I smile and tell Harris I'm getting inside.

"Okay, a member of security at The STEELE Tower will give you access to my penthouse. He'll meet you at the concierge desk. I'll be there as soon as I can. Oh, wait, hold on… I have to take this call. I'll see you soon," Harris says, then ends the call.

I glance at the mobile and shake my head as I slip it into my purse. The text alert dings.

Sorry I had to rush. Can't wait to see you. H.

I sit back against the sumptuous leather seat and grin.

"Thank you," I tell the security guard as I step into Harris' penthouse. The guard bids me a good evening and returns to the private lift.

I still can't believe Harris allowed me into his personal space, unattended by him. However, I will not snoop. Instead, I drape my coat on the bench in the entry and place my purse on top. Mobile in hand, I walk to the living room. The delicious aroma of food fills the air.

Someone beautifully decorated his home with masculine touches of leather, rich colors, and a well-stocked bar. I make a beeline for it. Naturally, the selection includes the Jackson Corporation labels. My fingers graze an impressive storage box made of the most rare and most expensive African Blackwood. I know it all too well…

It contains Jackson Corporation's Scotch blend the master distiller worked on for the past sixty years. It's a limited-edition run for an astronomical one-million pounds.

Over six months ago, bent on my revenge goal, I uncovered the launch plans and other details. Even though I couldn't get the recipe, Chet Stewart agreed the intel I stole was worth the hefty sum he paid to me. He didn't make me privy to how he plans to use the information to Stewart Scotch's advantage and sting Jackson Corporation.

With a shudder at the thought of Chet, I move on to another bottle. I pour Jackson Special Blend Scotch into a Waterford Crystal snifter and stand in front of the floor-to-ceiling windows. Hopefully, the amazing view of New York City lit up at night from the fifty-first floor will chase away the terrible memories.

I take a healthy sip of the Scotch. The burn is just what I need.

"I'm more impressed by the view of you, Kitty Kat, than you can ever be of the Manhattan skyline at night."

Lost in thought, time passed. Harris' warm breath on the side of my neck as he whispers in my ear causes me to shudder—this time in a good way.

"I missed you, Kitty Kat," he rumbles, nuzzling my neck. "Did you miss me?"

Without missing a beat, I place the snifter next to my mobile on a table and turn around to face him. My arms go around his neck as I stand on tiptoe to bring his face closer to mine.

"More than you can even imagine, Harris Steele," I murmur against his full lips, then nip the bottom one.

He growls, bends his knees, and tosses me over his shoulder. A swat to my ass only covered by a wisp of silk from my dress makes me yelp and flail my legs. He bands his arm around my thighs and strides from the room.

"You will show me just how much, naughty lass," he

rumbles. "First, I feed you, then you feed me. After, we eat what Lucien has for us."

"Yes, Harris," I purr.

* * *

"Good morning, sleepyhead."

A lazy smile spreads across my face at the sight of a sexy, rumble-haired Harris staring down at me. I reach up and cup his stubbled cheek. He leans into my hand as his eyes close. He sighs contentedly.

"Good morning to you, early bird," I whisper as my fingertip drags across his lips.

He kisses the tip of it and smiles.

"Move in with me."

My eyes pop as my mouth forms an O.

Harris chuckles.

"Is that a yes or a no?" He asks as his thumb lifts my chin to close my slack mouth.

I blink.

He ducks his head and murmurs, "Don't leave a guy hanging, Kitty Kat."

Then he lifts his eyes to gaze at me from beneath his thick, ebony eyelashes. The absolute sexiness of his vulnerability seals the deal. I squeal and push him to his back as I straddle his hips and plant kisses all over his handsome face.

"Yes. Yes. YES!!!" I shout.

Harris beams at me with a beatific smile that makes his

dove gray eyes shine. He sits up and kisses the tip of my nose.

"Good Kitty Kat," he says. "Let's do this now. Then you can thank me properly later."

I giggle and slide off his lap.

After we shower, he arranges for movers from STEELE International's operations department to meet us at the flat I share with Vivian. The team will pack my things up and bring them to Harris'—*our*—flat in just a few hours.

I tease Harris about how spoiled rotten he is to get this done last minute on a Saturday morning. He just shrugs. I call Vivian, and she squeals louder than I did at Harris' proclamation. She promises to help instead of going to her Pilates session.

The movers make quick work of boxing my clothes and the items I decorated my room with while there. Harris and Viv sit in the family room chatting it up like old friends. Some help they prove to be I laugh to myself as a mover carries the last box from my room.

"Okay, my little helpers, time to go," I tell Harris and Vivian.

"Oh, my, done so soon?" She asks with her hand to heart and wide-eyed, feigning surprise.

Harris grins and stands from the sofa.

"Well done," he says and wraps his arm around my waist.

I roll my eyes and nudge his side with my elbow.

We ride a lift down to the lobby while the movers finish on the service lift and at the service entrance.

"You're sure you have everything?" Viv asks before she gets into Harris' Rolls-Royce SUV.

He turns to me questioningly.

I run through my mind's eye of the room. Then I remember the last gift my father ever gave to me. A hand-crafted music box. He received it as payment for one of the rare inventions he created that actually worked. I cherished it from first sight.

"Hold on, I forgot my music box. I'll be right back," I say, spinning on my heel.

"I'll come with you," Harris offers.

"Not to worry. It'll just take me a minute," I say as I wave him off over my shoulder and rush inside.

As I pass the utility closet, I grab the step ladder and head for my former room. I left the music box on the top shelf of the walk-in closet. It hurts to look at it sometimes since it reminds me of my Da and how he passed at such a young age from a heart attack. But I keep it close.

A smile plays at the corners of my mouth as I open it to listen to the playful tune. I close my eyes and remember the day he gave it to me.

"You really think you're special now? Don't you? Well, we have unfinished business, lass."

My blood runs cold in my veins as goosebumps break out over my entire body. My precious music box crashes to the floor. The tune dies out on impact.

Chet Stewart!

How the bloody hell did he find me and get in here?!

I spin around to find him dressed as one of the movers,

even down to the gray coveralls and matching cap. The hat set low on his head to cover half of his face.

He snatches it off. His eyes shoot icy daggers at me, and I freeze when he pulls a handgun with a silencer from his pocket.

My heart stops as I stare open-mouthed at the jet black metal aimed straight at my chest. I realize the dark stain on the neck of the coveralls must be blood from the mover who wore them.

Oh. My. God. Chet has gone mad.

He glares at me with such animosity, the air gets sucked from my lungs.

"You ruined me, my family, our company. You will pay, Kat *Jackson*!"

* * *

Harris & Kat's Story Continues: *Honor My Desires*

**Turn the page for the Steele & Jackson Family Trees,
Author's Note,
and a Preview of *Honor My Desires***

THE STEELE FAMILY

STEELE INTERNATIONAL, INC

Multigenerational, multibillion-dollar business luxury real estate development and management corporation

Headquarters & Family's Primary Residences:

The STEELE Tower, New York City

A modern, gray-tinted glass fifty-seven story mixed-use skyscraper on southwest corner of Fifty-Seventh Street and Fifth Avenue within Billionaires' Row

Global Offices:

- The United States of America (New York City, New Jersey, Chicago, California, Miami, Las Vegas)
- The Caribbean (St. Maarten, St. Barth's, St. Lucia)
- The French & Italian Rivieras (Nice, Cannes, Positano, Capri)
- Monaco (Monte Carlo)
- The United Arab Emirates (Abu Dhabi, Dubai)

STEELE FOUNDATION: A STRONG AND SUPPORTIVE HOUSE

Builds and manages attractive, affordable housing for urban, lower-income families

Available for download at **bit.ly/STEELEFamily**

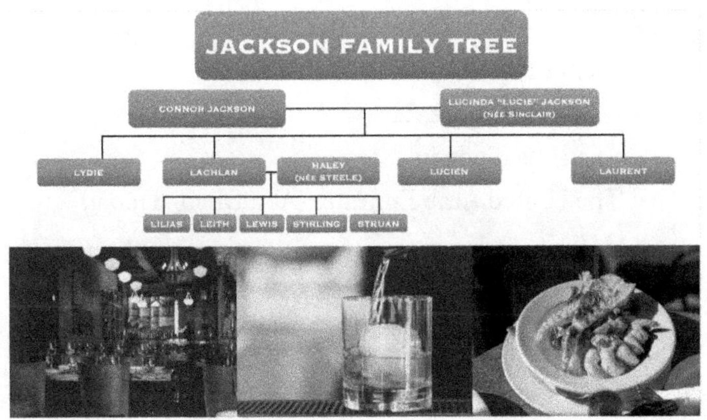

JACKSON CORPORATION

Multigenerational, multibillion-dollar business fine dining,
distilleries, and vineyards corporation

Headquarters:

Jackson Town House, Aberdeen, Scotland

A landmark property built by the founders of Aberdeen granite
on Union Street; the second largest granite building in the world.

Global Offices:

- The United Kingdom (Aberdeen, Scotland; London, England)
- The United States of America (New York City, New Orleans, Miami, Chicago, Los Angeles, Napa)
- The Caribbean (Puerto Rico)
- France (Paris, Cannes)
- Monaco (Monte Carlo)
- Australia (Sydney)
- The United Arab Emirates (Abu Dhabi, Dubai)

JACKSON FOUNDATION: ENJOY LIFE
RESPONSIBLY

Operates alcohol treatment centers for lower-income individuals
and support for their family members

Available for download at **bit.ly/JacksonFamilyTree**

Author's Note

Thank you for reading Part II of Harris and Kat's sexy, steamy romance! I hope you enjoyed the continuation of their of sizzling, second chance billionaire romance. If so, I'd love to hear your thoughts, please share a review at **bit. ly/CLBooksSI-JC5Review** and tell your friends.

Click below for what's up next for this darling duo:

Honor My Desires Harris & Kat Part III **Click Here**

At **CharmaineLouise.com** take the *Four types of lovers. Which are you?* **Quiz** to match your Sexy Fantasy: sub, Voyeur, Dominatrix, or Dominatrix sub Switch.

Follow me on social media including my CLBooks Coterie Fan Club below or on your favorite channels below and subscribe to my newsletter at **bit.ly/ CLBooksNewsletter** for a **Free Book.**

Fulfill Your Desires.

xoxo

Charmaine Louise

bookbub.com/authors/charmaine-louise-shelton
facebook.com/CharmaineLouiseBooks
instagram.com/charmainelouisebooks
tiktok.com/@charmainelouisebooks?
goodreads.com/charmainelouisebooks

Tease My Desires Lachlan & Haley Part II

Grant My Desires Lachlan & Haley Part III

Intrigue My Desires Harris & Kat Part I

Decode My Desires Harris & Kat Part II

Honor My Desires Harris & Kat Patt III

A Trilogy of Desires Lachlan & Haley Parts I-III

A Trilogy of Desires Harris & Kat Parts I-III

Series Extras

Series Playlist

Visit CharmaineLouiseBooks.com for the complete list.

"Hey, Kitty Kat. Have dinner with me tonight at my penthouse. I'll get one of Lucien's restaurants to send over food. But you'll be dessert. Hmmm… Maybe some fresh whipped cream and a couple of sweet maraschino cherries on top. Licked clean, naturally. Sounds tantalizing enough for you?"

I smirk when Kat's gasp comes through the mobile. I can picture her alabaster cheeks flushing rosy red. Not as vibrant as her Titian hair, but just as silky to the touch. The pupils of her eyes more than likely dilate with lust, leaving only their rims a dazzling emerald green. Her little pink tongue darts out to moisten her lush lips as the air rushes past them.

My cock twitches in the trousers of my bespoke Saville Row suit at the vision of my sexy Siren aroused.

Katrina Roberts cum Katrina Jackson. Yeah… *Jackson.*

The woman who nearly toppled both the Jackson and

the Steele clans with her scheme of vengeance in alignment with Chester *Chet* Stewart. Kat—an unknown cousin of the Jacksons—partnered with Stewart Scotch, Jackson Corporation's top competitor and historical clan rival amongst the world of Scottish nobility.

And I—Harris Steele, tech wiz extraordinaire—didn't see it coming. At. All.

Too busy enthralled by that redheaded Siren to see the signs of her betrayal until it was almost too late. Three months of the closest to a committed relationship I've ever had in my thirty-two years, and it ends with her admittance of misdeeds.

Lachlan Jackson—my cousin via our mothers being best friends and my brother-in-law—as CEO and Chairman of the Board of Jackson Corporation may have chosen not to press charges. He only banned Kat from Scotland.

But I banished her from my life. For fourteen weeks, that is. Unable to resist her Siren's call, I initiated a week to fuck her out of my system. All it did was make me crave her more and realize more is just what I want from Kat Jackson. My Kitty Kat.

She redeemed herself with letters of apology to each member of my family and conducted herself in the manner of one who wants to make amends. She even donated the money she garnered from giving Stewart intel on Jackson Corporation to the Aberdeen Children's Center, where she volunteered.

I'm far from a weak man and gave her hell. But there's no point in wallowing in the fiery pits when I can luxuriate deep in her warm, welcoming core. Especially when we both acknowledge what we shared over those three months was real. Despite her initial reason to use me as a smokescreen to access the Jacksons as part of her attempt at their downfall.

Ah well…

So here we are post the Seven-day Fuckfest, a surprise trip to Maui for Valentine's Day—don't think I'm not a romantic—and a week of me in Buenos Aires for business. And I want to have My Kitty Kat cum for dinner. Yup, pun intended. And in my penthouse at The STEELE Tower on Fifty-seventh and Fifth Avenue in the midst of Billionaires' Row in New York City. My sanctuary where no women besides those of my family have crossed the threshold.

Harris Steele—Alpha male billionaire playboy—falls for The One. Hard.

The last man standing of The STEELE Quaternity— dubbed such by the media as the most sought-after of the world's eligible billionaires and heirs to STEELE International, Inc. Handsome; six plus feet; ebony hair; shades of gray eyes; powerful Alpha Doms and males. I've followed in the footsteps of my three older brothers Sebastian, Malcolm, and Roger. They succumbed and married the women who captured their hearts—Lola, Starr, and Leonie, respectively.

I once laughed and called my brothers suckers. Now, they'll laugh at me. Again. This time for good. If My Kitty Kat behaves like a good little kitten.

"Oh, Harris," she starts breathlessly. "That sounds more

than tantalizing. I'd love to have dinner with you… And be your dessert."

I growl as her response ends in a sultry purr. My cock throbs in approval.

"Excellent, Kitty Kat. I'll meet you in front of your apartment building at seven tonight," I say, ignoring the twinge in my gut from her use of the four-letter word even regarding food. I'm not all the way there yet. We end the call, and I sit back in the leather chair of my Gulfstream G650ER.

"The pilot is ready for takeoff, Mr. Steele."

I turn my gaze from the window to the flight attendant and smile as I give my consent to leave Buenos Aires behind.

As much as I enjoy being the co-head of STEELE Technology and Cyber Security with my fraternal twin Haley, I can't wait to head home. Home where My Kitty Kat will be soon.

"I APOLOGIZE, Mr. Steele. There's no getting around this accident. Shall I have a STEELE driver collect Ms. Jackson?"

A glance at my Audemars Piguet The Royal Oak Complication watch confirms we'll be late picking up My Kitty Kat. I agree with my driver, Alonso Masa's recommendation. Once the STEELE driver is outside of her apartment building, I call to let her know.

"Hi, Harris," she says breathlessly. "I'm walking towards the lobby door now."

"Hey, Kitty Kat, I'm stuck in traffic. So I won't be able to pick you up. I sent a STEELE driver with a silver Mercedes-Benz S 580 for you. He's out front. Do you see him?" I tell her.

"Yes, and I'm getting inside now," she responds, in an attempt to hide her disappointment.

Join the club. I'd rather have met her, too.

"Okay, a member of security at The STEELE Tower will give you access to my penthouse. He'll meet you at the concierge desk. I'll be there as soon as I can. Oh, wait, hold on… I have to take this call. I'll see you soon," I say, then end the call.

It's from a potential client another client referred to me while in Argentina. I can't ignore it. While I answer, I pull up the message app and shoot a text to Kat. Hopefully, it'll lessen the bluntness of my hang up.

Sorry I had to rush. Can't wait to see you. H.

By the end of the call, I've secured a new client for his company and his personal accounts. I send a quick text message to Haley as a heads-up. She sends back a grinning emoji. Then follows it with a reminder I'm behind her in our monthly new business quota by two.

We're the youngest of the Steele siblings and a surprise to our parents being three years younger than Roger. As the Dynamic Duo, Haley and I have made it our mission to make our mark on STEELE International and to contribute to our family's multigenerational, multibillion-dollar company.

Consequently, our division generates a sizable amount to STEELE's bottom line and brings in clients for the other divisions—Retail Properties, Entertainment Properties, and Residential Properties. Each of our brothers runs a division, with Baz also being the CEO and Chairman of the Board. STCS has become an indispensable part of STEELE International.

I snicker and shoot back an eye roll emoji, knowing it'll get Haley riled up.

We're hella close and love each other to death. She's as protective of me as I am of her. I'm sure she'll be okay with Kat and me getting back together since Haley instigated Kat and me talking weeks ago. Based on my conversation with my Dad Morgan and my mother Shelley's message, I'm sure they'll be open to it, even if warily. *Remain open to love. It can surprise you whence it comes.*

I keep my parents' words of wisdom in mind as I walk through the living room of my penthouse to where My Kitty Kat stands staring out the floor-to-ceiling windows.

"I'm more impressed by the view of you, Kitty Kat, than you can ever be of the Manhattan skyline at night," I say. My warm breath tickles the side of her neck as I whisper in her ear.

She shudders.

"I missed you, Kitty Kat," I rumble, nuzzling her neck. "Did you miss me?"

She places a snifter next to her mobile on a table and

turns around to face me. Her slender arms go around my neck as she stands on tiptoe to bring my face closer to hers.

"More than you can even imagine, Harris Steele," she murmurs against my lips, then nips the bottom one. The scent of Jackson Scotch wafts across my face.

I growl deep in my chest as I bend my knees and toss My Kitty Kat over my shoulder. A swat to her ass only covered by a wisp of silk from her dress makes her yelp and flail her legs. I band one arm around her thighs and stride from the living room.

"You will show me just how much, naughty lass," I rumble. "First, I feed you, then you feed me. After, we eat what Lucien has for us."

"Yes, Harris," she purrs like a good little kitten.

Off to a great start.

Once inside my bedroom suite, I carry her to the bed and place her on her feet. My hands skim the sides of her body from her shoulders to her thighs. With a flick of my wrists, I divest her of the skimpy, silky number she wore to tease me.

My Siren gasps and covers her DDs with her hands. More than her palms can cover, the luscious tits spill around them.

"Do not cover yourself from me, naughty lass," I admonish as I grasp her wrists and bring them over her head. I dip mine to envelop a puckered rosy nipple into my hungry mouth.

She groans and undulates her body.

My other hand drops to cup her round ass to still her

movements. I want her to focus on the pleasurable sensations without distraction.

I continue to lave, nip, and to suckle her delectable tits until they're heavy with her need. Another flick of my wrist and I snap the thin material of her G-string to bare her pussy to me. My fingers skim its wet seam collecting her cream.

Her pupils dilate as she watches me slip the glistening digits into my mouth and swirl my tongue around them. My groan of appreciation makes her tremble and close her eyes as she sways.

I scoop her up and toss her into the middle of my king-size bed. Her eyes pop open, then half-mast as I kick off my shoes and strip out of my suit. My muscles ripple as I stalk towards her and lower onto the bed between her spread thighs.

My Siren widens them for my broad shoulders as I bow before her dripping fount. Her cries of carnal ecstasy as I devour her sweet pussy heighten my desire to fuck her raw.

But first she must be ready to take my ten inches. My fingers join my lips and tongue to drive her over the edge again and again. Not until her cream pools beneath her ass do I plank over her sated body.

She can only move her eyes languorously as she watches me take her legs and wrap them around my hips. She gathers the strength to tighten the hold as I align the purple, swollen head of my cock to her warm, welcoming core.

A single thrust seats me deep within her pussy. She screams as her body adjusts to my girth and length. Her inner walls clench to draw me further inside.

I throw my head back and howl.

"So fucking good, Kitty Kat…" I groan. But remain still until she's ready for the ride.

"Harris… Please…" she begs as her hips squirm for much-needed friction.

Who am I to deny her?

My hips meet hers as I flex my ass and withdraw before pounding back into her quivering sheath.

Her head lolls as her mouth forms a perfect O. No sound slips past her lips. Only from her lower ones, as her wetness squelches from the driving force of my thrusts.

My grunts add harmony to the erotic symphony we create. Her high-pitched wails as she cums undone for me build to a crescendo. I erupt with an almighty roar.

My climax triggers another for My Siren. She keens as her pussy clamps down on my cock to milk it of every single drop. Her fingernails dig into my biceps to anchor her from flying into the stratosphere.

But I'm gone. Lost in the throes of passion.

I return to My Kitty Kat's soothing caresses and her whispered words. My face nestled between her pillowy mounds, my heartbeat slows. I wrap my arms around her waist and roll onto my back.

She cuddles into me as her head rests on my chest over my heart. She slides her hands around my flanks to hold me close. With a sigh, she settles.

"I missed you, too, Harris Steele," she whispers.

A satisfied smile curves across my lips.

"I missed you, too, Kat Jackson," I respond.

Her stomach growls louder than I did moments ago. She giggles and turns her face into my chest, embarrassed.

"Not very sexy, huh?" She asks as her shoulders shake with mirth.

I smack her ass and sit up.

"No. And not good for my ego," I respond wryly. "Guess it's time to feed you, Kitty Kat."

She bites the corner of her lower lip and nods. Then she lowers her gold-tinged eyelashes.

"We can always return for that dessert you promised," she purrs.

My cock twitches, ready for more.

"Abso-fucking-lutely, Siren," I swear.

Yeah, it's good to be home. With My Kitty Kat.

***

Click the Link Below or Visit books2read.com/u/ b5lD97 For Your Copy

Honor My Desires Harris & Kat Part III

I dedicate this novel to those who deserve a second chance and to those who give it to them.

Fulfill Your Desires.

xoxo
Charmaine Louise

WELCOME TO CHARMAINELOUISE — THE SENSUAL LIFESTYLE

GLITZY. GLAMOROUS. STEAMY.

CharmaineLouise New York, Inc. invites you to indulge in *The Sensual Lifestyle* through **CharmaineLouise Books** and **CharmaineLouise Intimates**. CLBrands immerse you in *Sexy Fantasies* with CLBooks contemporary romance novels and give you *Sexy Under Things & Loungewear* with CLIntimates.

Charmaine Louise Shelton the Founder, CEO & Author of CLNY loves all things classic, elegant, feminine, and of course with an erotic edge! Favorite outfit of choice is a cashmere cardigan, leather pencil skirt, and seamed silk stockings with stiletto heels. Sexy Fantasy Type: sub with a dash of Voyeur. When not writing and designing, Charmaine Louise travels and spends time with her Maltese buddies, ZIGGY and Jynger.

CharmaineLouise — *The Sensual Lifestyle*

~ Visit online at **CharmaineLouise.com**

~ Subscribe to **CharmaineLouise Newsletter**

~ Find us on Facebook **@CharmaineLouiseNewYork**

~ Instagram **@CharLouNY**

CharmaineLouise Books *Sexy Fantasies* launched summer 2020. Sizzling, contemporary romance with your soon-to-be favorite Alpha Doms, Powerful Billionaires, and the women they lust after and love for second chances, insta-love, enemies-to-lovers, and more.

Want to chat it up and share your thoughts with other CLBooks Lovers? Read our blog, join our Charmaine-Louise Books Coterie Fan Club and follow us on my author pages and social media to be in the know about the book release dates, exclusive content, giveaways, contests, and more!

~ **Purchase your eBook and paperback novels from my Author Page by clicking here!**

~ Read and subscribe to our blog *The World of Sex*

~ Connect on **Amazon Author Page**

~ Goodreads Author Profile

~ <u>BookBub Author Profile</u>

CharmaineLouise Intimates *Sexy Under Things &* *Loungewear* debuted in 2003. Inspired by the sensuous sirens and sylph swans of the past and present, the hand crochet cashmere and silk collections are for the sexy: hence, the line names Ginger — Bombshell; Diana — Showstopper; Jackie — Timeless; Lena — Classic. Also known as The Movie-Star from Gilligan's Island; Ms. Ross The Boss; Mrs. Kennedy Onassis; Ms. Horne.

Do you thrive on seduction and being sexy lounging at home? Read our blog and follow us on social media to receive the tips, the latest additions to the collections, private sales, and more!

~ Read and subscribe to our blog *The Art of Seduction*

~ Find us on Facebook **@CharmaineLousieIntimates**

~ Instagram **@CharmaineLouiseIntimates**

Fulfill Your Desires.